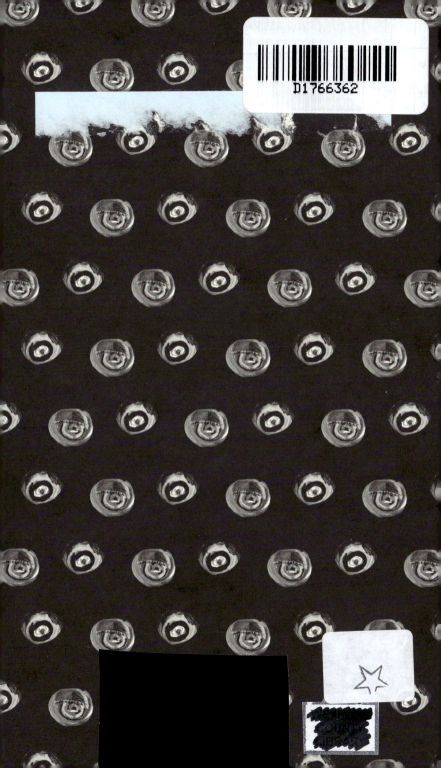

D1766362

GraveLarks

GraveLarks

by

JAN KŘESADLO

translated from the Czech by
VÁCLAV Z J PINKAVA

JANTAR PUBLISHING 2015

First published in London, Great Britain in 2015 by
Jantar Publishing Ltd

First Czech edition published in Toronto by '68 Publishers in 1984 as
Mrchopěvci

Jan Křesadlo
GraveLarks
All rights reserved

Original text © Pinkava Estate
Revised translation, editing and cover art © 2015 Václav Z J Pinkava
Illustrations © 1999 Jan J Pinkava
Jacket art by Jan Křesadlo © Pinkava Estate
Cover design by George Pinkava
Jacket and book design by Jack Coling

The right of Václav Z J Pinkava to be identified as translator of this work has been
asserted in accordance with the Copyright, Design and Patents Act, 1988.
No part of this book may be reproduced or utilised in any form or by any
means, electronic or mechanical, including photocopying, recording or by any
information storage and retrieval system without written permission.

A CIP catalogue record for this book is available from the British Library.
ISBN 978-0-9933773-0-3

Printed and bound in the Czech Republic by EUROPRINT a.s.

www.jantarpublishing.com
www.kresadlo.cz

CONTENTS

LIST OF ILLUSTRATIONS

GraveLarks began life as *Mrchopěvci*, the first novel written by Dr. Václav Jaroslav Karel Pinkava (1926–1995) under his pen name, Jan Křesadlo.

At the time, Pinkava was the Principal Psychologist and department head of a provincial psychiatric hospital. He had emigrated to Britain in 1969 from post-Soviet invasion Czechoslovakia, where, due to his bourgeois origins and staunch anti-Communist party stance, he worked at the periphery of clinical psychology, in the diagnostics and experimental treatment of what was then known as "sexual deviation". He was an authority in his field, and despite his political non-allegiance, a Prague High Court expert witness in sex crime cases.

Of much relevance to this volume is the fact that Pinkava was actively involved in research into homosexuality and was an active proponent of its decriminalisation – this happened in Czechoslovakia in 1961, six years earlier than in Britain.

Another event worth noting is that in 1949, Pinkava stood trial accused of helping to organise an armed uprising with an expected sentence ranging from 25 years to execution. Having miraculously won, even after two appeals by the prosecutor, he was nevertheless removed from his studies at Prague's Charles' University. He was readmitted much later, but was allowed only to study psychology; then a pariah subject. Meanwhile he'd been a labourer and on military service where he made friends with Roma servicemen, and swiftly learnt their language.

Time passed and in the summer of 1980, when there was not enough going on at the Psychology Department of Colchester's (since closed) Severalls Hospital, Pinkava took time out to write his distinctive first novel. In the original manuscript, he called it "a bizarre romanetto". It was written in the fortnight from 21st July till 5th August in 574 pages of what seems to others a largely unintelligible scribble of a manuscript. It took a further ten days to turn it into 183 pages of typescript. On a whim, Pinkava then sent the text to Josef Škvorecký (1924–2012) who, in addition to being another exiled Czech, was a noted author and academic. Also, Škvorecký ran *Sixty-Eight Publishers* in Toronto, publishing Czech literature that was unavailable or banned in Czechoslovakia at that time.[*] Škvorecký loved the novel, but not the tamer, original ending. After some corresondence, Pinkava agreed to bring the ending to a darker and more graphic climax.

Thus, at the belated age of 58, Pinkava had his first novel, *Mrchopěvci*, published in Canada; in the title year of Orwell's dystopian creation, and a few years before the formal end of the Cold War.[†] It won him the 1985 Egon Hostovský Prize.

While eagerly publishing his follow-up novels, Škvorecký sought to have Křesadlo's prizewinning novel published in English and his effusive recommendation for a future English edition, written in 1987, is re-printed in this volume.

The first English edition was not published until 1999, well after the fall of the Berlin Wall and the Velvet Revolution in Czechoslovakia. For that Czech/English version, the translation was the work of three of Pinkava's four children and his prospective son-in-law, and put together to a very tight publishing deadline. The publication was not without its faults.

From that original quartet, his oldest son, Václav, a professional translator, has completely revised the text, returning to the original typescript to conform with the author's nonconformist text layout, as well as re-introducing some hitherto omitted snippets. It is this revised text which we present in this volume, with additional explanatory notes and a glossary of terms, where they might be needed.

I must point out the scale of the challenge to render this novel into English.

The original – with its Czech language antics, often playfully idiosyncratic changes of 'register', interspersed with Romani and its

---

[*] Sixty-Eight Publishers, Toronto was established in 1971 for the purpose of publishing the prose and poetry of exiled Czech and Slovak writers banned in Czechoslovakia. In all, 220 titles were published including works by Milan Kundera, Škvorecký himself and even Martina Navrátilová, the tennis champion. It ceased publishing in 1989.

[†] Petr Hanuška, 'Vzájemná korespondence Jana Křesadla a Josefa Škvoreckého', *Česká Literatura, Volume 44 (number 6), 1996.*

pidgin Slovak and Hungarian cameos, Sudeten German, French and Russian, as well as segments in Latin and, most saliently, in classical Greek, – is just not an easy novel to translate.* It is a magnificent satirical conceit to transpose the life of the fifteenth-century *bohemian troubador* French poet, François Villon, into the singer, poet and *Bohemian-with-a-capital-B*, Zderad. Fifteenth-century Villon is re-imagined here as a talented social misfit, exploring the Czech twentieth-century notion of escape from oppression, through *emigration within*. A particular triumph of translation is the rendering of Zderad's Villonesque ballade from the Czech into English in the typical rhyming scheme, including the envoi, on the subject of mankind's 'universal prostitution'.

The fine illustrations in this volume are by the author's second son, Jan, who wrote and directed the Pixar Oscar-winning 1997 short film *Geri's Game* and was the originator and co-director of Pixar's Oscar-winning 2007 film *Ratatouille*.

Josef Škvorecký would often identify Křesadlo, and not the better known Milan Kundera, as 68 Publishers' greatest writer, even calling him "entirely unique"†. However, Škvorecký is not Křesadlo's only high profile admirer to contribute to this volume.

Peter Pišťanek (1965–2015), the award-winning Slovak author of the *Rivers of Babylon* trilogy, often spoke of his admiration. In his lifetime, he published a number of articles about Křesadlo, collected here in the *Afterword*. In his allegorical piece, Pišťanek boldly places Křesadlo on a pedestal as "the greatest post-war Czech writer".

Pišťanek also alludes to Křesadlo's favourite armchair crusade: Milan Kundera. Křesadlo despised the former Stalinist and later professional dissident, as a morally challenged pseud. He would use pejorative allusions to Kundera for the names of his *anti-heroes* in later novels. Křesadlo did not limit venting his creative spleen on

---

* *The Secret Life of Cyprian Belva* [Skrytý život Cypriána Belvy, Prague, 2007] the quasi-sequel to *GraveLarks* contains long passages rendered in Glagolitic text and his science fiction odyssey [Austronautilia – Hvězdoplavba- Malá kosmická odyssea, Prague, 1995] comprises of 6575 verses of Homeric Greek, with a parallel Czech translation in hexameter.

† http://www.ce-review.org/00/37/interview37_skvorecky.html

Kundera alone. This particular novel's *antagonist* bears an undeniable resemblance to a former university classmate who – swimming adroitly with the changing tides like numerous others – enjoyed great Party patronage and became a well known academic philosopher. As Křesadlo reminds us, there are multiple sources of inspiration for the resulting 'psychophysical organ transplants'.*

To date, a further fourteen novels and three collections of short stories have been published in Czech. Still more works, including a collection of sonnets and a couple of opera librettos await publication. Together with his daughter, Eva, and originally under a different pseudonym, he translated a collection of poems by Czech Nobel Prize winner Jaroslav Seifert, which was published as *A Wreath of Sonnets* by Sixty-Eight Publishers' offshoot Larkwood Books, in 1987. He also wrote numerous articles for many science journals on general and specialist themes in psychology and on mathematical logic, with several non-fiction books published; not forgetting his artistic and musical creations.

History has not stopped in the thirty-one years since the original publication. The 1950s, satirised in GraveLarks, can seem hazy today, with terms like *dissident, Stalinist* or *Cold War* difficult to place. The new reader may find some helpful context in the reasons why the author chose his pseudonym, Jan Křesadlo.

Pinkava felt that if he published under his own name, he could bring his relatives in Czechoslovakia to the unwanted attention of (and random interrogation by) the secret police. Thus, a pseudonym of some sort was needed. His choice is telling: the name Jan is common enough and also significant in the history of Czech patriots and martyrs.† Far less common is the surname. The word *křesadlo* has more than one

---

* Milan Machovec (1925–2003), philosopher and philologist who taught at Charles University, Prague.

† In particular Jan Hus, the church reformer executed in Constance in 1415 and his opposite number, Jan Nepomucký, metaphorically resurrected during the counter-reformation, himself an early victim of the very Czech art of defenestration in 1393. Other noted name-holders include Jan Masaryk, who "accidentally fell" from a window at the Czech Foreign Ministry after assisting the fledgling Czechoslovak secret police with their enquiries in 1948; and more recently, Jan Palach who committed suicide at the top end of Wenceslas Square by setting himself alight in January 1969 and Jan Zajíc who did the same in February 1969, both in protest of the Warsaw Pact invasion of 1968.

meaning. It is a *flint-and-steel* fire-starter, which, in vernacular Czech, is regularly used as an idiom for a *troublemaker*. Crucially, the word *křesadlo* also contains the Czech soft consonant ř. Pinkava was very patriotic, and the letter ř, as in Antonín Dvořák, is uniquely Czech.

In choosing his pseudonym, Pinkava gave notice that he was a dissenting émigré writer, not shy of stirring up trouble for the regime and mindset that forced him and his family into exile, while raising a wry smile among his original Czech readers.

I trust this book, in this rendition, will make you laugh, even as you savour the writing and cringe at the story portrayed. It is, in the true sense of the word, awesome.

Michael Tate, Publisher
London, August 2015

FOREWORD

To Whom It May Concern   11 June 1987

    I consider Mr. Jan Křesadlo's /Dr. Václav Pinkava's/
novel published by my firm, the Sixty-Eight Publishers,
Corp., and entitled in the original Czech <u>Mrchopěvci</u>
to be one of the most original, shocking, truthful and
artistically very interesting works of contemporary Czech
fiction. It is profound, ironic, witty and - what is rare
in today's writing - it betrays a learned author who,
in spite of the width and depth of his knowledge, has
remained an acute observer of <u>real</u> life and <u>real</u> people.
It is not often that one finds, in fiction of any nation, a
portrayal of the Stalinist fifties that has been executed
with so much freshness, incisiveness, charming cynicism,
accuracy as Mr. Pinkava's novel. It is also devoid of any
sentimental seriousness and it makes excellent reading
even for those who are not interested in the political
background against which the macabre story is played out.

    I think that an English-language publication of this
novel would be regarded by those who know what literature
is all about as a discovery.

Josef Škvorecký
Novelist and Professor of Literature

PREAMBLE

The characters of this book correspond to real-life characters in that they likewise have a head, two arms and other body parts. They even have corresponding emotional states, I hope. They live in the same environment that afflicted fifteen million real people, too. So it would be quite a miracle if they didn't resemble some actual people.

But writing about real people, however useful, wasn't the purpose of this book. In keeping with the accepted rules of the trade, the main characters are complicated transplants of psychophysical organs, with care that the resulting mishmash be unrecognisable. As far as the character of 'the Man' is concerned, he is of course fictitious, but similar types do exist in real life, believe it or not.

Our 'Man', like Marxism itself, stems from three sources. His work, fate, hobbies etc., are all modelled on a real comrade, but all are infernally inflated, as if you were making a tiger out of a pussycat. This also applies to some of his personal preferences, which were modelled on a once existing person, in reality a simple bricklayer. The place of action is inspired by a report which once appeared in a foreign newspaper.

The dustman Döme is taken from life, but his criminal activity as described is completely fictitious from start to finish. I feel honour bound to stress this very much, just in case someone recognises him and starts causing trouble.

Figures of worldwide or state-wide significance, not directly referred to in the book, might take on various low-level forms of camouflage as appropriate (e.g. comrade Stalin). The same goes for incidental characters that just flit by and don't do anything embarrassing.

This book could, in places, be considered disgusting. Partly this comes with the spirit of that age, and partly I hope the disgusting bits aren't seen as an end in themselves. I also hope that they are balanced by other, more positive factors. This sort of concoction is in any case characteristic of life on this planet, which we've attempted to reflect here, to some extent at least, in all its true complexity.

The Author

Многие меня попросят
и теперь, пожалуй, спросят
Глупо так зачем шучу?
Что за дело вам! Хочу!

Пушкин : Царь Никита

Many folks take me to task
lately, even dare to ask:
Why this idiotic scheme?
What's your problem? Mine's the whim!

Pushkin : Czar Nikita[1]

I

Once upon a time…

It was after the year 1948, but still long before the period of the 'thaw,' as in so many other émigré novels.

The Comrades were still honeymooning with their imported Behemoth, pandering to its every wish and whim.

They outlawed most things, and those they couldn't ban they at least disfigured and ruined.

Even so, they left a few things alone, either till they got round to them, or till they got the point of them. Often their advisors hadn't had things quite like it at home, back in Asia, so it never occurred to them there could be such things in Europe.

Among these, for example, were our burial rites and connected practices, a fact which happens to be important for this little narrative.

Those that weren't around at the time for one reason or another should kindly note, that while the general standard of living was already dropping below the contemporary standard in the 'West,' it was still much higher than in the USSR and most of her other European satellites.

Apart from all this, despite being early summer – it was raining almost as though we were in England.

———

On the fringes of the City's vast burial grounds, which lie to the east of its centre, there are quite a few pubs. Since time immemorial people with a role to play in the act of burial have been regulars there. As we write these lines, four men were sitting in one such, their job being to provide four-part singing at those funerals where the bereaved had asked for it.

They were drinking tea with imitation rum, for the day was wet and cold, and they were waiting for the next funeral at which they were due to perform.

The expanse of the cemetery might well be likened to a great green lake, or small sea, and this foursome to shipwrecked sailors thrown up on its shores. In a slightly different sense they really were all washed up, because singing at funerals is no career at all.

The first tenor[*] had a head as bald as an ostrich egg, or perhaps Telly Savalas.[2]

He was quite decently dressed in a leather coat left behind by the Germans, and a turtleneck sweater. Once he'd had a good singing voice, but he'd spoilt it all through excessive drinking. Apart from funerary singing[3] he was a chorus reservist at the operetta, but his fate there had already been sealed because he had a tremolo like the vox humana stop on a romantic organ.

His face, which was strangely reminiscent of the bald-headed Pharisee in Titian's "The Tax Coin," was thickly embroidered with apoplectic veins.

He sat in silence, slowly sipping his tea and ersatz rum.

Let's call him Tůma.

The next man strongly resembled a parrot, or a caricature of a music teacher.

He was very short and had a limp, which of course wasn't apparent right now whilst he sat at the table. His walking stick with its rubber end was hanging by the handle's beak from the back of an empty chair.

He had thick spectacles and steely-grey hair that flowed down to his shoulders in a manner highly unusual for the period. The crown of his head was, by contrast, bald.

His face was also artistic, in a caricatured sort of way, with its delicate hooked nose and a childlike mouth.

He was, as they say, 'clean shaven', i.e. he sported three-day-old grey stubble.

This last applied, with necessary modifications, to the rest of the quartet too, as beards only came into fashion much later.

His hands were conspicuously tiny.

His peculiar appearance was a last reminder of those far-off days

---

[*] It was a male quartet proper, consisting of two tenors and two basses. There was no male alto, which survives only in Britain, her colonies and ex-colonies.

2

when he'd been a musical infant prodigy and a worthy focus of hopes run wild.

He was very bitter and cynical, detesting the Church and her hierarchy, although, truth be told, it was she who fed him, albeit meagerly.

In the quartet we're describing, his role was that of accompanist and first bass.

Why he wasn't more successful is difficult to guess, considering for example that he didn't drink.

One might expect, with a degree of optimism, that hidden in a drawer at home he could have some outstanding pieces: Compositions in a style far ahead of their time, féeric quartets, entrancing symphonies and the like, which would even now vindicate his bungled existence.

Unfortunately this was not so.

His church music, some of which had even been published, did in truth have virtuoso organ parts, yet otherwise it was as barren as a hollow nutshell.

He sat motionless with his greasy artistic hat in front of him, which resembled the excrement of some long since extinct giant animal; that of a Dinotherium, for instance.

To cap it all he had the improbable, Latin-sounding name of Turgo.

The next fellow had dark brown hair, which was only just greying at the temples and was groomed in a conventional manner.

He was lean and bony; his face, as if carved out of a piece of hardwood, wore a permanently troubled, almost weepy expression, crinkled as it was with numerous wrinkles running diagonally down it.

A gigantic Adam's apple, protruding from his sinewy neck, supported the supposition that he was the second bass of the quartet. From the side you could see he was almost totally chinless.

His hands, cradling the cup, seemed huge, yet unaccustomed to physical work. He wore a conspicuous and obviously cheap ring with a red stone, or more likely a piece of glass, set into it.

His shoes were like the drawers of a chiffonier.

To the Czech ear his name matched his face well, for he was called Krůta.[4]

He was listening with reverence to Turgo[*] who was in the process of explaining the difference between the "short" and the "split" pedals on old organs, in an irritated parrot-like squawk.

It was obvious that Turgo was a kind of foreman or boss here.

Like Turgo, Krůta too held the thankless and miserably paid post of church organist, in his case on the outskirts of the City.

Even so he was doing relatively well.

He had a motorbike on which he travelled to his engagements, and thanks to this increased mobility he was able to earn more than the others, who were condemned to use public transport.

Somewhere on the City's edge, indeed, beyond where it actually ended, he had a little cottage, possibly inherited from his parents, where he kept various small domestic animals such as rabbits, chickens and goats.

As opposed to Turgo, who was a fallen virtuoso, Krůta had only quite modest organ-playing skills, for he had started out as a locksmith. That, however, had long since ceased to matter amid the continuing decline of church music-making.

He was acquisitive and always on the make, but in a pedestrian and not very lucrative, small-time way.

Apart from organ-playing, 'carcassinging', petty black-marketeering etc., he was likewise an odd-jobbing locksmith, mechanic, tinker and so forth, on account of his overall dexterity.

His relatively good economic standing was reflected by the fact that, like Tůma, he had a leather jacket.

His rustic nature also showed up in his being religious, in a common-sense, un-philosophical way, looking upon the figures of the Catholic pantheon as fetishes, intended to bring him material gain.

His lachrymosely crinkled face was the result of a chronic personal condition, of which more later.

———

Let the fourth man, and our particular focus, having left him till last, be called Zderad.

He was still a youngster.

---

[*] Or perhaps to Turgono (from the Latin Turgo, Turgonis).

A kind of lunar and languorous pallor covered his regular and generally agreeable features, of a somewhat southern type.

He had dark hair, with the first hint of a future occipital tonsure, or bald patch around the crown.

His frame was solidly put together, but sagging.

His broad shoulders were covered by a modest, greasy raincoat.

As is apparent from the context, he occupied the remaining part within the quartet, namely that of second tenor.

It's true he had a pleasant and, as yet, still steady, somewhat flute-like voice, reminiscent of a decorous owlet, but he could neither reach the low- nor the high notes properly.

In a mixed choir he was able to remedy this imperfection by stretching his range with falsetto, yet could not last too long, forcing first tenor against three other gravelarks, without cover from above.

He was therefore permanently relegated to second tenor, which is always the pariah of the male chorus; for, if need be, virtually anyone can take the part, with the possible exception of those in possession of extraordinarily full and deep bass voices.

He was an outsider in other respects, too.

The youngest of the quartet, he had no income from other sources, and was a former intellectual to boot.

In times of plenty he'd never imagined making a living of any sort through music, and for this very reason his fellow degraded professionals looked down on him.

A few years ago the revolution's horror-machine happened to catch him in its cogwheels and eventually spewed him out, albeit without major disfigurement, but with enough scars to last him the rest of his life.

In the process of being spat out, Zderad grabbed onto the grave-larking raft, which he clung to firmly, since it was still marginally better than digging, or deburring castings in a factory; even though, if truth be told, it earned him even less.

————

The 'interment industry', for some reason overlooked by the revolutionary Humiliators of Space-time,[*] offered a kind of dreamy, melancholy asylum.

Large city cemeteries are in general pleasant, tranquil institutions.

Compared to ordinary parks, they have the advantage that most people don't come here for a stroll with their families, since you're not allowed to holler, play football, or ride a push scooter. Dogs are, in our central European tradition, also excluded.

What you will find here are beautiful old and sagacious trees, somehow calmer and more dignified than those in normal parks, not besieged by ice-cream men or peanut sellers.

Undisturbed, birds and small animals live here in their incredible diversity of species.

Here, one can go for long walks, without meeting needlessly many people. The more remote corners are devoid of straying feet, for long hours or even days at a stretch.

Numerous works of stone-masonry offer to educate in many respects, and the subtle melancholy of impermanence breathes forth from the inscriptions.

There are no posters to be found, exhorting one to "vigilance and alertness" and the fulfilment of the Five-year Plan.

Here, the slogan "The Soviet Gravedigger – our Model" cannot be erected, simply for reasons of personal safety.[†]

Similarly, it is difficult to fight for "more and better" funerals.[‡]

Owing to the fact that "Lenin still lives and will live on"[§] we are not confronted with his Tartaric features here.

An analogous situation also applies to morgues, funeral chapels and to procedures accompanying the various types of ceremony.

Life, throbbing with "Joyous Production Plans," pulsates beyond the cemeteries and looks on them from afar with superstitious fear;

---

[*] This refers to the heroes of the Soviet revolutionary song: "We shall humiliate space and time, we young masters of the Earth..."

[†] Once in a mental asylum, in fact, in the psychiatric teaching unit of the University, the inmates erected a placard "The Soviet Madman—our Model," which was of course hastily removed. This really did happen.

[‡] In contrast to the universal formula of the fifties: "For More and Better X," the X being some kind of product or service or the like.

[§] From a poem by Mayakovsky.

a wonder it doesn't subconsciously make the sign of the cross.

Flocks of "Christ-almighties," which festive citizens let loose from their mouths only surreptitiously and secretly, here proudly jut up in their immobile, immutable physical form.

The taboo of Death is stationed at the cemetery gate, with a blazing sword like Archangel Gabriel at the Gates of Paradise.

Most of the time, it efficiently repels all the revolutionary busybodies.

In a cemetery there is no sense of time, or rather, not much of one.

Let us make one last observation; our narrative is set in an epoch when it is not yet fully appreciated or discovered that cemeteries might be used for the purposes of human rights demonstrations and their subsequent dispersion.

Therefore, as of yet, everything said about the cemetery hereto, held true practically without exception.

––––––

Zderad had instantly appreciated this situation, by an intuitive act of cognition, without any discursive reasoning.

At that time the term 'emigration within' had not yet been publicised or probably had not even been invented.* Nevertheless if there is a place and occupation from whence it is best and safest to ignore the merry present day, it is undoubtedly a cemetery and all things connected with it.

From this we may infer that Zderad was quite an intelligent young man, and practical in his own way, yet rather eccentric, as he tended to apply his discernment in an untraditional, un-Czech and materially fruitless manner.

––––––

At the time of writing, the quartet of funerary singers we've just described was sitting in the pub, drinking tea with ersatz rum and chatting; Turgo holding court about short and split pedals, whilst

---

* A Czech or perhaps generalised Soviet colonial term: Such an émigré withdraws inward and ignores the political realities around as much as possible. One of the most famous and radical "inner émigrés" was the poet Vladimir Holan who never left his house for over fifteen years.

and meanwhile, outside, it was bucketing down.

Zderad had before him, as well as his tea, a piece of manuscript paper which he was covering with notes, pausing from time to time to whistle and hum.

The widow of the 'dear deceased' had ordered the somewhat suspect and dangerous song "Ach synku, synku,"* which had finally been permitted, albeit with a certain embarrassment, by the Communal Funeral Services.

Given that the song had become obscure, and thanks to the typical organisational muddle, Turgo had forgotten to bring the respective song-sheets (if indeed he'd had them). Furthermore, the quartet members knew no mutually compatible four-part arrangement by heart. Having been reprimanded by his comrades, Turgo took umbrage in a hysterical, artistic way and refused to arrange the song on the spot, although he could have done it very well, and usually did when the need arose.

Zderad thus took up the task, partly because he seemed to be the most capable one after Turgo, and partly because he wanted to show that he could be useful in, and worthy of, such exalted company.

Zderad had never attended courses in harmonising, but he had clucked away in choirs since his grammar-school days, so that all the respective turns and tricks jumped into his head in a quite automatic and natural way. Frequently he had no idea about the names of the respective chords and harmonic connections, yet he was perfectly capable of using them all without any difficulty or mistake.

This is not to say that he was especially gifted in this respect. Such talent could be (and I hope it still can be) found in the Czech Lands round every corner.

Having traced a treble and a bass clef with a self-assured flourish on two staves, one beneath the other, he joined them together with a fat baroque bracket, writing the time signature ¾ twice, stacked one under another.

After that, inspired by the apoplectic lustre of Tůma's head, he

---

* This folk-song "Oh sonny boy" used to be a favourite with T.G. Masaryk, the first president of Czechoslovakia and a much-loved public figure. The song was therefore more or less taboo with the communist régime. It is not an exclusively funereal song but may be sung at funerals.

made a quick decision, and added two flats in each stave:

Krůta could take the bottom E-flat with ease, whilst the top A was getting progressively more and more inhumane to ask of poor Tůma.

The preambles over, Zderad attacked the arrangement with great gusto:

At that time Zdeněk Nejedlý's[*] star shone at its zenith, and therefore the more Wagnerian and Victorian anything sounded, the more Socialist-Realist, and "closer to the people" it was.

Zderad was now putting this uncompromising and unequivocal principle of "anti-bourgeois aestheticism" into Practice, which, as we memorised at school, is the only Test of Theory.

A chromatic parody quickly grew beneath his hands, aglow with the whole gamut of colours, like stuffed parrots under the glass bell in the parlour of a patriotic industrialist during the last days of the Austrian Empire.

After all, most of the gravelarks' repertoire was of this type, thus underlining the ossified tastes of the gouty old petrefact in his ministerial chair.

Having perpetrated the last plush obscenity on the penultimate phrase *"Daddy asks i-if you've"* (G minor, E-flat minor, B-flat major, G-flat major, B-flat major again) Zderad concluded the final cadence *"finished ploughing?"* reasonably traditionally and handed the paper over to Turgo.

The myopic Maestro lifted the paper to his nose with severity and scrutinised it carefully.

He had most probably intended to reject the greenhorn's arrangement, but they were pressed for time.

"Fine," he therefore uttered unenthusiastically, "let's have a go at it, quietly."

The carcassingers gathered behind Turgo's shoulders and struck up a soft pianissimo.

---

* Zdeněk Nejedlý was an old musicologist of granite views who happened to be a communist, and so became the first minister of education after the coup. He dictated musical taste to the whole country. For personal reasons he suppressed Dvořák and adored Smetana and Wagner. He explained his decision in Marxist jargon. This was especially funny, as his taste was extremely conservative and "bourgeois".

The sad, clean, clear folk melody prevailed even against the Wagnerian plush, in the same way that the view of Prague Castle miraculously stands up to any number of postcards and commemorative mugs, without being degraded by them.

Everyone in the pub knew what it was basically all about, a phenomenon we refer to as 'a common cultural heritage'.

The barmaid shed a tear.

At the back of the room some lout lifted his attentive and vigilant, doberman-like muzzle.

But before he had decided on taking action, the quiet funeral song expired with the last tonic chord, which Krůta on his own initiative propped up with a still quite decent bottom B-flat.

The funerary singers then rushed out into the rain in the general direction of the cemetery.

The thug with the doberman-like head carried on sniffing for a while, but then calmed down.

Either he took the activity to be permitted, or he simply did not want to get soaked.

"… the quartet of funerary singers we've just described …"

II

Roughly to the northwest of the cemetery seas are slums, or at least there were, back then.

Incidentally, I doubt that the Comrades have got rid of them since, although it has most likely been part of the Plan for the last thirty years or so. The erection of monuments, mausolea and representative edifices is surely more important, and besides: *"Vremya ne khvatit."**

Although, quite frankly, anything is possible.

The slummy streets bear the names of ancient dukes and rulers and similar personages; however this doesn't help them one jot.

If you walk directly north from the northern wall of the most beautiful graveyard, you'll arrive at a pond where toads congregate for orgies in March.

Later we find tadpoles there among rusty pots and waterweed.

Beyond the pond, rather more westwards, we find bulging bald squatty hillocks, lacerated with various craters.

In these craters, by way of contrast, it is people who creep together, largely during the summer months, and exclusively in the dark.

From the top of one of these hillocks you can see into a courtyard formed by three houses, built roughly in the shape of an incomplete square.

There, deep below us, we see a well, a yard with a carpet-beating frame and a feeble little garden consisting mainly of ivy.

A series of galleries, partially made of wood and with only half the original windowpanes, wind round the inner walls of the houses, forming about three levels. From the galleries one can then enter the slummy dens.

In contrast to Krůta's relative affluence, we find on one of the doors here an enamel tablet, on which is inscribed in calligraphic

---

* Время не хватит. There's no hurry. A famous Russian phrase akin to "mañana" script the name:

Zderad

Here, alas, it is his lot to dwell.

Zderad's abode consists of a single room, shaped most appropriately like a coffin.

You see, the two shorter walls are not, as one would expect, part of a standard rectangle, but are shaped like a symmetrical anisoscelic hexagon, just like the shorter sides of our coffins when covered with their lids.

The longer wall is barely fifteen paces long.

The width of the room is about four or five of the same units of measurement.

Apart from the door, the room has two more openings; a window onto the balcony and another, slightly larger one, on the opposite end, looking onto the street.

The room is divided roughly in half by a sort of curtain, running along a slightly rusty rod on equally rusty little rings.

In the half nearer to the door is a miserable looking cooker and an assortment of kitchen jumble including a table and a couple of chairs.

In the other half are two sofas of sorts, each one along a wall, and a baby's cot of the familiar wooden cage variety.

All our senses are struck by a feeling of poverty, yet less pronounced than that which existed before World War II, or that which still exists in the Soviet Union.

Indeed in the year 1945, a Red Army officer visited another dwelling in the same house and concluded that this was the home of an "inzhenier" – a technical graduate. He left behind a red haired daughter called Nadia, but in this instance it was not a case of rape.

At that time, though, Zderad was still living in a decent citizen's flat with his parents in an entirely different quarter of the City.

*"Time drew the curtain and changed the world,"** however, and all that

* "Čas oponou trhnul — a změněn svět!" A quotation from the real Neruda, the real poet, i.e. Jan Neruda (1834–1891 in Prague), poet, novelist and journalist, a poor man of

remained of that period of Zderad's life, apart from memories, was that little enamelled tablet outside his door.

———

The weather cleared towards evening.

The scent of wet verdure emanating from the graveyards and empty building plots wafted all the way here.

The sky was as mild as a cow's eye.

Zderad was lying on one of the sofas, doing nothing.

His wife, a relatively presentable young woman of freckled complexion and strawberry-blonde hair, with a minor hip luxation on the right side, was away attending some meeting, for she made her living by teaching at secondary level and therefore had to cultivate her "cadre profile".*

Their child, a curly-haired three-year-old boy called Záviš, was away at his weekly boarding crèche, nursery school or kindergarten, depending on what it is called when it's for three year olds, which I forget.

Zderad was pleasantly alone.

This world, although not worth much, is definitely not the worst of all possible worlds, and does provide pleasant moments, even for those whom it treats with total contempt most of the time.

At that moment, the sweet melancholy of resignation had descended upon the slums, and was filling up Zderad's den to the brim, like some invisible liquid.

An archangel with a fish's tail was, it seemed, practising on his

---

a poor background, no diplomat, no waffler, no snob, no Stalinist, no political creation, no tuxedo revolutionary, no thief of names.

* Cadre profile – a communist invention to control people. Every employer has a 'cadre department'; (separate from the personnel one) presided over by a 'cadre referee' or officer who keeps files on people with respect to their political reliability. The profile influences everything: chance of employment, promotion and general status. A teacher's profile is particularly sensitive. The files were difficult to keep until recently, when the West sold its computer technology to the Soviet bloc. The cadre profile goes with you to your next post and the police keep a copy of it in order to prevent possible bribery of the officer to keep out damaging information. Not much use until the recent advent of technology.

translucent Last Judgement trumpet, to improve his embouchure technique for that particular gig; but instead of severe fanfares he was producing something akin to sensuously wailing blues.

Shadows of swifts swept across the pale, rose- and green-tinged facing wall of the coffin dwelling, and their vertiginous shrieks alternately came, and went.

Stretched out in his lair, Zderad was projecting to his inner eye the scenes of his prematurely done-for life, the flavour of which – nevertheless – was, in essence, sweet.

The bitterness and sourness which had previously tended to fill him had retreated into the background, and now merely added an agreeable flavour, akin to that of herbal teas.

Images were rising from the depths of his memory and floating past, like reflections on water.

His entire life to date was mirrored in them in a simplified and condensed form, hinting that perhaps it did have a meaningful flow after all, albeit incomprehensible to the limited human intellect.

It is said that this is how scenes of a lifetime parade before the mind's eye of the dying, taking, in objectively measured time, the merest instant.

————

Perhaps it would be interesting to follow this stream of phantasms, and thus initiate the consumer into Zderad's history and inner world.

One method of achieving this is to relate the memories drop by drop, mixed in with depictions of immediate events.

This literary method, although outstanding, is not going to be deployed here, as we feel it would not be appropriate.

A certain impatience also prevents us from giving Zderad's past in detail in one sitting, and therefore, we shall restrict ourselves to a mere outline, as we did when describing his habitation.

We disagree with those thick novels where the histories of all the main characters are narrated in great detail, often covering several generations beginning with grandpa, whilst the action proper is shrunk into the last third or fifth of the book. Apart from the fact that the consumer is taken for a ride, we consider this modality of literary production a trifle boring.

Zderad watched himself growing up in an average and reasonably well-off family as a talented lad, justifying the best possible expectations.

He saw himself sailing relatively smoothly through the Protectorate[*] and emerging at the other end, heading for better tomorrows.

Then there was a crash, and down came the curtain.[†]

With the feeling that this was impossible, and that it could only be a dream, Zderad watched the total destruction of all his destinies up until then.

His father, a tolerable despot with outdated opinions, disappeared one fine day just like a paper kite that's broken free of its line.

And, just like a kite disappearing skywards pulls its tail away after it, so Father had pulled away with him everything which had constituted Zderad's life, present and future.

Drastic accounts of communist dungeons are common these days, and you're no doubt sick of them; we ourselves have no plans to wallow in them either. It should be noted, however, that Zderad's father was picked up one fine day in his office, and later it was announced that he had committed suicide while in investigative detention.

No one ever learnt why he was being investigated or what the investigation was about.

Zderad's mother didn't survive it.

Zderad's sister vanished without a trace.

One could maintain the more humane and agreeable hypothesis that she managed to escape to the West. However, the strong contingent of sadists within the rank and file of State Security also lends support to other alternative interpretations.

In the process of class purification, the little property that Zderad's family had possessed also disappeared somehow, as did Zderad's studies, naturally.

National service then followed.

Probably owing to some administrative mistake, Zderad was not

---

[*] The Protectorate of Bohemia and Moravia: a satellite state of Nazi Germany, created out of the western part of Czechoslovakia by Hitler in 1938.

[†] In 1945 the democratic Czechoslovak Republic was re-established, only to become a Soviet satellite less than three years later, by means of a coup, with the tacit consent of the West.

sent to the Blackies,* and served normally as a private with a rifle and so on, merely for the prescribed two years.

In due course, Zderad found himself, all but destitute, outside the barrack gates.

———

It was during this phase of his life that Zderad entered his present, quasi-posthumous state.

The agony ceased, and was replaced by the calm of a sweet, living death.

Some philosopher, whose name, nationality and historical niche Zderad had long since forgotten, seems to have asserted that mental vibrations draw together the props required for our external fate.

Perhaps there's something to it, as, from that point on, Zderad's work started to manifest the corresponding traits.

In his mind's eye he sees himself on the surface of a lake, which bears the name 'Posel'.

A little tin boat, driven by a small diesel motor, is chugging dreamily, and on the horizon the ruins of an old castle are emerging.

With its steel jaws, the boat bites at the reeds; Zderad then pushes the cut reed-stacks to one side with a pitchfork.

A heron floats silently to its roost, dragging its feet across the faint azure of the sky.

In the reeds a carp munches with its jade jaws, and Jano the Slovak at the tiller intones an obscene song.

In the evening, day shift over, when the lake has filled with stars, Zderad slips into the water and slowly swims across.

After a warm sunny day, it is then that the water is at its most pleasant,

---

* The Blackies have nothing to do with racism (which doesn't exist in the Soviet bloc, of course). They were soldiers serving with the auxiliary technical corps. They served without weapons and worked on building-sites, in mines etc. They had black epaulettes, hence the name. They could be kept there indefinitely, and frequently were, owing to the legal status of the armed forces. The corps also served as a kind of alternative prison for those whom it would be difficult to indict and to sentence, and who weren't important enough to justify the effort. Many priests, for instance, spent many years with the Blackies.

and a mere kilometre of comfortable swimming can't tire a strong young man.

Yet, before he takes off for the smooth expanse, Zderad finds a piece of plank in the willows and strikes it sharply against the surface of the water.

On hearing that signal, at the other end of the lake, Sylva lowers herself into the water; a short half-hour later they are on the little island.

This world is really not the worst of all possible worlds.

————

— "Posel," Zderad can hear aloud, within himself.

" Ὕπαγε, νίψαι ἐς τὴν κολυβήθραν τοῦ Σιλωάμ
(ὃ ἑρμενεύεται, ἀπεσταλμένος) … "*

"What are you blabbering again," says a grumpy female voice. "You woke me up."

————

Zderad came to with a start and realised that he had dozed off, and that it was already dark; Sylva had returned from her meeting and gone to bed on the other couch.

Although he was not hungry, he realised with some regret that she hadn't bothered to wake him up for supper, presumably because that night there wasn't any, — and that the romance of the lake had long since vanished.

In fact it had fizzled out extremely quickly.

Anyway, Zderad had become aware of this while still a labourer with Fishing Industries, National Enterprise.

The mystical Naiad, who used to emerge on warm nights from the depths of the lake, turned out to be a quite prosaic farmer's daughter, who was studying at a teacher training college, and regularly spent her vacations at home in the village on the other side of the watery expanse.

————

* "Go wash in the pool of Silóam, (which is by interpretation, sent.) He went his way therefore, and washed, and came seeing." Quote from St John IX,7; Posel means "envoy" or "messenger". The lake had a biblical name, as do many places in Bohemia.

When he first saw her in daylight, and for the very first time in her clothes, Zderad was amazed by her evident ordinariness.

The fact that her face was swollen with crying and pregnancy and that she was accompanied by her father, an austere and unpleasant Evangelical, also known as a Ram or Helvete, contributed to this, of course.

He also noticed that she walked with a limp, a feature which had not been apparent, either during swimming or on their reed-bed on the island.

It was probably precisely this defect which had driven her into the arms of an impecunious unskilled labourer without a future.

From the very beginning, Zderad had never attempted to hide his misfortunes from her, although he could have easily pretended that he was a student, or that he had some kind of intellectual profession.

Many sages have frequently, and very appropriately, stressed that it is practically impossible to assess the class profile of a stark naked person. The story of Mr. Božetěch, as told by one of our literary greats, is a case in point.[5]

He would tell her practically everything, as they lay under the moon and stars, listening to the nocturnal voices of the lake, because, apart from the main aim of their meetings, there was also his pressing need to talk to someone intimately.

This candour, or what the worldly-wise would call idiocy, also made it possible for them to find him easily, once the autumn weather had interrupted their meetings.

On the other hand, he himself knew nothing about Sylva, perhaps not even her name, as this was more convenient for his romantic foolishness.

The brutal materialisation of the nymph shook him.

It showed that the dreamy postmortality of his existence was actually extremely vulnerable and could be smashed into splinters at any moment by so-called objective reality; which was unpleasant in itself, and also from the viewpoint of the situation which had arisen.

The daytime, prosaic Sylva also had other shortcomings:

Her intelligence could not be judged to be terribly high, and she made up for this lack with an irksome, schoolmarmy instructiveness. Unfortunately, at the same time she was bright enough to be aware that Zderad was naturally superior in this respect, and later she frequently enjoyed showing him that this didn't impress her in the slightest.

Apart from this, like all freckled reddish blondes she had a tendency to sweaty redolence, which fact had also not had a chance to reveal itself in good time. (Let us add, that the imperialist decadence of antiperspirants was, at the time and place of our narrative, still a thing of the future.)

On the positive side of Zderad's instant encumbrance we could go on to say that Sylva was a very strong woman, both physically, and in so-called character. This was borne out by the way the above situation had arisen.

Under the circumstances, it was also highly disadvantageous, since she clung on like a leech, while fending off all objections to him, including those of her own family.

Once exposed, Zderad's aquatic affair became quite the local sensation around the lake and environs – another reason why it was impossible for him to slip the noose.

The whole affair could of course be viewed with understanding, and even envy, but this didn't help, indeed rather the opposite.

Pedestrian, timid spirits always launch themselves with rage at anything which parades their own boring nothingness before their eyes, provided they may dare to do so, which in this case they certainly could.

Sylva's rustic relatives also showed characteristic obduracy.

The outcome of all this was Zderad's present situation:

A bizarre, dead-end job in the city, a tired, irritable and by no means de-luxe wife, a coffin-dwelling in the slums, and a little son they could not properly care for, and therefore had to leave to the tender mercies of socialist education in the weekday nursery.

This fact caused Zderad chronic worry because he had once read books on psychology, and therefore knew that separation from parents has an adverse effect on little monkeys, and therefore, most likely on children, too.

———

"It's nothing, go back to sleep," said Zderad morosely, albeit apologetically, to keep the peace. "I dozed off. I had a bad day.

It rained. The money I got today is in the jug. Forty crowns.

I kept some for the tram and for food.

Wake me up in the morning when you go to school. I have to go to the other end of town.

I had to tell you this, sorry. I'll just get undressed. Don't be cross with me for waking you up."

Sylva only muttered something.

Zderad got up quietly and with great caution, so as not to make any noise. In darkness, he changed into a slightly tattered pair of pyjama trousers and a kind of shirt which he used as a top, which had long ago become a shadow of itself.

Then he buried himself in the blankets.

Bitterness and sourness, mollified at the hour of sunset by sweet resignation, now swamped him like the deep waters of Lake Posel, icy and reeking of mud.

He sighed, whispered a coprolalic oath, and entered the inner spaces of his mind.

He appeared to be lying in the rain on the edge of a dense, dark emptiness in which his outstretched arms could reach nothing.

After a while he finally went under and for a few hours his consciousness was smothered in the arms of merciful sleep.

———

He was woken up by the sound of a hollow ringing purl, which he at first mistook for the alarm clock.

The "Preamble" states that this book is somewhat disgusting in certain parts, and this is about to happen now.

If you wish, you may easily skip this section, with minimal detriment to your understanding of the plot.

One of the disadvantages of living in slummy dens is the shortage of hygienic facilities.

Note that when describing Zderad's coffin we never mentioned a water-tap, or bathroom, or anything similar.

Water had to be drawn from a single tap outside in the corridor, and every morning and at other peak times there was a queue for it.

The fact that in the house in question every gallery or floor had its own tap was a relative luxury. It was the same with the toilet – there was one lurking at the far end of each gallery.

Owing to the fact that slums are frequently inhabited by small-time criminal specimens (large-scale crooks, as we know, usually inhabit villas or mansions), it is advisable to lock the doors of the coffins carefully every night. Unlocking them repeatedly during the night would disturb other members of the household and the neighbours. It is also inconvenient to traipse outside at night, depending on the weather, of course.

These circumstances give increased prominence to the age-old institution of the chamber-pot, which, as we know from the relevant literature, was already known to the ancient Romans.

The morphology, sociology, history-of-art aspects, and other scholarly and scientific features of chamber-pots are fascinating; unfortunately they have no place in the given context.

Some rare specimens made of fine china, adorned with ornaments and jocular inscriptions, are frequently shown to tourists at former, or still functioning, seats of nobility at home and abroad.

After this digression the origin of the ringing purl becomes clear, without any need for explicit explanation.

The image of a woman pissing into a chamber-pot aroused Zderad sexually, a fact which is probably of no great surprise to the average male reader. Anyway, there is a book written by a Swiss psychiatric know-all, which, under the inconspicuous title of "Trieb und Kultur",* deals with nothing but this somewhat distasteful, yet real, side of the human and animal psyche. Under the pretext of science it also features a lot of pornographic pictures of micturition.

However, he did not dare to turn around and open his eyes in order not to startle his lawful wife or offend her finer feelings.

---

* Drive and Culture

Women are no doubt also lecherous, but they often insist on various rituals and tokens, which, pitifully, men have to observe if they wish to achieve sexual intercourse.

Instead, he pondered about whether or not to make a sexual advance on his wife after the physiological process was over.

Poor wives are, as a rule, morose and worn out, betrayed in their hopes and so on, and they submit to their husbands only out of fear; for the randy primitive knows how to force submission, disregarding the emotional devastation it causes, neighbours' gossip, and so on.

In Zderad's case, however, the combination of an educated mind and a proletarian pocket was highly non-conducive in this respect.

Despite his considerable desire, he did not want to risk rejection and thus deliberated whether he shouldn't rather imagine a mountaineering caper up a church spire or an overhanging cliff, and then fall asleep again.

This excellent psychological technique to counter sexual arousal had been advised to him by a certain Jesuit, in the days when he still went to confessions and took the Holy Church as gospel.

As is often the case, lust won, and groping with his hands, Zderad stumbled across the gap to his conjugal bed or couch.

Surprisingly, Sylva received him without protest, albeit without passion, and they cohabited to the accompaniment of the fanfares of dawn.

Zderad, however, remained blithely ignorant of the significance of this fact.

III

"Where's Tůma?" said Turgo in his parrot-like way.

"I bet he's pissed again, the idiot – he's totally unreliable.

We'll wait five minutes.

Luckily there isn't as much going on here as at the Central so it doesn't matter.

If he doesn't turn up then we'll have to start without him.

Zderad, there's nothing else for it – you'll have to take the first. I'll take it down a semitone for you.

Krůta, you sing it the way you know it, or from the score.

And I suppose I'll have to improvise, so that when there's a third it doesn't sound empty. And the organ will help. The singing's just in the chapel and old Voves has no ear for music. He won't have a clue whether there's four, three or two of us singing. So we won't tell him and we'll split the money.

At eleven we're back at the Central, I suppose the fool will turn up there. Let's go lads! What an idiot!"

Promoted to first tenor, Zderad had an unpleasant feeling of butterflies in the stomach.

In reality it was no big deal: there would only be a couple of people in the chapel, it was no fancy funeral, the priest had no ear for music and the organ was the only accompaniment, so he really couldn't make a mess of it.

First come the responses – that was only unisono, then some kind of "Silent grew thy lips and features," there was only an A, so that would be A-flat, he could manage that from time to time.

— Even if it did crack, it was no big deal anyway.

— We are no opera singers, just gravelarks, the bums of the music trade. So why the stage fright, damn it?

He felt as if he was about to leap out of his skin. And there was nothing happening. He wasn't hungry. Sylva had even made him an unusually good breakfast that morning. Bread with goose-fat and liver, obviously from home ... it looks like the old Ram is softening up after all – and that night, for the first time in ages – that usually helps against anxiety.

— And he had slept well, too.

— So why the devil feel such tension? Even his palms were starting to sweat – a thing unknown.

— Darn it!

— Really, a man has so little control over his own body and soul.

———

Then he saw Him.

Directly under the organ loft as they were going up.

In fact, he had somehow forgotten about Him.

Yesterday, as far as he could remember, He wasn't around.

He used to turn up before, but Zderad kept telling himself that it must be some crackpot who had nothing to do, had a disability pension and liked going to funerals.

It was strange, though, that with the number of City funerals there must be, He so often appeared in the same places as Zderad, but maybe He just liked male quartets.

Maybe, though they weren't the only funerary singers.

Zderad himself knew of at least another three groups.

Anyway, it was possible.

What was strange, though, was that Zderad noticed the Man in the first place.

The world is full of people, after all.

He always stood like that; either in the chapel or at the grave, to one side among the gravestones.

There was nothing special about Him, except maybe those watery eyes, yet something about Him made Zderad feel sort of tense and faint. He always felt the Man was staring straight at him.

Every time, before He appeared, Zderad felt a strange, icy anxiety. Sometimes, even before the Man appeared, anxiety and tension would presage his arrival.

All that would still have been all right, but once, the Man had even followed him, at a distance.

At the time Zderad had turned, and headed straight for Him.

Then a tram had got in the way; and when it had gone, the Man wasn't there anymore.

"Maybe I'm imagining it," Zderad thought. "I've got a persecution complex. I'm beginning to crack up. Maybe He wasn't following me at all, just happened to be going in the same direction."

— (So why had He disappeared so quickly?)

— Ah well, like the saying goes *'let the horse decide, he has the bigger head for it.'* Let's just leave it at that.

Let us not forget that Zderad was a young man, and as such he was still quite light-hearted, despite his unfavourable fate thus far.

He satisfied himself with the idea that it was only a strange coincidence and did not think about the Man much more.

— A snout?

— What could He do to him, now?

— After all They didn't even sentence him back when … even though at the time it looked as if They were going to.

— Once he was ruined, in terms of "class," it seemed that he was of no further interest to Them.

— And anyway, They must have watched him closely during his two years in the army and must have realised that he was harmless.

— But then, not even the devil would trust 'em. The Lord and devious minds move in mysterious ways. But what about the fact that He's turned up here as well? A place They don't normally come to?

———

On his way up to the organ loft, Zderad had to pass right by the Man, and he had the feeling that the cadaverous horror which was wafting over him was much stronger from close by.

The Man was unashamedly staring at him, there was no doubt about that.

He must have been over thirty, closer to forty, and fairly large.

It is difficult to describe His facial features, as there was nothing distinctive about them.

He was blond, of that washed out, pale variety, with hair and skin of almost the same, yellowish, maggot-like colour.

Although most fair people darken with age, this does not usually apply to this particular type. The Man's hair was still completely straw-coloured, or tending towards ashen in hue, but He didn't have much left.

His mouth was wide, soft, with something frog-like about it.

His nose was inconspicuous, most probably straight.

In contrast, His ears were distinctive, round, and although they were not large, they stood out, somewhat like those of the Good Soldier Švejk in Lada's illustrations.[6]

The most striking thing about Him, however, was – His eyes.

These sort of eyes occur most often in a certain category of spotted dogs and rabbits, and often they only have one such eye while the other one is dark.

The eyes of some fish are also similar, as are the eyes of albinotic jackdaws and buzzards.

The eyes were watery-looking, blue-grey, frog-like in shape and appeared to be blind.

The Man's posture was a little hunched, as if slinking; like a timid dog, and yet, there was something threatening about it.

— Like a hyena.

It sounds cheap and exaggerated, but that's how it was.

It is interesting that some forms of artistic kitsch really do occur in nature, such as for example golden and scarlet sunsets.

I challenge anyone to explain to me why it never offends good taste in the original.

However, if you prefer, the Man did not carry himself like a hyena.

He was always dressed rather well; conspicuously so for the time and place of our narrative.[*]

— 'What the hell!' … thought Zderad as he stepped up to the railing

---

[*] In the Soviet bloc of the fifties, good clothes were considered bourgeois and nearly a crime i.e. as far as ordinary people were concerned. Later the official doctrine became more tolerant of fashion, but by that time normal people could not afford good clothing any more. Thus, if one saw a conspicuously well-dressed man in Prague, he was either a foreigner, or a star of some kind, a public figure, or a secret policeman. The foreigner would not speak Czech, or at least not good Czech, the star one would recognise. If neither applied it had to be one of Their boys.

of the loft.

The Man was now standing slightly more to the front, nearer to the altar, and was staring, quite openly staring, at the loft.

But at that moment Turgo struck the organ keys and the funeral ceremony began.

———

The effort involved in singing the first tenor enabled Zderad to forget the Man.

He also didn't take any notice of Him after, at the Central Cemetery, although He was there again, and again He was staring in that watery and albinotic, buzzard-like way.

Tůma, you see, did not turn up even there, and his temporary substitute had his mouth full of work in order to sing in an unnatural range.

They cursed Tůma, but were ashamed of themselves later.

By that time, Tůma was already in the bosom of the Lord, for he had suffered a fatal stroke; that morning.

———

Tůma was later replaced by a man called Kukula, a tiny individual with a beautiful voice, who really did deserve a better deal in life.

He was also, like Zderad, a former intellectual, because he was a failed priest.

He had, however, left before the advent of the Joyful Present, so in his case the ascendance of the Just World-Order had no direct influence on his downfall.

After all, he could always say that he had parted company with the Church, comrades, and this would in fact have been an advantage.

But it would appear that it hadn't occurred to him to do this, or that he was too stubborn to do anything of the kind.

Although he was highly musical, in other respects he was a bit of a fool, and one could not have a conversation with him about anything, as Zderad found out very soon, to his disappointment.

All this is just a digression anyway, as Kukula is not an important figure in our little narrative, although he must of necessity continue to appear.

By way of another digression, let us make the observation that Tůma's funeral occurred without the assistance of our gravelarks.

We don't even know how his burial took place. But what is certain is that he couldn't have afforded a funeral with singing, and his life-long colleagues didn't consider him worth losing what little money they could earn elsewhere, at the time of his funeral. The youthfully idealistic Zderad had made a timid suggestion of this nature, but it got him nowhere.

This sort of thing happens very frequently, and I hope it does not surprise you.

Expressions of friendship, loyalty and so on, move us precisely because they are unusual and unexpected. The utter, however meta-phorical, ritual defecation of the gravelarks upon Tůma's coffin was an event to be expected with the highest probability, and that's why it leaves us completely unmoved.

———

The events concerning Tůma and the mild curiosity aroused by Kukula enabled Zderad to forget the Man.

Indeed, He had also stopped appearing the very day after the tenor's stroke.

Zderad's mind was in fact occupied by other, more intimate events, which he followed with relative pleasure.

It seemed as if Sylva had somehow come back to life.

Although she seemed to have to attend more meetings than usual these days, she didn't complain of tiredness and dissatisfaction and was even quite nice to her husband.

Their marital life revived to such an extent that beneath the mechan-ical routine one could almost recognise glimpses of their long-gone lakeside romance. She was even somehow prettier, which Zderad attributed to the revitalisation of their relations.

Suddenly, as if by magic, there seemed to be enough to eat in the coffinous den, something which had never been the case before. This, it seemed, was being sent by the old evangelical Ram, or rather his horrified wife.

It was to be hoped that eventually they would soften completely and shower the undesirable son-in-law's family with even greater mounds of homestead plenty.

Apparently, he was still fiercely resisting all attempts to be made to join the farming collective, though at the time no-one really knew how collectivisation would finally end or what course it would take, and so Zderad didn't worry about the possible, and objectively probable fate of his father-in-law; because he knew nothing about it.

He even hoped that, in time, he would be forgiven, and invited in person to partake of the 'Egyptian jars of buttermilk'.

Zderad ascribed the change in his wife's behaviour to an improvement in her relations with her parents, and didn't think much about it.

The days rolled on like golden rounds of peasant cake, and the nights blossomed once more with velvety blooms.

This world really did not seem to be the worst of all possible worlds.

————

That day it was warm but cloudy.

It is on such days that ants usually swarm, if it is late summer of course.

Zderad finished his day's stint, pocketed his meagre wage, and set off for home.

On the way he had to avoid a crowd of people, possibly leaving from another funeral, and so he made a detour along the footpaths between the graves.

At that moment the Man tugged at his sleeve.

He stepped out soundlessly from behind a tombstone, stretched out His hand and stared insipidly:

"I am to speak with you."

The given phrase was still used in some quarters, but to a normal person instantly brought to mind the language of the old school reading books. That is how Death addresses the Peasant in an ancient ballad to be found there:

"I am to speak with thee,
    thou needs must come with me."

30

With this sentence, the Man, perhaps unintentionally, added a further measure of eeriness to His sudden materialisation, and Zderad's knees nearly buckled under him.

His entrails were filled with degrading fear and the blood drained from his face.

The Man's mouth stretched in a malevolent smile, which there is no sneeringly taunting word for.

"Don't be afraid," He said, "I only want to speak with you.

Go to" … and here He gave the number and letter designating a square on the plan of the cemetery chessboard – "and wait there." "Don't turn around. I will come after you.

But – don't run away! Or They will lock you up" …

The final words evoked a new explosion of horror, and, as if in a trance and on shaking legs, Zderad set off for the selected place.

He lost his way a couple of times, although he knew the cemetery perfectly, and had to double back.

Finally he stopped, breathing heavily, as if he'd been through some great physical exertion.

The place where the Man had sent him was in the old, practically deserted part of the graveyard.

Rows of family tombs of former patrician families, in a variety of historical styles, stood back against the wall.

The inscriptions on all these were in German.

Thick, neglected bushes screened them off from any unlikely passers-by.

No one looked after these tombs, because their owners had been deported,[*] but naturally, no one demolished them or removed them either.

They were left to themselves, disappearing ever more deeply under vigorous vegetation, presenting a picture of romantic decay.

Zderad could hear his heart thumping like the accompaniment to the sounds of birds and insects. He was sweating profusely.

---

[*] After the end of the war, practically all the German inhabitants of Czechoslovakia were deported to Germany following the former annexation of the border regions by Hitler, under the pretext that they were German, (which had served as the pretext for launching World War II.)

"The place where the Man had sent him…"

Then the Man appeared again, just like a ghost.

He grinned once more in the same way, then reached into His pocket and produced some kind of photograph.

Without a word He handed it to Zderad.

Raising it to his eyes, Zderad discovered that it was not a picture but a photocopy of some kind of text.

It took some time, however, before his hand steadied enough for him to inspect it.

Meanwhile, the Man seated himself comfortably on a sarcophagus and lit a cigarette He had taken out of a silver case.

The lighter was also classy.

He pushed the cigarette case toward Zderad, who didn't even notice. Finally, he'd managed to control his shaking hand enough to be able to see the text through the spots before his eyes:

It was an ordinary, now obsolete, type of photocopy in the negative, i.e. with white letters on a black background.

The letters themselves, though, were not so common, particularly on photocopies, at least in the geographical zone of Czechoslovakia. Namely, they were Greek.

As soon as Zderad managed to see the text, and to recall its origin, he was seized by an uncontrollable terror.

The fact is, he became aware that he was most probably done for, and that the Man had practically absolute power over him.

———

Since the Spring of 1968, when the death of Jan Masaryk was being discussed in the media for a while, this kind of fear has been known by the euphemistic term "deadly anxiety," especially in connection with an intimate relic.*

---

* In 1948, Jan Masaryk, the son of the first President of the Czechoslovak Republic, T.G. Masaryk, was forced out of a window by the KGB, thus simulating suicide. The circumstances of his death were briefly discussed by the media in the "Prague Spring" of 1968. His pyjamas, kept by a relative as a kind of relic, showed that he'd soiled himself in the process, which the media discussed with the utmost ineptitude and poor taste, in evidence that he'd been forced out. It was referred to as a "token of deadly anxiety".

Zderad, however, was not quite so unfortunate, for, having dropped the photocopy on the sarcophagus, he managed to jump into some kind of white flowering thicket, just in time.

The man, seeing Zderad's reaction, was very pleased.

His watery eyes showed a small spark of life and He revealed His broad, yellowed teeth.

He picked up the discarded photograph and stepped up to the bush, which He parted with obscene curiosity.

"Go away!" Zderad started shouting angrily, but stopped when the Man waved the photograph meaningfully.

Gradually "deadly anxiety" came to mean "shitting one's pants".

IV

It was dark.

Sylva was away again, probably at a particularly constructive meeting, for it was already almost midnight.

The street-lamps were casting a greenish glow on the walls inside the coffin-dwelling.

Zderad was lying on his bed, but he could not sleep.

His head was burning.

All kinds of feelings were alternating within him like the stop combinations on a large church organ.

He was utterly confused.

At times he thought that he must be going mad or that he already was mad and that the whole thing was a hallucination.

The situation in which he found himself was completely incredible.

It would seem that Zderad had a particular affinity for life's bizarre situations, as we have already seen from the way he acquired his wife, and even from the way he earned his very thinly-buttered daily bread.

An event of the sort that had just happened, however, went beyond all his wildest imaginings.

In view of its most peculiar nature, there are grounds for concern how best to describe it adequately.

———

He had no idea how he had managed to get home that night. He had not eaten since midday, and yet he was not hungry.

He could dimly remember that on his way home he'd had an attack of vomiting, and spattered the grid of some drain or other. An old woman who'd seen him had launched into a loud diatribe on drunks.

Later he had to rush from his den and dash to the end of the gallery another couple of times.

He felt thoroughly sick.

He longed to take a bath but that was a very complicated matter in his slum dwelling.

It was done by collecting water from outside in saucepans, heating it up on the cooker, and then filling the tin bath; and then there was the problem of getting rid of the dirty water afterwards.

This was customary at Zderad's abode every Saturday, with Sylva acting as the major part of the work-force.

Right there and then, Zderad did not feel up to it. In a stupid way he also thought that it could attract the neighbours' attention, and that he could somehow give himself away by bathing at an unusual time, which was rubbish, of course.

But Zderad was incapable of thinking clearly.

He therefore did nothing, and felt sticky and dirty in the extreme. He suffered considerably.

Perhaps the simplest way of attempting to recount the events is to begin by relating the content of the mysterious photocopy, which the Man had shown to Zderad. Written on the shiny, stiff photocopy, white on black, was the following:[7]

Στᾶλιν ἄναξ, ἀγαμαί σε. Σὺ λευκαλίθῳ ἐνὶ Κρέμλῳ
ἑζόμενος κρατέεις πάντων Ῥώσσων Τατάρων τε
καὶ πολλῶν ἐθνῶν ξείνων ἀμενηνῶν κραταιῶν.
Ἐν κονίῃ ἕρποντες θεὸν ὡς εἰσορόωσι.
Σοὶ δὲ μέγας στρατός ἐστι βροτοκτόνος ὃς δ' ἐνὶ
                                              Χώραις
ἀλλοδαπῶν φορέει ὀξὺν καὶ κῆρα μέλαιναν.
Ἄνδρας συλεύουσι βιάζουσίν τε γυναῖκας
ὡρολόγους γὰρ κλέπτουσιν τοὺς ἄνδρας ἀγαυοί
ἐν καρποῖς φορέοντι τὸ γὰρ μέγα θαῦμα ἰδέσθαι.
Ἄλλοι γὰρ ῥ' ἐκάμοντο ἰδυίῃσι πραπίδεσσιν
σὺ δ' ἐλθὼν αἴρεις ὅτι τοι κράτος ἐστὶ μέγιστον
Χεῖρας δεδριθὼς παμπόλλοις ὡρολόγοισιν
ἑζόμενος ὁράας χρονοδείγματα κύδιι γαίων.
Πάντες δειδιότες κυνέουσι πόδας τε πυγήν τε.
Αὐτὸς γὰρ κρατέεις, ἢν δή τινας οὐκ ἐρίδησας
πέμψας Σειβέριην εἰς λάγερα ἢ ψύχωνται
δεσμοῖσι στυγεροῖσι δεδημένοι ἧι θάνωσι
Ῥωσιακῆς γαίης πάντες ῥ' ἄνδρες τε γυναῖκες
εὐχόμενοι στυγέουσιν ἐπεὶ θεὸς ἐσσι μέγιστος
Ἥλιον δ' αὐτόν φασι σόν τ' ἔμμεναι ὄμμα
καὶ Στάλινος πόρδην φασὶ ψολόεντα κεραυνόν.

Translation:

> *Ruler Stalin, I revere you. Sitting in the white-walled Kremlin,*
> *you rule powerfully over the Russians and the Tartars and*
> *countless heads of many nations.*
> *Crawling in the dust they look up to you as to a god.*
> *You have a great army, killing mortals, which brings*
> *destruction and Black Death to the lands of foreigners.*
> *They kill men and rape women,*
> *they also steal watches worn by valiant men*
> *on their wrists, which is a wondrous sight.*
> *Other men forged them with ingenuity,*
> *and you, having come, then take them, for you are all-powerful.*
> *Having covered your arms with many watches,*
> *you sit admiring your time-markers, exulting in your glory.*
> *They all kiss your feet and arse in terror.*
> *For you alone do rule and, those who displease you,*
> *you send to the land of Siberia to a camp where they freeze,*
> *bound in miserable chains, or die.*
> *All the men and women of the land of Russia*
> *pray to you in terror, for you are the supreme god.*
> *The Sun himself, they say, is your eye*
> *and Stalin's fart, the smouldering thunderbolt.*

The few readers who are able to understand the Greek text, as well as the majority who have read the translation, will no doubt see that, at that time, this otherwise innocent little poem was practically a death sentence for its creator.

The author of the poem, as the intelligent reader has already no doubt spotted, was none other than Zderad.

Hence the 'deadly anxiety' which our hero suffered, when the blanched Man suddenly presented him with it.

It is unlikely that this bizarre story will ever come into the hands of some bewildered Western intellectual, whether in the improbable form of a translation or even in the original, that is, prostrate beneath the spectacled gaze or the shadowy beard of some eccentric Slavist.

Should this highly unlikely event be taking place, however, we would tactfully like to point out that Zderad was by no means abnormally cowardly, and that the consequences of this schoolboy exercise in Homeric hymnology could really be quite unimaginable. To be precise, they were, on the contrary, sufficiently imaginable to be shocking. People had been beaten to death for much less than the said idea; that Stalin wears many watches stolen by the liberating army, or that the Soviet citizens consider thunder and lightning to be the manifestation of his flatulence. Let the vaguely lefty academic invertebrates recall Solzhenitsyn's letter,[8] and what it led to. OK?

———

Zderad had conceived the above doggerel before the year 1948 as a grammar-school pupil, and had long since forgotten it.

He did not even know how it could have found its way into the Man's clutches.

The photocopy was, however, clearly written in his handwriting, which could be identified even in the Greek, and what is more, it had the completely unequivocal Czech heading:

Ode to Stalin
Z. Zderad, 7a

To be candid, Zderad had also written one other poem on a similar subject, which was a little bit worse, even.

That one was written in the Aeolic dialect in the first Asclepiadic metre, and dealt with how the Soviet nations will get plastered, when, by the will of Zeus, the Generalissimo[9] kicks the bucket.

That poem reflected Zderad's professional and political growth, both in the formal and material sense; from the simple hexameter in the Epic dialect, which is easy because it presents a rich variety of alternative forms and turns of phrase, so that getting the right rhythm is easy, to the Aeolic dialect and to the complicated Asclepiadic metre: The ideological content itself had also become more risqué.

It was quite possible that the Man also had this other text in His possession, and that He hadn't come forward with it straight away, so as to gradually ramp up the torture of His victim.

———

We had left Zderad at the moment when he was forced to disappear into the thicket, in order to preclude the degradation of soiling himself.

There is a warning at the beginning of this book that it will be somewhat repulsive in places and we repeat it here.

The time has now come for the decent citizen to hurl the book to the ground with a loud "What the?!" or to consign it to the flames, most probably in the open fireplace of his distinguished middle-class residence.

————

The Man, his yellow teeth gleaming, tore into the bushes and rejoiced in Zderad's humiliation.

The events that followed were somehow condensed in Zderad's memory into fleeting, simplified and absolutely improbable images, which nevertheless filled him with a variety of strong and almost totally unpleasant feelings.

— He remembered how he squatted there in a humiliating manner, while the man stood over him, gazing with pleasure, uttering various sarcastic comments.
— He also remembered how he was forced to perform the necessary and highly private ritual in front of the Man, who had declined to leave the bushes and had even offered him some paper serviettes for the purpose, which Zderad had had to accept, as the alternative was even more humiliating.
— He remembered how he'd momentarily thought about belting the Man and knocking him off his feet, and then we'd see.
— Then, how the man had obviously read it in his eyes and how He'd growled that if He wasn't home by evening, He'd made arrangements for a certain envelope to be delivered to State Security.
— How Zderad had hesitated, and backed down.

————

Looking at the whole event with detachment and from a bird's eye view, we know that this was where Zderad had blown it.

If he had risked the possibility that the Man was just bluffing, and had belted Him one, the whole thing might have developed differently and there would have been no need to write this bizarre story.

Let us also make the observation that it will never become clear whether the Man did have any goings-on with the StB[*] or whether He was just putting on an act in this respect. Of course, as we shall see, He was on good terms with Them, but the question was, how far would that have gone.

If Zderad had not co-operated at the beginning, the Man could have carried out His threat anyway; with, no doubt, a realistic hope of success. Yet it is possible that He would have thought better of it, because He could have been taking a risk himself.

To shop someone because he'd said that Stalin is a bastard, in Czech, is a lot easier than persuading the relevant gorillas that some carcassinger had, years ago, written a Greek poem of anti-Marshal blasphemy.

By doing this, the snitcher himself could have ended up in the spotlight of investigative attention, which might not have been pleasant; because, in His own way, He had a lot to hide.

There was, of course, another, faster, more drastic possibility, which did not even occur to Zderad, with his fudgey soul.

In Zderad's defence, let us add that he was completely incapable of thinking in this way.

After all, it is a good rule in our part of the world to behave so that we do not clash with anyone, if at all possible; because it is highly likely that the other guy may be involved with Them, in some way or other.

————

Now, Zderad recalled how he'd stifled his aggressive impulse, and how he suddenly found himself in front of one of the deserted patrician tombs with a German inscription.

— How the tomb was in the pseudo-gothic style.
— How the Man had suddenly produced a large, ornate key from His pocket and opened the narrow gothic door, how He had pushed

* StB – "Státní Bezpečnost". The Czechoslovak equivalent of the KGB.

Zderad inside and how He had locked the door behind them again.

— How he'd struck a match and lit a candle in a candlestick.

— How the tomb had turned out to be a complete small chapel, though empty and plundered, with the coffins apparently lower down in the crypt.

— How—

At that moment Zderad's stomach heaved again, and he was forced to make another dash along the gallery.

The description of the rest of Zderad's memories is a highly difficult and delicate matter.

Because, as soon as the door of the chapel had shut behind him, and the candle had begun to burn bright, the Man had unexpectedly fallen to his knees before Zderad, uttering a stream of repulsive endearments.

Although at that moment it was already clear to Zderad that homosexual prostitution was required of him, in order to save himself from denunciation, the events that followed by far exceeded the limits of his knowledge of sexual pathology.

What the Man was doing to Zderad obviously had sexual motivation and meaning, yet it was a matter of definition whether it could be called a form of sexual intercourse at all.

In the Austro-Hungarian Empire there was an anti-homosexual law, and it was basically that same law which was still in force at the time of our narrative in Czechoslovakia. Codified laws were always more-or-less upheld in the country, outside of political matters, unlike the Soviet Union, and this may still be the case.

So, if I am not mistaken, according to the old Austrian law, the man was not even committing a crime.

However, many queers preferred to confess to things which they had never done in reality, and for which they were sent to jail, rather than describe the actual deeds and leave the courtroom free, but in monumental disgrace.

Sometimes they didn't even know that their act was not punishable by law, and maybe they thought that they would be quartered or burnt alive for what they had done.

This matter was that kind of oddity.

Frequently, the Austrian citizens did not even confide to their attorneys, and insisted on some lesser, but still quite disgusting versions.

Only after the sentence had been passed, reduced through the selfless efforts of their lawyers, did some of them admit that their activities had been much worse, that if only the Judge had known—

*"Aber das ist doch straflos,"** Dr. Buxbaum would say with amusement, pocketing his fat 'palmare' and departing to entertain his colleagues that evening, with the necessary discretion, of course.

———

If we still can't, in all honesty, guess at what we're talking about here, let us make use of Czech literature:

As experts will confirm, the defrocked priest Jakub Deml admits to a highly peculiar passion.

He states, with rare honesty, in his literary diaries that he longs "to kiss women's thighs."

This description is grossly euphemistic.

From various clues and hints, however, it is unfortunately clear what the poor man really meant.

I still don't understand, though, why he wanted his readers to know this strange fact about himself.

Well, the man, who actually resembled Deml a little, had the same longing, but for men. OK?

———

The details of the bizarre act kept returning unpleasantly to Zderad's mind. He remembered —

— How the crypt had reeked of mould and perhaps even cadavers, how he had stared at the candle flame, gripping the cold edge of the altar mensa.

— How a moth had committed suicide in the flame.

— How the Man below him had whispered and mumbled, distasteful and ridiculous, and how at the end He'd grunted and sobbed.

———

* "But that's not even penalized"

— How He'd kept wiping His mouth afterwards with the paper tissues: so that's why He had them on Him.

— How He'd looked malevolent and shame-faced and how He'd kept brushing His knees and straightening His tie in a vain attempt to restore his lost dignity.

— How He'd left, looking more like a beaten dog than usual and how His damnation almost visibly trailed behind Him like a plume of thick purple mist.

— How, before that, He had mumbled that He would be back.

———

Finally, Zderad fell into a miserable half-dozing state which mercifully deepened into sleep towards dawn.

———

He woke up late.

At first he felt fine.

Then the awareness that something wasn't quite right emerged.

Finally, that awareness took shape, and that shape was the Man.

Zderad crawled out of his bed in a pitiful state.

It was already almost ten.

Luckily that day the carcassinging didn't start until afternoon.

He sat on the edge of his sofa and deliberated what to do. The event hung in the air like a huge transparent boulder.

For a while Zderad tried to convince himself that he must have dreamt it all, but he still had that bitter taste in his mouth after the repeated vomiting.

— "It looks like it must be true," he said to himself with distaste.

The panic and confusion were over, and Zderad was capable of thinking almost normally again.

The first thing he realised was that even this must not be allowed to break him.

He therefore brought in some cold water and washed thoroughly in the tin bath.

He got rid of the taste in his mouth with toothpaste.

That brought him round.

He got dressed, had something to eat and started deliberating on how to get out of this.

— Maybe the best thing would be to move.

— But if the Man was with the secret police, or if He had any contacts with them, He would find him very easily.

— It would also mean finding a new flat and job, and that was totally impractical at that moment in time. Sylva could easily announce that she wasn't going anywhere.

— A teacher is glad to have a place in the City – and just as their relationship is beginning to improve a little. And he would have to explain why to her, and that would be totally impossible.

While thinking about all this he became aware at the back of his mind that he hadn't seen her since yesterday.

— After all, since he slept badly all night, he wouldn't have slept through it if she had come in.

— Or perhaps he had. Now, of course, she was at the school.

— And another thing, to find a weekday nursery for little Záviš – there are long waiting lists.

— No, it wouldn't be possible to move.

— How about attack being the best form of defence, and shopping the Man?

— But what if he's one of Them? The homosexual murderer Haarmann[10] was also "Herr Geheimagent". People like that are protected even in less monstrous regimes.

— Besides – what he did – eugh – maybe it isn't even an offence; Zderad seemed to remember that someone, a lawyer or somebody, had told him that when the act doesn't have anything to do with the sex organs.

— Of course, there is the tomb – desecration or whatever you call it, but our masters don't care about that anymore. He can't say that he was forced to do it either, or he would have to say why – and that would mean crashing down with him.

— Writing funny poems about Stalin, even though it was in Greek and eight years ago, that's something like a capital crime.

— He was finished.

The Man had him by the balls, and he knew it.

— This was an educated person, who must know Greek well.

— That's clear both from the fact that He could understand the thing, and from some of the sarcastic comments He mumbled as He stood over Zderad writhing in the bushes.

— Zderad dimly recalled some ironic praise for his unusual knowledge of the Homeric dialect; and had the feeling that the words Oxford and Dublin came into it somewhere as well.

— Here was a Man-of-the-World.

— A type of gentleman, rare in this country.

— Our philosophers have almost always had worn-through elbows and struggled on in middle schools or libraries; even a potential Chair at the University would never elevate them very far up the social ladder.

— So He must be financially well off, and it doesn't look as if these are just the remnants of a capitalist past; which makes it worse, of course.

— Clearly, in all the relevant respects, He stands high above Zderad, the shipwrecked cemetery singer.

— In the cool light of day, his disgusting degradation beneath Zderad is bound to be highly unpleasant for him.

— One day, simply as a result of yesterday, He will destroy Zderad, whose existence would otherwise continue to remind Him of his own absurd damnation.

— Tiberius' azure grotto.[*]

Zderad felt the wave of cold horrifying terror wash over him again. An unformulated and unformulable idea seemed to be emerging from the mental boulder of anxiety, like a huge and hideous fledgling from a gigantic egg.

He did not allow it to take shape, however.

He realised that the horror which he had felt about the Man from the moment he had started appearing always came with that combination of compassion and revulsion that we feel when we come into contact with revolting cripples.

It was strange that he had felt like that without knowing anything about the Man.

— A case of extrasensory perception? What use is that?

---

[*] A place on Capri where Tiberius strangled young men for kicks.

— But what now?

First, Zderad deliberated, he will have to find out who the Man actually is.

Even if this information leads him to feel completely helpless and hopeless, it will at least remove the mystical horror resulting from the freak's anonymity.

For the moment the Man had the advantage, because He clearly knew Zderad and his life circumstances.

This was obvious from the way the whole situation had developed.

The way to start could be by finding out how the Monster had got hold of his poem, and how He'd gone about finding the author.

That kind of detective work would require time and money, and Zderad had very little of either.

Then a self-evident solution came to him.

His mood improved, as if by magic.

But then it sank, way below zero again.

He had become aware of another gross side to the whole thing.

————

Oh, the complexity of the human soul!

Yesterday Zderad was sick as sick can be and his deep revulsion manifested itself repeatedly and physically.

Yesterday's experience had, however, also contained an aspect which so far he had carefully circumvented in his thoughts, but which had now pushed its way through into his consciousness, because the circumstances dictated it.

St. Jerome in his letters to the holy maiden Eustochium spends a lot of time and energy advising her how to preserve her virginity and the technicalities of the topic.

It is not our intention here to blasphemously investigate the motives of the hermit, venerated by the Church; whose authority, albeit fraudulently, was instrumental in the preservation of the Slavonic Mass in Croatia.*

————

* Because St. Jerome came from Dalmatia, where, of course, there were no Christian

46

One of his theses is that a violated virgin does not sin and does not lose her moral status of virginity, as long as she does not feel pleasure at the time.

This was what Zderad remembered when the memory at last brutally forced its way into his consciousness:

In the greenish mouldiness of the tomb, he had realised, with surprise, that the superficial mechanical irritation of an extremely private part of his body was capable of evoking waves of feeling usually associated with a different, albeit not remote, part of his anatomy.

Contributing to this was the awareness of a temporary, and thus all the more raging dominance over the Monster, who a moment earlier had completely ruled over him, tugging at the invisible fetters of fear.

The cruel mental pleasure of unspeakably obscene power over the horrific blackmailer had fused with the sepulchral lover's revolting but effective caresses, spiced with His muffled sobs and grunts.

The posterior of the stinking mandrill, which is incredibly obscene, offends the more sensitive visitor to the Zoo, yet it shines with a symphony of delicate and pronounced hues of greens, reds, blues and purples.

Metallic shining flies, for example of the genus *Calliphora*, which revel in excrement and carrion, are of a similarly glorious coloration, as are many species of dung beetle.

Thus, the radiance and glory of Being permeates all its levels.

Uninfluenced by the spectacle it was illuminating, the flame of the candle burned with a beautiful and glorious brightness and, at the same time Zderad's lust also flared up in spite of himself.

Pulsating, it glowed colourfully, with ever greater strength, until

---

Slavs in his day, the Croatian priests succeeded in due course to fool the Pope into believing that the Glagolitic script was invented by him and not by the heretics Cyril and Methodius. This is why the western or Glagolitic Slavonic rite survived there, whereas in Bohemia it was wiped out. It was later put to music by Janáček in his Glagolitic Mass, etc.

it finally exploded in cosmic fireworks.

This recollection, which finally and irrevocably emerged in Zderad's memory, filled him with a feeling of extremely painful embarrassment.

He tensed under the impact of this new suffering, closed his eyes, mumbling something, trying to submerge the memory again into his subconscious.

Finally he came to, soaked in sweat.

It was clear that the Monster had won after all.

Another wave of deep shame glowed scarlet.

Zderad got up mechanically and approached the chair on which his worn jacket hung limply.

He reached into the pocket.

It was there.

He pulled out the banknote, smoothed it out, and intently studied its complicated graphic curves, for a long time.

He had not seen one for ages.

But he did not destroy it.

V

Time passed and the astronomical horologe now showed full summer.

It is surprising how nature cares nothing for the affairs of man, whether public or private. It even tries, and quite successfully so, to take no notice of interference in her own order.

Veterans of the two wars, and you could find plenty of those in the City, sometimes told of birds singing during the shelling and trying to nest in bombed-out buildings and so on.

Even in the cemeteries, summer shone in golds and greens as if there were no Party Rule in the Homeland.

Nature was also blind to Zderad's own personal misery.

The school holidays erupted.

Sylva disappeared to her parents, who, it seemed, were willing to take her in, and took little Záviš with her.

Zderad stayed in the City.

The rules governing the status of funerary singers dated back to the Austrians, who held holidays to be of little or no importance, especially for the lower order of beings.

Like labourers, the graveyard singers were on piecework.

Zderad was therefore forced to stay in the City to continue earning just enough to keep himself, thus taking the financial burden off Sylva's shoulders, since she earned slightly more, enough to keep herself, the child and the coffin-dwelling.

Apart from that, Zderad was still unwelcome at the family homestead, and to tell the truth, he would not have had enough for the train-fare, or, at least, that's what Sylva thought.

In fact Zderad had more money now than he'd had for a long time. By his own standards he was almost rich.

He couldn't very well show this bounty to Sylva, though, because that would have led to questions, and he had to content himself with giving her all the money he earned from singing.

The source of this unexpected income is by now obvious to us, and we fear that the formerly likeable Zderad has been rejected in the reader's mind.

After all, right at the beginning he should have turned the Monster down, possibly even beaten Him up, and taken the risk that he and his family might be annihilated, over a silly schoolboy verse, in a dead language growing more and more exclusive.

We also know that it might have come to nothing.

"Die rather than sin," is the maxim of St. Aloysius and many other Fridolines. In contrast, let us quote the southern Czech proverb that "a poor man can't afford to be honourable," which seems to be a truism of cosmic proportions.

Let those consumers who succeeded in getting out, albeit after some time, inspect their own consciences.

"MILLE MODI VENERIS"* says Publius Ovidius Naso, and let us add "SCILICET VENALIS".†

The formulation of that idea, with its quite superfluous classical exhibitionism, bears the unmistakable hallmark of Zderad's psyche, and is indeed one of his own aphorisms, with which he tried to sugar his degradation.

To submit, under threat of annihilation, to the carnal desires of a mental cripple, is a clear and tangible case of prostitution, yet not one of the worst kind.

We also note that the nature of the required act was precisely the opposite of the one more or less perpetrated by the majority of us in the homeland, albeit only symbolically and allegorically.

So let's keep our hats on, shall we?

———

Nevertheless, we hesitate to admit, that Zderad was somehow beginning to get used to his situation.

According to Marxist-Leninist lecturers, capitalists are also immoral

---

* Many are the ways of Venus i.e. Love.

† Likewise of commerce.

because of the corrupting influence of their wealth.

Zderad bought himself a few shirts, socks etc., cotton trousers and sandals known as 'Jesus creepers' for summer comfort.

When it came to dressing up, he couldn't make up his mind between a leather jacket and a new suit, but refrained from purchasing either, for the sake of secrecy.

In so doing he displayed much greater foresight than the managers of the MASNA chain of state-owned butchers', who glutted on flashy cars and went to jail in droves at the time.

At present, I'm told, by usually reliable sources, corruption in the homeland is so total, that these phenomena take place practically in broad daylight; and nothing happens to anybody, because they're all in it up to their ears.

For the first time in ages Zderad had enough protein (though supplies from the farm had ceased coming in since Sylva's departure), and he put on a little weight, which the Monster commented on with delight.

Occasionally he even allowed himself the luxury of a beer or two. He even started smoking now and again, even though he knew that, in so doing, he was damaging his only operating asset.

Among other things, you see, the Freak used to bring him expensive foreign cigarettes.

He was not dependent on that, however.

In fact he could have packed in carcassinging altogether, and he would occasionally fail to turn up, under some pretext or other. Graveside singing was thus becoming more or less a cover occupation.

Despite the occasional fits of shame, which would attack him unexpectedly – maybe in the street, like a sudden toothache, stopping him in his tracks, whereupon he would sweat for a while, eyes halfclosed – he even started to enjoy life a little.

Whenever he was able to get away, he would go to the lidos* and, revelling in his own youth and strength, he would swim long distances against the current, often under several bridges and against the flow

---

* A section of river pontooned-off for recreational use.

of the weirs, as far as the Water Tower.

He even went to the cinema several times, but he found the Joyful Reality being rammed down the audience's throat too depressing, and gave up this form of entertainment.

Turgo and Krůta, who both had better relations with the authorities, offered him opportunities to stand in for organists several times, and he came to enjoy the voices of the City's various instruments as he gradually got to know them.

He discovered, however, that he had such deep-seated religious conditioned reflexes that he felt almost like a blasphemer as he played the sacred instruments; though he would quickly get over this religious obstacle by indulging various arguments and sophistries.

His interest in literature was re-awakened, and he would stand outside the KNIHA, National Enterprise bookshop windows, looking for something to devour.

But there was less and less good stuff to be found and soon there was practically nothing.

It should be pointed out that desertification at the time was almost total, and that the better writers of the future were at that time still in a state of embryonic latency. Some, though not all of them, were writing and publishing true and earnest byzantine odes to Stalin, only in the Czech and Slovak languages, of course.

The antiquarian booksellers were much better, and beautiful old books, the remnants of various eliminated ethnic and social groups, were to be had for next to nothing, because, comrades, who'd want to read them?

Zderad had to make a conscious effort not to part with too much of his money, so as not to give himself away to Sylva with his excessive bibliophilic opulence once she had returned from the holidays.

He kept his books in a wooden trunk, which, once covered with a clean, though much patched table-cloth, was also used as a side ta-ble. Meanwhile, Sylva's 'Makarenkos'* and other Soviet classics were

---

* A. S. Makarenko – Soviet educationalist, considered an authority on bringing up children during the Stalinist era.

housed in a glass display cabinet, obtained with their joint official earnings at considerable financial sacrifice.

As it was only possible to lift the lid after removing various vases and ornaments, Zderad's library was relatively secure – but could he trust her?

In this way Zderad acquired a copy of Erasmus' Greco-Latin Bible, which only had the title page missing, and had probably escaped the attention of second-hand book dealers as a result of this. Likewise he also obtained a first edition of Kafka's "In der Strafkolonie," because the comrade sorters clearly did not know what it was.

After these intellectual excesses he felt even greater pangs of conscience with regard to his family than after his meetings with the Monster; so that he would send even his whore-money to Sylva's country address, and lie about unusually large numbers of first-class funerals and a great deal of filling in for other organ-players, now that it was the holiday season.

But the greater part of the money he put aside for a rainy day.

———

He still had not relinquished his plan to escape the Monster's grasp.

So far all his attempts at finding out the Freak's identity had drawn a total blank. From various clues he'd discovered that the Misfit owned a car, but he had never managed to see it long enough and close enough to get the number.

Naturally, Zderad had absolutely no idea about makes of cars.

Once, when the Monster was beside himself with His filthy grunting, Zderad looked through the jacket which lay discarded on the altar, but he found that the careful bastard had left His citizens' ID card at home.

Perhaps the Comrade was even exempt from carrying one. He found nothing else in the pockets.

Several times Zderad attempted to follow the creature, but He'd always vanished, as if into thin air.

Later, He hinted that He could perhaps still tell the Comrades how good Zderad was at Greek, if he kept on trying to tail Him.

———

Although he tried to rationalise it away, Zderad suffered particularly because the sepulchral séances were never without his own intimate contribution.

This indeed made him the Monsters cohort, and ghoulish lover.

Had he been able to remain totally unaffected, he would have been able to feel a certain mocking superiority, which is the secret of professional whores or frigid wives.

However, the Monster's indescribable caresses were so provocative,

—

Nevertheless, Zderad was pleased to note that he was also beginning to get used to this side of things and his moral dilemma was somewhat eased.

Let us add, more explicitly, that the Monster belonged to the rare kind of perverts who do nothing with their partners' genitalia, nor try to get close to them with their own.

The Monster remained faithful to His deviation, which we might, along the lines of masochism, sadism, rétifism etc. label as demlism, in this case of the homosexual variety.

If we are not mistaken, a man of these inclinations is known among the Czech boys by the term 'buližník', and the activity which he performs is called "buližnická".*

Despite its morphological identity with a word denoting chert, a type of mineral (a form of quartz), this word is of quite different origin. It is a calque, i.e. a word made up of parts taken from various languages, unrelated to one another.

Or at least, this is a possible explanation.

The suffix '-ližník' is of Slavonic, i.e. Czech origin, and its meaning is evident (being derived from the verb "lízat" meaning "to lick"). The other, preceding part is the word, "bul" is of Gypsy origin, and designates the part of the body impinged by the activity concerned. So the word should correctly be written "bulližník," in contrast to the decent mineral, "buližník".

---

* ... a word which is a substantified adjective, an activity, like, for example, "čekaná," 'lying-in-wait'.

Apparently, one accepted English term for the activity in question is "rimming," which makes the active party, presumably, a "rimmer".*

Rimmers are further subdivided into occasional and exclusive.

The Monster, probably luckily for Zderad, belonged to the latter group.

As soon as Zderad had become used to his customer to the point where he was neither shocked nor uncontrollably aroused by him (the two had originally been linked) he was able to lie to himself that he had the genuine whore's superiority.

The situation thus appeared to acquire a certain bizarre stability, to the near-satisfaction of both sides, and Zderad would catch himself lacking the inclination to do anything about it.

He had been corrupted.

---

* This may have nothing to do with Rimmon, the ancient deity worshiped in Damascus, as in to "bow down to the house of Rimmon" (2 Kings 5, Verse 18) – to compromise one's convictions – More probably the word comes from the Latin "rima," chink, or the old English for peritoneum, "reoma". Or it could just be derived from "rim". If the more erudite etymology is correct, this may disclose the private predilections of scholars. An alternative and more euphemistic English term is "honey-potting".

VI

It is about ten o'clock in the morning, on a Friday.

A red squirrel and a black one are chasing one another through the cemetery trees, a small blood-red mite runs around the stony labyrinths of the gravestones, houseleeks are starting to bud, bees are buzzing from flower to flower and so on.

The graveyard is pulsating with the joy of life and at this moment Zderad is engaged in his cover occupation.

A widow in mourning leans on her son's arm, crying, the priest sprinkles the grave with holy water, and the gravediggers have already put the straps around their shoulders.

The white handkerchiefs contrast aesthetically with black attire.

The last farewells are underway, and the quartet intones the favourite song of the deceased:

[:O'er the lake of Stachov,
Ruffled by the breeze,:]
[:O'er the lake they're flying,:]
[:Flocks of wild grey geese:]

In his choice of song the dead shoemaker displays unusually good taste, of a clearly archetypally superindividualistic origin.

The beautiful, simple, mildly melancholy melody, has been piously arranged by Kukula, not forgetting to make use of the 'waldhornquinten' harmonies to which the melody lends itself to in the "ruffled" bit, and the first of the repeating flocks.

The main harmonic tricks occur in the second tenor and Zderad is performing them with gusto.

It is not Lake Stachov, which he doesn't know, that emerges in his mind's eye, but the wide and glistening surface of Lake Posel, which we've heard of already.

He contemplates the fact that he not only has enough money to take up his detective work, but also to drop in on Sylva's birthplace, to surprise both wife and son and possibly even to establish a friendly relationship with the old Ram; after all, he might have mellowed by now, since there is no place for illegitimate children nor divorces in his mindset.

The second "flaa-aa-ying" glides into the tonic through a plagal cadence and Krůta's deep C drones softly. No doubt about it, he's the best bass of all the carcassingers in all the graveyards.

Kukula's bass voice glistens like a goldfish reflecting in a shoemaker's brass ball, and all would appear to be somehow as it should be.

It is as if the widow's wailing is but a small detail in an incomprehensible but nevertheless vaguely benign space-time horologe.

The coffin has slid into the grave, clods of soil fall, thrown by the mourners, and the dead cobbler takes his leave of the world through the mouths of the four singers:

Not wild geese but goslings
Can you hear the call?
Where've you gone to, fine girls:
Pretty, one and all?

Not wild geese but ganders
Can you hear the call?
Where've you gone to, fine lads
Where to, where at all?

— Where to, where at all —

Zderad picked his battered briefcase off the ground, bulging with everything necessary for a short trip to the country, and shot off for the train.

The lads will look after his share of the money until Monday.

He would be loath to miss a good connection.

He suddenly felt the way he did back in his childhood, when going for outings by train with his parents.

Ostensibly in an attempt to take a short cut, but, in reality, out of boisterousness, Zderad leapt over graves, and finally, vaulted over the low cemetery wall.

Off we go!

———

— *"Où commence par une croix de bois la route qui mène jusqu'à Dieu, bordée de tristes petits pommiers qui s'en vont indéfiniment par deux,"*[11] the educated Zderad says to himself with his inner voice as he takes pleasure in scanning the scenery, which looked as if it had been cut from the poem by the French Consul to Austria, residing in Prague.[*]
— Autumn might be better suited to the mood, but even so, those little appletrees making their way two-by-two up the hill cause the appropriate metaphysical tugging at the heartstrings.
— In the end, it cannot be denied that the chap had indeed been a poet, even though he knew next to nothing about us, and mucked about with the little he did know, a fact which is amply clear from those four poems of his; in gratitude for which, the Catholic intelligentsia to this day bows down to the Pilsen night-wick[†] of his Gallic ésprit.

---

[*] 1909–1911, Paul Claudel

[†] The Pilsen night-wick — although by then obsolete, due to the advent of electricity.

— Mind you, they're themselves well out of fashion now, in exile, or in jails, whilst a different array of western Slavs goes through similar prostrations before the Soviet Union.

— And, *là voilà*, there it is, *"un long clocher comme une fleur d'oignon,"* though it is a church tower, not a belltower, as such.[12]

While making these literary and historical deliberations, Zderad was gradually ascending the long hill and sweating considerably.

His briefcase was heavy, the sun was baking, and the relevant corner of the homeland, notwithstanding the bits the poet got right, was not quite as *'tout plat'* as he described.*

Due to which, Zderad was in an irritable and unforgiving mood.

———

The closer he got to the church and, he assumed, to the parsonage, the more foolish all this peregrination was now beginning to seem to him.

He was, as they say, clutching at straws.

He had resolved to do something about his situation, come what may.

The Monster, you see, had been getting progressively more and more distasteful.

It had started when He brought a large suitcase to one of their rendezvous. It was difficult to steer the trunk through the narrow gothic door of the tomb or mausoleum, and just as they were trying to do this, voices could be heard beyond the curve of the path. Luckily they were inside just in time, otherwise those people would have probably raised the alarm about grave robbers.

Out of the trunk came a bridal gown and – o horrors – a top hat and tails for Zderad. It must have been on hire, or otherwise it would have cost a fortune.

Zderad could have theoretically remembered such a lamp from his childhood. A jar was filled with oil and the Pilsen float with a wick placed on top of it, and lit. The result was a feeble light.

* Though Claudel spent time here, making him an expert, he must have only seen the Elbe floodplain, or the wheat-fields of Haná. Going up Brdy mountains would have broadened his horizons. Bohème, Bohémien, c'est la vie.

In view of the Homeric Ode to Stalin there was no alternative and Zderad had to go through a sort of wedding service.

The Monster wore a floral wreath over a blonde wig as befitted a cross-dresser, (by the festive candlelight, sHe looked the part, all too much). sHe spoke in a suitable contralto, and was moved to tears. Occasionally the wig would come off and, wearing a cassock, He became the celebrant.

Then there were the rings:

Zderad never wore his later, which was understandable (he didn't have a real wedding ring, because at the time he and Sylva couldn't afford it), but he had to put it on for the rendezvous.

The ring was very fine, and massive.

There was no inscription on it, the Monster was too cautious.

In additon, the Monster had brought a sort of improvised wedding feast, including a bottle of champagne and two seemingly rare small chalices, such as might be used for a Mass.

Embarrassment became betrothed with revulsion when He finally asked Zderad to piss into one, and then drank the foaming liquid with gusto.

Fortunately, His perversion remained otherwise unchanged:

The consummation of their "wedlock" ended in the usual rimming fashion; and He didn't even ask Zderad to kiss Him on the lips beforehand. Zderad breathed a huge sigh of relief.

When he looked back on it, he himself was surprised at what a man will do out of fear and – let's admit it – for money!

That time the reward was especially juicy:

A "wedding gift," the Monster had said.

———

"Out of the trunk came a bridal gown ..."

This had not yet exhausted the freak's fantasies.

The time after that, He turned up, as normal, without a suitcase, but as soon as they were inside the tomb He stripped, and appeared in black lingerie and stockings.

From His briefcase He not only produced a wig and high heeled shoes to complete the illusion, but also a cane.

He told Zderad that "sHe'd been unfaithful" and "begs to be punished" whereupon Zderad had to administer with the cane. The Monster yelled for mercy and promised to be good, etc.

It was therefore high time to extricate himself, as Zderad firmly decided, the instant the freak limped off.

Things were beginning to get worse and worse.

Who knows what He would come up with, next time.

What Zderad didn't know, however, was that the sudden blossoming of the Monster's erotic fantasies was connected with external circumstances, and later, external circumstances would once again dampen them somewhat.

———

On the bed in his coffin-dwelling, he considered for a long time how to get hold of the fatal Stalinist apotheosis, for it appeared his serfdom hinged on it.

He magnanimously glossed over the financial aspects, for now.

At that time the slummy hovel reeked of all manner of gutter and sewage smells, and Zderad felt as if he was imprisoned in a gigantic cesspool.

Like most people in times of great difficulty, Zderad also turned to the God of his boyhood, begging to be released from his present curse.

It crossed his mind that the surly Spirit demanded greater suffering of him, even death, through his honourably refusing the Monster, and bearing the consequences.

This alternative did not appeal to him one bit, so he prayed fervently to have the ordeal commuted to something milder, even though he knew that such a request was heretical, from the point of view of the doctrinal teachings of his childhood.

When he emerged from prayer, he was richer for the experience.

He appreciated the religious zeal of prostitutes.

He fell asleep very late.

His dream was extremely peculiar.

———

He dreamt that he was at some kind of religious festival, perhaps to do with the Blessed Virgin, but possibly not Catholic but some kind of Orthodox; Armenian perhaps, judging by the exotic and strange paintings and details of embroidery on the garments.

"He dreamt ..."

The festival seemed to be taking place on a bridge of sorts.

The participants of the festival were not people, however, but quasi-human animals, as if from The Island of Doctor Moreau.

Since they had originally been of quite different sizes, they presented a monstrous sight due to their disproportion.

There were small hamster- and rat-men, slender cat-men, dog-men of various sizes, from the small to the larger-than-life – clearly derived from St. Bernards and wolfhounds – and finally giants, stemming from horses, cows and camels.

The kneeling cameloids were still grotesquely taller than the standing people derived from smaller animals, and they were also taking up an enormous amount of room.

They sang in bizarre voices, corresponding to their original animal cries, but on the whole it harmonised reasonably well.

The Monster was at the altar and it appeared that he was conducting the Mass.

Somehow or other Zderad found himself at the altar.

The Monster cut his garment open at the front with a ritual sword, to the applause of the assembled creatures, just as Italians applaud the Holy Host.

Having exposed the length of Zderad's body at the front, He held a chalice for him to urinate into.

Zderad refused to do this.

The Monster therefore turned to the altar and held up the text of prayers for Mass in a gold frame, several of which can usually be found on an altar.

He pushed it towards Zderad.

Of course, once again it was the Ode to Stalin, printed in ligature as it used to be done in the past, with a parallel Latin translation:

"TE DOMINE STALIN ADORO, TU CREMLO ALBOSAXO, RUSSIS ET TATARIS DOMINARIS OMNIBUS SEDENS."

Zderad, however, grasped the Monster by the throat, who began to transmute, like Proteus in the grip of Menelaos. Finally, He stopped shape-shifting, changed back into a man, and that man was BRVA.

At this point Zderad awoke, feeling that perhaps he was

onto something.

———

Brva was Zderad's old classmate from the grammar school.

He was very kind and gentle, but extremely stupid.

The religious instruction master helped push him through the school year-by-year, since Brva intended to become a priest.

Zderad used to help Brva out with his studies, particularly with Greek and Latin, in which Brva seemed to be particularly obtuse; which was of course highly unfortunate for his future theological studies.

Zderad even used to visit Brva's home. Brva's father was a concierge in a decent part of town.

They lived in a basement flat, and Zderad recalled that, at the time, the abode seemed miserable and lugubrious.

It was of course much better than his own present-day coffin-dwelling.

Brva was not Zderad's only client:

Zderad had a whole cohort of academically retarded and morally fallen pupils, though by rights he should have kept in with the élite of the class.

Perhaps the fact that he was drawn to the relative dregs was already some portent of his fall-to-be.

During Greek and Latin composition, he took care to guide his flock of black sheep through the rocky mountain-passes.

He would always do his own work first.

He was always the first to finish, way ahead of the other better pupils.

Instead of handing in his exercise book and waiting outside the classroom, he would spend the rest of the lesson preparing cribsheets for his protégés, with special allowance for the style of each individual.

So as not to give the game away, he would leave in a few relatively minor mistakes, since it was inconceivable that pupils like Brva or Garbušek could hand in flawless work.

By mimicking individual styles and stupidities, and by the skilled colportage of the finished chits, the rest of the lesson would pass by, in a way which was both amusing and generally beneficial.

By now, most of Zderad's former protégés were Doctors and Professionals, enjoying at least some degree of esteem, and earning decent daily bread without the aid of physical prostitution.

As far as Zderad knew, Brva had become a priest after all.

Now he recalled, that once, when he was sitting with Brva in their basement flat, struggling with something from Homer, Mrs Brva had brought them some sort of homemade fruit wine or something. It was just before Christmas, or maybe just after.

Zderad kept drinking, until he got fired up and began showing off to poor Brva.

It was then that he had penned the Ode to Stalin in order to prove his Greek erudition... the magazines which came from the Soviet Union and from the home-grown communist press were already beginning to provoke such a reaction, even though the Joyful Dawn was yet to come.

Brva had kept the poem, out of awe.

So Brva was the key, albeit not a promising one.

— Let us find Brva then.

According to the last news he'd had, Brva had started as a chaplain in the parish of X.[13] That was convenient, because the village of Mlno,[14] on the shore of Lake Posel, was basically on the same route.

It was possible to undertake the trip using the money earned through degradation.

— Let us go forth!

———

Zderad was walking on toward X, calling himself a variety of names. The last news he'd had about Brva was well out of date; the trail was very cold. Possibly Brva had long since gone, given the peculiar things that happened to priests in those days.

At last he stopped on the village green, with its typical duck pond, and found his way to the parsonage quite easily.

He pulled at the ancient bell pull by the door, on which a brass plate read:

VINCENC PLICKA
PARSON

and waited.

After some time, a mature bespectacled woman came to the door, domestically dressed in an apron, with all the typical appearance of a parsonage "Miss".

She looked Zderad up and down with some misgivings.

Zderad stammered out his wish to find Father Brva and added that he was a former schoolmate.

The woman's face became very sad:

"Father Brva is not with us any longer. You see he – perhaps you should speak to my brother. ... He's in the orchard with the bees. Come in—"

"Miss" led him through the garden to the back door of the building and disappeared around the corner into the orchard.

"Vince," she called, "there's a gentleman here looking for his old schoolmate, Zdeněk."

"I'll be right there," answered a far-off male voice. "I'm almost done – just the lid to put back."

At this, the Miss reappeared, at a gallop, furiously waving her arms around. She burst through the door and pulled Zderad in.

"A bee was after me," she said apologetically, out of breath, when they had stopped, in a small anteroom with a brick floor and smoky walls, on which hung even more blackened paintings of saints.

"My brother will be here in a minute. He's a beekeeper, you see," she added superfluously with a kind of maternal smile. "Sit down while you're waiting."

Zderad sank into a wicker armchair, and waited.

The parsonage anteroom was pleasantly cool with a somewhat damp, but pleasant smell of apples, wax, and perhaps incense; the air was calming and conciliatory, clearly religious.

Soon, he saw walking past the window, with the rolling gait portly people have, a large figure, clad from head to toe in white overalls.

On his head the Parson wore an olde-worlde beekeeper's straw hat, from the rim of which hung a veil, tucked in under the collar of the overalls. In his hand he held a smoker, with which he was puffing ferociously all round, and at his body. Around him swarmed a cloud of distinctly angry bees.

He passed the window, and a moment later, the opening and closing of a door and heavy footsteps could be heard somewhere inside. Then a door into the anteroom opened and the Hierarch entered. He was still in the overalls but his head was now visible.

It was massive, covered in thick, tidy grey hair.

His face was heavy and fleshy, like a farmer's, with good-natured but somehow sad furrows around the mouth and eyes.

These in turn were dark and wise, equally sad, and benevolent in a resigned sort of way.

"One of my colonies is very vicious," he said without introduction, in a deep, slightly nasal voice somewhat resembling a trombone, or as though the bulbous-beaked Chinese goose *Cygnopsis cygnoides* had learned to articulate speech.

"Friends keep advising me to put them down with sulphur smoke – but I can't –

I tried to catch the queen to change her for a gentle one, you know? Because when you exchange the queen for a docile one from a docile colony, then her progeny will also be docile, you know? But that's the second time I haven't found the vicious one. She's there all right, the brood-chamber is full, but she gave me the slip again somehow. It's a big colony, you know.

So, I've drawn another blank. My sister is complaining she can't go into the garden – what can I do? I'll have to try again sometime.

And what brings you to these parts?"

The last phrase did not sound like an affectation, coming from his lips. He looked at Zderad mildly and ponderously, but piercingly, as if he could see right inside him.

Confused by this X-ray scan, Zderad once more stammered out his inquiry, and the necessary details about himself.

"Well, come on in," said the Parson.

"Something rather strange happened there, you see. Let's find a quiet place to talk about it. Perhaps you could clear up a few things for me as well."

The Parson led Zderad into a small room, which looked just like rooms do in all older, wealthy country parsonages, in the same way that the priest himself was a typical example of a good village parson.

He disappeared again for a moment, and returning without the overalls in just shirt and trousers, he poured Zderad some rowanberry wine – or some such, sat down opposite him at a little table with a doily, and once again scrutinised him wisely and heavily with his dark eyes.

"So you are Mr. Zderad" he trumpeted again quietly.

"Young Zdeněk – father Brva – told me about you, how good you were at school, and in particular at Greek. But he said you used to needle him about the truth of scripture – you shouldn't have done that."

Zderad became confused again. It was quite true of course. Zderad often enjoyed showing Brva his own intellectual superiority, even by pointing out the absurdities of his faith and muddling his head that way.

He had thought at the time that stupid Brva was letting it in one ear and out the other, but he was brought up sharply when he realised that in doing so he had touched him and tortured him more that he had intended.

"And what are you doing now – at the University I suppose?"

Zderad felt the usual taste of bile in his mouth and aggressively confessed that he was only a funeral singer.

"Oh, why's that? – Ah, I see. – Still, be glad you're free at least. While a man has a full belly and a roof over his head he has good reason to be content and praise God!"

Zderad had long since acquired this wisdom – even though he did not praise God for it – but alas, his current situation turned it all to naught.

He felt a strong urge to tell the priest everything – he looked trustworthy – but in the end he changed his mind after all.

The thing was too revolting – apart from which – that wasn't why he was here.

"You know," the priest continued, like a trombone, "but don't tell anyone – dear Zdeněk died."

"He died" – the priest lowered his voice to a horrified whisper – "by his own hand! Just think – a priest – and here, in a village. We kept it from the villagers, even his family doesn't know – the doctor was helpful. …

We told them all that he died because his heart gave out. …

When a man hangs himself, his heart does stop beating – so we weren't lying, really," he added with the usual clerical circumlocution.

"And then – to do something like that – his heart gave out in a moral sense too, he lost heart as we say, don't we? So we didn't really lie.

The bishop gave permission for a Church funeral – that's common enough now, and we told his mother she couldn't see him – that he was decomposing already, poor thing. He looked awful – dear God". The parson crossed himself.

"We don't even know why – hard to tell.

There was a man who came to visit him out here, from the City, who he was or why it's difficult to say – we thought perhaps that he might be from the police or something – but we don't know.

Zdeněk was afraid of him. But he never confided in us. They used to go to the woods together – they used to be gone a long time – and Zdeněk – he was obviously unhappy about it, he would pray in the chapel long into the night – and he would weep – he was such a sensitive boy, but, you knew him.

He never confided in me, you know.

And I – I must say – didn't pressure him to; to be honest I was half afraid of what he might tell me, even though I can't think what it could have been.

I thought even – but then I know that Zdeněk liked girls – in all decency, you understand, but we are also only human – but he used to look, I noticed that. Lord knows…

He didn't come to me for confession – that's not usual practice – so I don't know – though, of course I wouldn't have said to anyone. …

He used to go to the late Ješina, on his bicycle, through the woods. Quite often.

Then Ješina passed away and no one took his place. Dear Zdeněk became sadder and sadder – and then finally it happened.

God have mercy on his soul.

You see, I thought, as a schoolmate of his, since you used to be friends, perhaps you could throw some light on it all?"

Zderad felt he probably could, but not to this old priest, who seemed too naive in that way that priests do.

Besides, he wasn't sure.

He just asked what the visitor had looked like.

"He's difficult to describe, he had sort of strange pale eyes – like – like the watersprite in folk tales.

That's why we thought he might be, you know – a secret agent.

But then again, that didn't seem to be it. He was dressed well and so on.

– But why the devil – *sit venia*[*] – should a man like that visit chaplains in the country."[15]

— So, it was clear.

But Zderad couldn't tell the priest what was what.

That was probably another mistake.

Had he told the truth, the old parson might have advised him.

It's an age-old fact that Catholic priests may look and talk as if they are clueless, but, in fact, often they are not so naive at all.

The Holy Roman Church is the foxiest of foxes, and a Catholic parson, unlike various other pastors, gets to hear the most peculiar things in the confessional.

Apart from that, Father Plicka also seemed to be reasonable in an ordinary, non-religious way.

He'd even let slip that he'd had the right suspicion – but – no – not that thing!

Had Zderad decided to speak then, he might still have got relief; but he didn't.

Instead the conversation turned to Brva, his studies, home circumstances etc., to Zderad himself, his wife on vacation, how he was on his way to see her, and later, when Zderad was rising to leave, the parson told him he'd better stay the night, as there would be no more trains to Mlno by then.

And that is what he did.

---

[*] "*Sit venia verbo*" – if you'll excuse the word.

Zderad sat in the slow train and cast his eye over the rolling, pensive landscape.

The verger, or someone, some codger, had taken him by horse-drawn carriage, old style, to a better connection for the stopping train – so he had been allowed a lie-in.

He'd had a good night at the parsonage, in a proper bed with clean sheets, provided by the "Miss".

He even had a bath beforehand – he didn't like the thought of crawling dirty into a fine bed. The parsonage had a surprisingly up-to-date bathroom, and an electric immersion heater.

He slept in the priest's own room – who, so he said, preferred to sleep in the apiary in the summer months.

The bedroom was pleasant, white, smelling of honey, wax and apples.

Above the bed hung a framed inscription, beautifully crafted:

> *"Better Celibate for Some,*
> *Than under a Woman's Thumb!"*

and he awoke in the morning to the sound of cockerels crowing, down in the village.

The supper which the "Miss" had prepared was simple, but tasty and filling.

It consisted of potato pancakes, known locally as "Tóčn" – in some quantity, with cranberry sauce.

And a bottle of missal wine.

The Parson, who'd had time to "size him up" politically, and decided he was safe enough (though he seldom spoke of these things) shared the local gossip.

He told him of his respected position both with the Party and the local National Executive in view of his services to collective beekeeping, and of how some farmers resisted forming collectives.

"I think they should, really," he trumpeted through his cold.

"If it were done properly – the farmers would all be better off!

They know their business round here, not like in Russia.

They could really do well out of it.

As you know, our nation has always pulled through by virtue of its rural roots.

Material welfare plays an important part – the Church has never denied that.

It's important for rural communities to thrive.

In the Thirty Years' War they cleaned us out, and look – by the start of the eighteenth century – the dark ages for Catholicism – the lords and ladies were issuing orders to stop farmers' wives coming to church in gold-stitched headgear, wearing garnets and such things."

The Parson chuckled.

"Well … and out of the farming classes – slowly but surely – came the intellectuals of the nation … first the priesthood – and now, you know the rest. … The Powers-That-Be have trodden us down again, sadly; but I think it can come round again. … Remember this, Zderad, the farmers always survive, whatever name they think up for them – and the language survives with them.

It's already under threat again. I ask you – 'the Battle for Crop-yield', no less! We always called it the harvest!

Or 'the Fish-level in Czech waters!' The fish-level? And other things.

We used to have teacher training colleges and now, Pedagogical Institutes!

Lord preserve us!

Well, we outlasted the Avars, the Huns, the Habsburgs, Hitler – much as he didn't last long in historical terms – and we'll outlast the Russians too, God willing.

And it will be the farmer who survives best again.

Down to earth, whether literally, on his patch, or the farmer within us all, who doesn't give tuppence for great big gestures. He just wants great big cabbages. He's dumb enough and idealistic enough to know the pigsty has to get mucked out in the end.

But then, no one expects idealism from them, they're supposed to be too dumb for that.

There, I seem to have said quite enough. Well, goodnight, and Franta will take you to the station in the morning."

"You know," he added "you and I, individual people may take the brunt – but the nation, the nation will not go under – it hasn't yet, anyway. Down there, hands in the earth, or in the compost-heap; that is our true element. Like the Bible says, God created Adam out of clay."

———

Zderad reminisced about the conversation and how the next day he'd stopped by Brva's grave with the Parson.

The inscription there read, simply:

P. Z. BRVA
Chaplain

– and the dates.

Houseleeks grew on the mound of earth, and radiated peace.

Zderad found it sad, but as if from a cosmically vast distance.

Brva's face, as he remembered it, seemed to rise out of the flowers, smiling timidly and kindly.

The way he used to smile under his desk, copying, while he, Zderad, the bighead, kicked him, hissing: "Get on with it you oaf. You won't even crib it in time at this rate, you blockhead!"

Now they were, kind of, both in the same boat, and Zderad, whose IQ had once caused a minor sensation at the Institute for Human Research, knew where he could shove it.

At least Brva had finished his studies, so there.

There was another thing he noticed on his friend's grave: Someone had put a picture there, a framed colour print of some Icon, fast fading and curling with the damp.

It was just a piece of paper, cut out of a book or magazine.

An Icon of a woman with a dark, stern face – a hermitess.

Zderad leant forward and could just make out an inscription:

'St. Mary of Egypt – hermitess'

— Mary of Egypt, the patroness of prostitutes!*

— So, the Monster's grimacing maw had even reached this place.

It was that very mishmash of sentiment and cynicism which made Him so nauseating. After all, these were the hallmarks of the Ruling Party, too.

And, of course, Zderad's mission was a total failure!

At least there was no more room for doubt. He couldn't quite see how the Monster had got Brva into his clutches. Surprisingly though, he found himself pitying the Misfit.

Naturally, he kept his discovery to himself.

The priest either knew enough or suspected enough, anyway.

He seemed as old as time, and as wise.

———

Perhaps Zderad should have grieved over his dead erstwhile companion, or been angry or afraid for his own future, but his mind strayed elsewhere, in a strictly personal direction.

When Franta dropped him off, he felt a bidding. Having seated himself in the station convenience he beheld a unique masterpiece.

Obscene graffiti scrawled on toilet walls are commonplace – here as elsewhere, but they seldom reveal any artistic talent.

An exception to the rule was to be seen in this station toilet; a near life-size picture of a woman, realistically drawn, in a posture known to primate ethologists as 'presenting'.

Some wayward genius had fallen by the wayside here, some unrecognised Rembrandt or Michelangelo of Closets had passed this way and filled the tedium of waiting with this creation.

The work was executed with an indigo pencil, which the artist must have sacrificed for the cause, and spent considerable time and dedication resharpening.

The woman was shown leaning on her hands against the same wall

---

* Owing to the fact that knowledge of hagiography is no longer common among the populace let us satisfy the readers' curiosity as to why St. Mary of Egypt is the patroness of prostitutes: according to Legend she wanted to reach the Holy Land but had no money for the ferry. She therefore bartered with the ferryman with what she had.

on which she was drawn, all correctly foreshortened to allow for perspective.

She was bent over, with her skirt hitched up; below her other, more relevant details, were stockings, attached to a suspender belt.

The artist had used a famous visual trick, familiar to visitors of stately homes and galleries. Like the crossbow archer in the diorama "Battle of Lipany,"[16] the focal point of this female form seemed to point straight at the viewer wherever he went.

For some unfathomable reason the ultimate obscenity were her knickers, rolled down to her ankles, which her outspread legs were stretching to breaking point.

All that could be seen of the head was a wavy perm.

Since the location was surrounded by a verdantly exhaling dense forest, it was hard to guess why the so-depicted would ever choose for the purpose of *coitus a tergo* this particular unromantic venue; unless the notion involved keeping out of the rain, or snow, or somesuch.

It seemed likely that the realism of the picture had saved it from the whitewasher's brush.

Zderad recalled this decoration now, feeling a strong desire to be with his wife.

The thoughts which turned his attention in this direction left no room for intruding ones, worrisome or otherwise.

The slogan in the Parson's bedroom now seemed like an infantile excuse.

———

He was now walking along the levee of the pond, reminiscing about the wilder days of his youth, and looked forward to seeing Sylva; and little Záviš, whom he saw too little of as it was.

He felt a little less sure at the prospect of the bony evangelical Ram, but he put that thought out of his mind.

It was early afternoon on a Saturday, and waterfowl sailed across the huge pond like a flotilla of small, predominantly white sailing boats, reminding him of the "Silesian Bard," Petr Bezruč.[17]

Strolling towards him in the distance, along the long straight road bordered by old bushy willows, a close-knit family was evidently on its way to a suitable beach or section of the bank.

The man was dressed only in swimming trunks and he had a child, wearing a little white hat, on his shoulders.

Walking beside him was a woman, also dressed in nothing but a bikini, which was green.

She had reddish blonde hair, and skin of that pale golden hue particular to those blondes, who are capable of basking; and it could be assumed that, on closer inspection, she would be covered in freckles.

In fact, she resembled Sylva, to a considerable degree.

She was carrying a large bag, probably containing food, a rug and so on, and she was leaning a little to one side.

Let us add, so as not to do the man an injustice, that he was also carrying something, as well as the child on his shoulders.

It even seemed as if the woman was limping a little but that was probably caused by the combination of the bag and the bumpy road.

A little later, when Zderad emerged from daydreams and speculations (he daydreamed almost constantly about practically anything), the distance between him and the ordinary little family had greatly reduced.

The woman began to resemble Sylva very much indeed and a few paces later Zderad even recognised the little face of Záviš.

The man with them was stocky, very hairy, even on his shoulders, with the beginnings of a beer belly; not just pushing fifty, by any means.

He was swarthy, almost completely bald, and of the sort of crude-hewn, unpleasant type like comrade Václav Kopecký[18] or some of the secret police boys.

The People describe this type of person as 'another one of those commie mugs'.

For those who don't know what I am talking about, let us give a short description:

He had no distinguishing features to speak of, thick black eyebrows, pale, rather hysterical looking eyes and a wide but thin mouth. He was also fairly wrinkled.

By now Sylva had also recognised Zderad, and froze in surprise.

It looked as though she went white, then flushed; then she put down the bag and began running towards her husband.

She embraced him unusually warmly.

"Hi," she was laughing. "Where did you pop up from?

This – this is comrade Burda, my headmaster. He takes great interest in the staff and so he came up to persuade Dad to join the collective."

This of course meant "look out" and "watch your mouth" and Zderad, who was well trained in this form of communication, did not have to be told twice.

Burda, understanding the situation, put down the child, who ran off towards Zderad.

An ordinary family reunion followed.

Burda suddenly found himself in the position of the outsider and stood with a rigid smile on his face.

He did not look at all pleased.

He offered Zderad his clumsy hand which was in essence the hard hand of a gentrified carpenter.

"Hello," he said in a common sort of voice which is difficult to describe.

"So how's the funeral singing going then?"

He was obviously so put out by Zderad's sudden appearance that he could not restrain a pugnacious put-down.

"It's going famously," said Zderad adding a proverb-which translates as: *"Can't get bacon from a cur, pigs won't give you fleece or fur."* The proverb in question was an old one, and pointedly obscure.

This confused Burda absolutely, and all he could do was clear his throat with embarrassment.

Zderad would have continued this style of conversation but Sylva gave him a pleading look. (Comrade Burda has come to persuade Dad to join the collective, hasn't he?)

So Zderad said something a little more normal, and emotions calmed a little, for the moment at least.

Zderad joined them in a completely natural way, carrying little Záviš on his shoulders and leading Sylva by the hand.

Comrade Burda, not knowing whether to simply go or not, followed them, his mouth more and more hard-set.

When they arrived at a small stretch of sandy bank (the sand had been brought in some time ago for day-trippers), they settled down and Zderad also stripped.

In those days the not-so-well-off wore boxer-shorts for underwear; and Zderad, who was no exception, was thus immediately dressed for the occasion to a respectable degree.

He then waded into the water; and after getting up courage, dunked under, like a duck.

The initial cold shock gradually melted away.

Zderad swam under water for a long time until the flashes of sunshine on the sand dimmed to nothing, until he could see nothing but green, then blue, then brown and the water pushed on his eardrums and became ice cold.

He then emerged, snorting like a walrus, and looked around.

Comrade Burda was sitting on the bank with his feet in the water, and little Záviš's white sun hat shone out by his side.

Sylva was nowhere to be seen.

Then he felt a hand on his shoulder.

He looked around.

The water nymph had returned after so many years and was smiling at him through strands of wet hair.

Zderad turned onto his back and swam on, holding Sylva's gaze.

They swam at length toward the distant curve of the horizon from which, after a little while, emerged the greenery of their nuptial island.

VIII

The morning was wintry and misty, before sunrise, and Zderad was dozing on a train.

He was returning to the City, to the cemeteries, the everyday world of his being.

The events of the past days and nights were swirling around in his head. In particular he kept coming back to his visit to the parsonage in X, and the fact that the Monster must have driven Brva to suicide.

It was of course quite clear who the "gentleman with watersprite eyes" was, and that he was most likely the one who put the Icon of Mary of Egypt on Brva's grave.

It was also basically clear now where the Monster had got hold of Zderad's Ode to Stalin. Maybe Brva even knew who he was; but Brva was dead, and the main question, namely the identity of the Monster, remained unsolved.

Zderad, however, did not feel that the trip had been totally wasted.

Amongst other things he had met Father Plicka, and he had a sort of feeling that that in itself was worthwhile.

The existence of the quiet, peasant-philosophical archetypal figure was in some way a counterbalance to the existence of the Monster, Burda and Zderad himself. While they themselves existed only in relation to the Joyful Present, the priest himself was of a super-temporary essence, an independent existence, which even Constructive Reality could not deprive him of.

In particular, Zderad was pleased with his visit to Mlno.

Surprisingly, the old farmer had been friendly, though in his stiff and taciturn way.

Zderad felt that he had Burda's presence to thank for this, for it was clear that the old man couldn't stand him.

Zderad's mother-in-law was a colourless, bullied person, but Zderad had the feeling that she quite liked him.

So this aspect of things was clearing up.

In particular, however, Zderad was grateful to Fate for enabling him to visit his wife, and did not admit to himself that the money for it had in fact been provided by the Monster.

Their first embrace on the island had also been very successful, on the emotional side. Memories had obviously played their part.

They would have stayed there longer if Sylva had not suddenly thought that Burda might leave and Závišek would become frightened or might even drown.

Burda was, however, faithful to the role of the reliable paternal comrade.

But he did not go back to the farm with them.

When she pushed Zderad into the house to see father, the situation was rather embarrassing, but the old Evangelical was visibly pleased when she explained to him that Zderad's arrival had put Burda off.

Zderad then exploited his visit to the full.

Apart from his natural needs, he also had the feeling that while with Sylva he was cleansing himself of the Monster and reasserting his normality.

In the early evening he took possession of her once again, this time in a very rustic way in the stable when she was giving hay to the horses, obviously inspired by the work of art at the train-stop.

The Persian miniaturist Abdullah is responsible, amongst other things, for creating a picture of Mohammed's ascension to Heaven. The Prophet, who for religious reasons has only a stain for a face, is surrounded by a great halo of flames. He is riding a rather non-descript mount, which could perhaps be a camel, most probably a female one, except that it has no hump. It does however have a beautiful woman's head wearing a golden cap or coronet. To emphasise the fact that this is a heavenly ride, the background is a deep azure, with stylised fluffy clouds and numerous angels holding censers and the like.*

---

* This picture could also be considered to be a decent allegory of heterosexual intercourse, especially one 'a tergo', i.e. the original pre-missionary position. Engulfed in the golden fires of pleasure the copulator is falling into the precipice of cosmic space whilst choirs of angels sound unexpectedly colourful harmonies. At the same time he gallops forth on the animal essence of his partner, which simultaneously has a human aspect, here symbolised by the human head on a camel or other animal body. Although

Apart from these lawful-entitlement games, Zderad also played with Záviš and noted that his time out of school was doing him a lot of good.

He also helped the old farmer out with chopping firewood thus working on improving his standing in the old man's eyes a little, and he attempted to overcome his mistrust of horses bordering on hippo-phobia, although only with relatively modest results, for which Sylva made reasonable excuses.

The night was, once again, very pleasant.

But when Zderad got out of bed at around five in the morning to go out into the yard he thought that he could see Burda's figure behind a fence.

On Sunday he was compelled to accompany the farmer's family to the Nonconformist meeting-house or chapel or whatever it was, which was situated in a converted barn at the far end of the village.

He listened to a boring and strangely malicious sermon, and also joined them at the Lord's Supper, at which time his basically Catholic soul reassured and consoled him that it was nothing, because the preacher was definitely not part of the apostolic succession.

Just to be on the safe side, however, he tried to evoke the most perfect contrition within himself with respect to his graveyard affair, although the firm resolve part was rather questionable.

They also sang some old Protestant chorales (the Czechs could never quite identify with the view that music has no place in reli-gion) and Zderad created quite a stir by producing various parts and harmonies for them. He thus seduced some of the Evangelicals to include a few thirds and sixths themselves, and after the service was over, everyone commented on how the singing was much better than it had been for quite some time.

After the mid-day meal, which was most substantial, as it consisted of two contrite hens that refused to lay, they went to the lake again.

This time nothing could go on, however, as they had to keep an eye on Záviš who was particularly cute that day.

They met Burda in the gate on their return, looking even more

---

dominated by the rider, she is at the same time mistress of the situation, as expressed by the said golden coronet. The personality of the rider dissolves, and hence the loss of facial features which are a mere stain of colour.

hard-mouthed, and the old farmer who was seeing him out was even more wooden than usual.

Owing to his staunch self-denial, however, he did not give any comment or explanation.

The night was once again clear and warm, and as soon as everything on the farm was silent, and Záviš was fast asleep, the couple took off on another astronautical trip in the man-made lake, unencumbered by any form of clothing.

When the east grew pale and mists rose from the water, Sylva turned to him, covered in crystal droplets and said:

"Zderad, remember, whatever happens. I am and always will be your wife."

Zderad kissed her and found that the drops on her face were salty.

Yet he did not know what she meant, as he'd automatically related her sentence to his graveyard secret.

Then he dried himself, dressed, drank the tea that Sylva made him in the kitchen, kissed his wife and sleeping Záviš, and set off through the lakeside mist to catch the morning train.

IX

It was about a fortnight later.

The neighbours were gathering on the balconies talking excitedly.

Some tried to pretend they did not know about it but nevertheless they poked their heads out of the windows and strained their ears.

It was around six-ish, the windows threw golden reflections on the opposite side of the slummy precipice and Zderad was just entering the building through the archway into the yard.

Shouting and dull blows could be heard coming from the ground floor – or rather basement flat, for it was above ground level in the yard but below it on the street side.

Hamouz, probably drunk, was beating his adopted daughter Nadia, whom we have already mentioned. She was in fact the daughter of a liberator.

Her mother had already been in hospital for about a week as a result of a similar happening, while the legal aspect of the thing was carefully hushed up.

Slum dwellers the world over do not confide in the police – who, in their turn, prefer to keep their work as simple as possible.

Perhaps Hamouz enjoyed a privileged position with them; considering he was a militiaman.

Zderad pushed through the crowd.

His heart was thundering and his feelings were simultaneously strong and mixed.

He had moderate sadistic proclivities, and the idea of a girl being beaten on her naked bottom by a brute with a leather strap (this could be guessed at from the sound) had a vaguely erotogenic effect on him.* At the same time, Zderad was beside himself with anger about this bestiality of his; which he had never asked for, which he

---

* The dirty old man Sigmund Freud devotes a whole treatise to this phenomenon in his "Drei Abhandlungen zur Sexualtheorie", 'three essays on the theory of sexuality', under the telling title: "Das kleine Kind wird geschlagen.", 'the small child, thrashed'.

hated, and which in some ways put him in the same category as the Monster and similar buddies.

This anger immediately turned against Hamouz via the mechanism of projection.

Zderad rattled the door handle of the cellar only to find that the swine had locked himself in his den with his victim.

"Hamouz," he yelled, "leave the girl alone, OK?!"

Nothing but thuds and wailing, in reply.

"Hamouz, open up and leave the girl alone, now!!"

Nothing again.

Zderad kicked the door.

"Hamouz, open up and leave the girl alone, or I'll go for the cops!"

"Fuck you, you dork – and go if you want – just make sure they don't keep you there yourself – you – you stiffsinger." roared the drunk's contemptuous and hollow voice from the depths of the basement.

"Hamouz!!!" screamed Zderad in his piercing trained falsetto, just like when he deputised for the first tenor — "you swine! Open up or I'll kick your hell-hole to pieces!"

This new voice sounded quite horrific and remarkably wild.

No doubt some of the readers have watched a fight between two tomcats.

Before they fly at each other they stand, humped, stretching to the greatest possible height, with ears flat on their heads; twitching their bristling tails, with which they shield their stomachs and flanks.

At the same time they give out a drawn mewing – the roar of miniature tigers. Some of them hoot in deep contraltos, while others whine in piercing trebles.

The pitch of the voice has nothing to do with their aggressiveness or physical fitness, and frequently the treble singer ends up ruling the ring.

Similarly Zderad's unnatural falsetto was almost more terrifying then if he had roared in the bass register.

He ran savagely up against the door, banging on it with his fists and kicking, but it didn't give.

Pulling himself together a bit he stepped back, took another run, this time using the full weight of his shoulder.

On the third try the rotten entrance gave way and Zderad flew into the hovel like a cannon ball.

In tense situations things often appear to happen as if slowed down. Perhaps this is because the subjective time of the participants has speeded up so that external events appear slower.

Zderad was thus able to clearly experience the whole situation, even though his flight through the air could only have lasted a fraction of a second.

"The girl was tied ..."

The girl was tied to the bedstead and obscenely bared.

The thick-set primitive, in a filthy shirt inflated by a huge beer-gut, was standing next to her with a cobbler's strap in his hand and with his hair on end.

The look on his face at that moment was one of stupefied fright.

Zderad flew at him and landed a huge and improbable blow on his jaw, like in a silent movie; shocking himself almost as much.

Zderad was left handed and Hamouz was not expecting a blow from his right.

It rang out like a shot.

The old man's head, equally improbably, swung to the side.

His dentures flew out of his mouth and clattered on the tiled floor.

Before he could collect himself Zderad gave him one from the other side, weaker, but even so, splendidly effective.

The brute flew into a corner, where he knocked over a wooden pail, and slumped down heavily onto its edge.

He must have hurt himself considerably because he howled.

Surprisingly, he was still holding the strap, and when Zderad rushed after him his bloodshot eyes bulged and he took a swipe at him.

Zderad moved, just in time, so that the strap missed his face, but it caught him on the shoulder.

That should not have happened; because from then on Zderad could only dimly recall the sequence of events.

It seems that he grabbed Hamouz by the neck with one hand, lifted him into the air, and with his other hand under the belt of his trousers (the instrument of torture was a different strap), swung him round, and with a massive thrust sent him into the midst of the onlookers, who were crammed into the doorway.

The hefty projectile scattered their ranks and landed in the yard, his mug down on the concrete.

He lay there for a while and then, sobbing disgustingly, raised himself; first to his knees, and finally onto his wobbly legs.

His face was horribly bloodied and grazed from the rough surface of the yard. He staggered back into the den, took a dirty jacket and class-denoting cap off a nail, bent down for his teeth; and without a word, crawled out through the arch, into the jungle of the slums.

As soon as he disappeared, the dead silence was broken by the squawks of the excited neighbours.

Zderad was taking all this in as if in a dream.

He realised that he was shaking macroscopically and felt that his face was drained of blood.

He leant against a wall, thinking that he would fall over.

He was very short of breath.

Some people seemed to be talking to him and someone was slapping him on the shoulder.

Someone was also trying to stick a grubby bottle into his mouth, but Zderad declined, because he realised that it must have belonged to Hamouz, and that they had taken it from his flat.

Meanwhile, some of the women had rushed inside and started taking care of Nadia.

They threw the men out and drew the curtain across the miserable little window.

Some do-gooder took to re-hanging the door and restoring the prolapsed screws on the fragile lock, covering up the hole left by the splintered wood with cardboard.

It was clear that public opinion was on Zderad's side even though they had up to now been exceedingly passive to Hamouz's sadistic sessions.

This is a common phenomenon, and the lore about strong personalities, untrue according to the theory (though not the practice!) of Marxism-Leninism, had once again been vindicated by experience.

———

By this time our hero had staggered back to his den and wearily slumped down at the table.

The excited crowing of the citizens could still be heard from downstairs.

His anger evaporated away, and Zderad began to feel afraid. Hamouz was a militiaman, probably a member of the Party.

Even the lowest-ranking arseholes in the hierarchy of the beloved organisation, had the power to destroy whoever they wanted.

The House Confidants, for instance.[*]

Zderad didn't even know who the Confidant in their house was. Maybe that was Hamouz as well.

There was of course the evidence that he'd nearly beaten his step-daughter to death, and before her, his common-law-wife, her mother, but of course you can use evidence in any way you like.

After all, that is the function of dialectics, the weapon of the pro-letariat, or rather the affluent pseudo-proletariat.

There were also the witnesses, but naturally they'll keep their mouths shut and disappear when they see the going get tough.

Or at least the majority of them will, and the Comrades will have no trouble dealing with the rest.

An assault on – or perhaps even attempted murder of, a militiaman – hmm – most likely a good twenty-five years.

But before they sentence him, they'll have a great deal of fun with him, probably with Hamouz in attendance – Zderad could feel the hu-miliating motion in his entrails just like at the time when the Monster first showed him the poem.

— The Monster!

— That could be the solution!

— It looks like He's one of Them, must be one of Them.

— You can see that from the affair with poor Brva, and from the nerve He has.

— It's obvious.

— He's one of them, and he's a gentleman, educated, with refined taste. (Refined taste! What? Given what he does? That's a good one!) Well – in some ways.

— He has a natural aversion towards "commoners" of the Hamouz type and, because He is a swine himself, it's not toned down with compassion.

— It seems He hasn't had enough of Zderad yet.

---

[*] Every apartment house or block of flats in Czechoslovak towns had an appointed "House Confidant" whose duty it is to keep a vigilant eye on the inhabitants. The atmosphere in the country is so cynical that this office is not even a secret one: for example if one applies for a permit to go abroad, the House Confidant has a lot of say in the matter. The House Confidants do tremendous damage because they are low ranking communists and thus petty, envious and uneducated, but still quite powerful.

— That's clear from that embarrassing nonsense of the "wedding" and things like that.

— He forced Zderad into the whole show, so He obviously doesn't feel that He is degrading himself before Zderad so much anymore. It looks like He wants to keep Zderad a bit longer.

— It's easier for Him that way too.

— So there is this possibility.

— If only it was morning already! Or better still, tomorrow night! That is when Zderad has the next date with his entomber.)

— But maybe Hamouz will arrive with the boys during the night.

— Or, early in the morning.

— They usually come in the early hours.

— If only he knew who the Monster was and where he could find him.

— (Well, well, look how things have turned out.) Don't be surprised, we're all just vulnerable humans.

— For Christ's sake! – They could even take Sylva! And Záviš!

— What about that Burda bloke?!

— Oh, my God!

— Easy, you've got to wait 'till tomorrow, panic won't help.

— The best thing now is to disappear somewhere and spend the night in pubs or somewhere.

— In the morning – he'd better not turn up for the singing, they'd easily get him at the cemetery for sure.

— He'll ring Turgo and tell him he's losing his voice, or rather pretend he is, on the phone.

— Venca of St. Nicholas can fill in for him.

— If he's not drunk that is.

— In the evening, off to the tomb and the Monster.

— There, you see, *man proposes and God* – well more likely the Devil – *disposes*.

— Damn it all a thousand times.

Zderad got up, and made for the door.

On the gallery on the second floor he saw a peculiar procession.

The caring women were pushing a pale, tear-stained Nadia along, holding her up on each side.

Poor thing, she could hardly walk.

The widow Hromádková must be taking her in.

It's most likely to be Hromádková.

At the sound of his footsteps they began turning their heads.

Hromádková said something to Nadia.

She turned her head, blushed a bit and – "Thank you, Mr. Zderad."

She smiled innocently and angelically.

"You swine!" a voice within him yelled. He realised that when he was beating Hamouz he had been roughing up a part of his own self.

———

"Derad! You hooligan! Wot you doink here?

Gyere igye, come here, sit down, old *kámoš*."*

Zderad turned from the bar of the smoke-filled 'Refreshments National Enterprise', towards the voice.

By the dim light of a bare bulb covered in fly excrement, he saw that the voice was issuing from the lips of a young, but very fat man in blue overalls.

The man's face resembled the underside of a well-browned round rye-loaf, both in shape and colour.

Stood before the individual was a glass of beer, and a semi-official looking cap with a black 'bakelite' peak.

Zderad cheered up, unwillingly.

Running from the long arm of injustice, he was thankful for any safe company.

Even if it was only the dustman Döme, his mate from national service days, a fleeting and occasional acquaintance in civilian life.

Döme spoke a strange mixture of Czech and Slovak, thus recreating the now officially non-existent Czechoslovak language.†

This newly created language was still giving him a lot of problems, of the morphological, phonological and syntactic kind, because he was not a Slovak but a Hungarian or rather, judging from his colouring,

---

* The speaker uses a kind of Hungarian-Czech-Slovak pot-pourri. Here we show it with a kind of half-breed English, which does not work nearly as well, but hopefully will give a flavour of the real thing.

† From a purely linguistic point of view Czech and Slovak may be considered to be two groups of dialects of a common Czechoslovak language, each group having developed an independent literary norm. For political reasons, this is no longer the official view.

of the Roma ilk.

How he'd managed to end up in the City, Zderad didn't know.

Zderad, his own metric pint in hand, made his way through the crowd towards Döme and shook him by his brown, dusty and surprisingly soft, small hand.

"How are you, Deradko, you hooligan?

You still sing funerals? You have a nice voice, I remember."

Zderad muttered something affirmative.

"How you sing to dze supreme commander as on church.

And Comrade Luttenant, Zderad, why you man sing as on church? What times we had, buddy.

Not good, but not bad."

Zderad laughed.

The story which Döme was trying to communicate in his broken Hungarian Czechoslovak concerned the prescribed song:

"To the supreme commander we now report with pride."

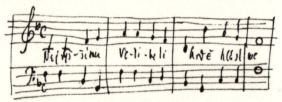

Out of boredom and a kind of passive aggressive impulse, Zderad had provided a kind of baroque 'basso giusto' to it, which suitably accentuated its hidden character of Jesuit-like ecclesiastical pomposity in text and melody. After all, Stalin, the supreme commander to whom we reported with pride, was originally a student of divinity.

With unusual intuition, the lieutenant aptly, though inaccurately, detected the ecclesiastical connection and commented: "Zderaaaad, maaan, you're singing like in church," which all those present found very amusing, including the comrade captain.

For a short while, Zderad and Döme took pleasure in their shared past experiences.

Soon, Döme saddened perceptibly, stirred the spilled beer around on the table with his finger and finally said:

"Now every woman is whore.

If she goes work, she also whoring.

For dze guy give him no peace. And dze guy, too, go work.

Ayayayay. Jeezuu."

It seemed that Döme had domestic problems.

He leant forward towards Zderad and said in a confidential tone:

"If you have young wife, you buddy mighty careful. For I have him old, and he no good eidzer."

Döme lowered his voice, looked around so that his oriental eyes flashed white in his brown face, and continued in a careful whisper:

"Because dze communisht, dzey bring him to it. If you, *leanyi*,[*] not give me – dzen – cadre reference! and he's finished, *kamarát*!"[†]

Zderad smiled. He was absolutely sure of his Sylva and found it hard to sympathise with the Gypsy.

Döme leant forward once again and self-importantly whispered his recipe for detecting marital infidelity:

"When your old woman come from work home, you touch him on his cunt. And if he nice, dzen OK. But if he caved-in – *az azaňát ištenét!*[‡] – he been fuckin. You don't believe? *Kamarát*! Dzis told me one professor doctór!"

Zderad guffawed.

Idiot, he thought, but at least I'm not alone.

They drank. Zderad was tired from the day's squawking, and then the set-to with Hamouz – the beer was going straight to his head.

He was trying to drown out his fear but wasn't managing somehow. If anything, it was getting worse.

The lash on his shoulder was hurting and he was loath to imagine what it was going to be like when the police lay into him for real, in the presence of Hamouz, relishing every moment.

More Gyppies arrived in the pub; it seemed to be their local.

They were shouting across at Döme in Gypsy and the linguistically

---

[*] Girl (Hungarian)

[†] Comrade, friend

[‡] Mother of God!

talented Zderad who had picked up this language in the army, noted to his surprise that Döme's command of Gypsy was as bad as his "Czechoslovak".

The Gypsies were talking loudly in their throaty language.

Zderad did not join in the conversation, which was very interesting; though probably only as uninhibited as it was, because they were not aware of his ability to participate.

It concerned e.g. the techniques of breaking and entering, and other methods of quickly and easily making *"lóve,"* or money, in English.

When the pub closed, Zderad got out of there with the Gypsies.

He declined their offer of a bed for the night politely and naturally in Czech. It was probably being made quite sincerely, but he was wary they might rob him or something.

Perhaps he should have shown them that he could speak Gypsy. They consider everyone who speaks their language to be a Rom, regardless of the colour of his skin.

This is understandable, as they have interbred with white travellers, and in some countries, like Britain, the Gypsies have entirely lost their original 'subcontinental' appearance.

Perhaps they would already have proved helpful, at that stage of his troubles, or at least would have made some effort to help. But let us not get ahead of ourselves.

———

Zderad spent the rest of the night at the cemetery, having first climbed over the decorative railings.

He managed to avoid whatever security guard there was.

Towards morning there was a light shower, and Zderad had the opportunity to savour the more unpleasant side of a tramp's life. It was also quite cold.

Before dawn he climbed over the railing again, walked aimlessly through the streets, bought himself a bread-roll and a sausage and spent the rest of the day at the lido on the River, or rather on a weir some distance from it, as he thought this would be safer.

He was in quite a good frame of mind, because, if what he feared

94

had happened, it was unlikely that a lot of men would be drummed up, just because of Hamouz.

It seemed more likely that the whole thing would be done on the quiet, with a handful of friends of the humiliated militiaman.

For this reason it would be practically impossible for them to find him in just one day.

In late afternoon he sloped off towards the tomb.

———

We are not going to describe how he broke the news to the Monster, nor how he accepted his assurance, that, if necessary, He would arrange everything; not even how he had to describe to the Monster the stupid details of the state of Nadia's injuries, or how he had to demonstrate how Hamouz went about it, on the Monster's own body.

The sad thing was, that even in these circumstances Zderad felt relief and quite genuine gratitude

Even at those times when he remembered that it was in fact the Monster who had caused Brva's suicide.

Zderad's moral corruption had thus reached a new level, without his being clearly aware of it.

———

Hamouz did not do anything.

He vanished for a few days and when he re-emerged he looked decidedly crestfallen.

He showed a creeping respect for Zderad.

He would address him from afar with the Arian greeting* of the new era: *"Toil be praised, comrade."*[19]

We will never know whether the cause was simply Zderad's honourable and noble deed, or whether the Monster had anything to do with it.

One might perhaps conclude in favour of the second alternative with regard to some symptoms that appeared during the next sado-

---

* The Arian greeting: In Nazi Germany with an outstretched right arm and the words "Heil Hitler" – its analogue in communist Czechoslovakia, equally enforced and hated is or was the greeting: "Čest práci, soudruhu" – meaning as given here.

masochistic rendezvous of the sepulchral sweethearts.

Once again we are not going to describe them, but nevertheless let us note that the Monster brought a truncheon to be used on himself and that Hamouz's name cropped up during its application.

But we cannot be sure.

Zderad was obliged to restrain himself, because he could not imagine what he would do if the Monster was unable to leave on his own two feet.

This was another of his mistakes, because in such an event he would have been able to find out more about him.

But maybe he no longer cared.

Zderad's corruption had progressed to yet another, higher level.

He had become aware of his new ability to terrify and terrorise people, thanks to his bizarre affair.

Likewise, the female rook which occupies a lowly social position in the flock immediately reaches the top of the hierarchy if she mates with a dominant male. Rooks will also sometimes form homosexual pairs, but, in contrast to humans, only if there are insufficient numbers of available females.

So much for the science of ethology.

Nadia stayed with the widow Hromádková and slowly recovered. She always greeted Zderad politely and blushed. He had clearly become her hero.

Some time later Hamouz's common-law wife returned, humbly crawled back into his den and a while later Nadia herself went back there.

Hamouz was quiet and deferent.

He did drink, probably more than before, but he did it quietly. He did not yell and he did not beat or threaten anyone.

Zderad's moral shares had a high value on the ideative stock-market of the slums.

He now had plenty of money, even though he could not make as much use of it as he would have liked, for reasons of secrecy.

Nevertheless, he did send more to Sylva.

He had now stopped visiting her, except for the occasional Sunday to Monday night, because the harvest had begun and Zderad had had enough of physical labour since his days as an assistant workman on the lakes.

This was not nice of him at all, but what can one do.

Comrade Burda was thus able to turn up in Mlno once again, but this never occurred to Zderad.

Neither did the fact that the Monster now had him hooked, even more effectively than before.

"INCIPIT ORATIO JEREMIAE PROPHETAE,"
    "Here beginneth the prayer of Jeremiah, the prophet,"
    "RECORDARE DOMINE QUID ACCIDERIT NOBIS INTUERE
ET RESPICE OPPROBRIUM NOSTRUM" ...
    *"Remember, O Lord, what is come upon us: Consider, and behold our
reproach."*
    The sound of the six mixed parts rolls under the vaults of the arti-
ficial caves of the church like a multicoloured nimbus cloud.
    We see our friend Zderad in the ranks of the tenors and Venca of
St. Nicholas flaps about on the conductor's platform.

We are present at a rehearsal of a more or less secret choir of Catholic
students and the author of the composition is none less than the
immortal Italian, Giovanni Pierluigi da Palestrina.*
    As in the case of funeral songs and other rites, here too, the lack
of experience and imagination of both the advisors and the advised
gives rise to the relative safety of the enterprise.
    Some of the singers, having come straight from some official func-
tion, are even wearing the blue shirt uniform of the Czechoslovak
Union of Youth, modestly hidden beneath their jackets.
    The wisdom of compromise, or double standards, enables the
enjoyment of a certain amount of culture.
    Zderad, however, is not entitled to hold the opinion that this is,
in fact, prostitution.
    Certainly not Zderad.
    At Venca's request he finds himself in the incongruous company
of the Youth-With-Prospects.
    Venca wants to have professionals in his choir, to pull it along,

---

* The Palestrina setting is of the first eight verses of Chapter 5 of the Lamentations,
with an opening and concluding sentence not to be found in the Anglican authorised
version.

and this for the modest remuneration of twenty crowns and a bar of chocolate (a manifestation of the bizarre qualities of Venca's mind) per rehearsal or performance.

Zderad, as we know, has had no need of it for some time now, but he likes to take part.

This is after all a different kettle of fish to the "Silent grew thy lips our dearest, when thy soul flew up on high."

For this reason he is even willing to undergo the bitter confrontation with these young people who have both a future, and a bit of fun on the side at the moderate cost of quite cute and innocent hypocrisy.

Had the avenging fist of the working class not come down by pure chance on his family, Zderad would be in the same position himself, or even better off by now.

He'd have some intellectual profession, regularly lighting-up the obligatory candles at the altar of the Marxist antichrist, and during his spare time he would perform and enjoy the recreation of real "culture," in a manner which escapes the vigilance and alertness of the self-centred, evil, abstract Spectre called, for some reason, The Working Masses.

As it is, he is finished; and, what is more, he has become a perverted prostitute.

It's bitter.

But now they are rehearsing another part of the splendid motetto.

"HEREDITAS NOSTRA VERSA EST AD ALIENOS DOMUS NOSTRAE AD EXTRAENOS" –

"Our inheritance is turned to strangers, our houses to aliens" – a male choir of four parts now laments and it is Zderad's role to pull along one of the two tenors, both almost equally high, because here Giovanni has let himself go and let loose his perfect imitative polyphony.

It is as if the faces of weeping fauns and half-human lions are emerging from the colourful renaissance ornaments, changing size in perspective as they come forward and recede again, through this music-illuminated space.

In the other tenor we can hear the handsome timbre of Kukula's voice, while Krůta is rasping somewhat in the lower bass.

For, indeed, nearly all the gravelarks are here, enticed by the prospect of extra baksheesh, plus chocolate, and a pleasant trip; and the huge feast in memory of the consecration of the local church of St. Wenceslas in X.

You see, Parson Plicka, as if he were outside his time, and just as if we were all in the days of the Austrian Empire, has asked "the gentlemen students from the City" to come and raise the cultural level of the festive services; and this is a rehearsal for the occasion.

Only the podagrous Turgo is missing, he is too old and cynical for all this, and perhaps he considers it unworthy of his artistic self. More likely, he is somewhat too ashamed, to stand before all this successful youthfulness.

"ORATIO JEREMIAE" has been included in the programme because of its topicality, albeit slightly out of place liturgically.

Now comes the trio of soloists.

"PUPILLI FACTI SUMUS" weeps a reddish blonde, together with a lanky bespectacled lad – a radish,* who at other times is probably in the Youth Union.

"We are orphans and fatherless"

"Our mothers are as widows," joins in another youth in plaintive imitation.

If truth be told, it is very simple, but the Devil knows, it really does tug at the heart strings.

The hopelessness of the Joyful Present is encompassed in it so fully and perfectly – who said Palestrina was incapable of "expressing emotion"?

And again the dark weeping of fauns and lions:

"AQUAM NOSTRAM PECUNIA BIBIMUS" –

"We have drunken our waters for money; our wood is sold unto us. Our necks are under persecution: we labour, and have no rest."

"AEGYPTO DEDIMUS MANUM" – the whole choir now cries out to the heavens the reason for their misery.

"We have given the hand to the Egyptians and to the Assyrians, to be satisfied with bread."

---

* Czechs use the word "radish" to describe someone who is red on the outside and white inside i.e. most of the populace of Czechoslovakia at the time.

"PATRES NOSTRI PECCAVERUNT" – the radish and the two lads complain again.

"Our fathers have sinned, and are not; and we have borne their iniquities."

"SERVI DOMINATI SUNT NOSTRI," the choir now proclaims its anti-worker tendency.

"Servants have ruled over us: there is none that doth deliver us out of their hand."

And again, the dense, colourful cloud of all eight parts.

"Jerusalem, Jerusalem, turn, turn again to the Lord thy God."

For a moment there is silence, for they all know.

It will always be a mystery how this Italiano, a guy who had most certainly never even heard of us, and of course, could not have known how we were going to end up, how, some four hundred years ago, he could have expressed it all succinctly and yet so perfectly.

And that bearded little Jew, the wretch who wrote the text, some time long ago in Asia Minor, when we didn't even exist at all.

It's clear that our misery is universally human, nothing special, and therefore, one day it will probably end. If we survive it, of course.

But this world is certainly not the worst of all possible worlds and, comrades, let us not blaspheme, we have not yet experienced the worst of it. In spite of all the misery there is still so called culture. "Вот, култура!"*

Even if it's all not worth a turd, and even if we all have to lie and cheat for a miserable mouthful and an unscathed body, we can still all publicly confess and cry about it together. And it can all be done with decency, dignity, unobtrusively and with propriety. Well, you tell me, who understands Latin these days?

And all thanks to some little Jew long since rotted away and an equally decomposed individual of the genus of ice-cream sellers.

Just think of it comrades!

"Right, now let's go through the Mass."

And now, blue as the sky over Rome, the famous MISSA PAPAE

---

* Russian: "Behold, culture!" The Czechs find Russian, which is a related language, rather funny in sound and turn of phrase, and frequently use it in a mocking way.

MARCELLI resounds with the sweet undertones of six part polyphony.

Venca had set it a little third lower so that now it suits Zderad beautifully and he can sing with gusto and without strain.

You can say what you like, but it's a good thing this darned Italian was born some time between 1526 or '27 (we don't even know that for sure) in the former Roman town of Praeneste!

For once the choir sings out according to those four-hundred-year-old instructions, Palestrina transports us as if by magic into weightless space, free of all matter.

Here, embodied only in our voices, we float, experiencing a kind of temporary assumption to heaven, having left our stinking souls and bodies deep down below us.

At such a moment it is possible – no, necessary! – to believe that our animal essence, emitting excrement and sexual products, is only a temporary prison.

And then, having descended once again, though we ourselves laugh at it cynically, nevertheless something like hope remains within us.

"The most dreaded of all curses, when God took away our singing."[*]

———

Zderad finally also descended, first from Palestrina's heavens and then also down the spiral stairs from the choir loft.

He did not stop to talk to anyone, neither to Venca nor the other two carcassingers, because that would bring the students into his view and bitterness into his heart.

He had yet to descend from the old quarter of the City, famous for its architecture, to the jungle of the slums, where he dwelt with his unsavoury and bizarre fate.

Because he had the time, and also because he was used to saving money, he decided to walk.

It was already autumn, and during his march a brownish dusk fell. The day had not been translucent as it often is in September, but covered by a day-long membrane of cloud.

---

[*] From a poem by Vítězslav Hálek (1835–1874) "A nejstrašnější kletbou jest, když Bůh odejmul zpěvy."

The lights of the City began to open their eyes.

But Zderad was not aware of them.

Another landslide was taking place in his soul as he became aware of his own bizarre misery and impotence.

Not only had he become used to the Monster and his unbelievable intimacies, but he realised that he appreciated the benefits which he derived from this.

For example, this year, after such a long time, he will be able to afford a decent winter coat.

He had intended to spend the money on Sylva but it seemed as if she didn't need it.

Recently she had been dressing quite elegantly and even had some kind of little fur coat, most likely only rabbit, hanging on a peg (they had no wardrobe) in the coffin abode, in a paper sack.

She said her parents had given her the money and Zderad had no reason to doubt it.

She also now wore quite expensive, provocative underwear, which Zderad naturally appreciated and also did not investigate in any way.

He could therefore afford a coat for himself, the only problem being how to explain to Sylva where he'd got the money.

Finally he decided that he would tell her he saved up for it, say from the money for his food.

He needed a coat and that was that.

Little Záviš's situation presented a worse dilemma.

He was back at his weekday nursery, although Zderad would now have been able to afford someone to look after him. But that would definitely give rise to suspicion.

So he left things as they were, for now, and suffered feelings of guilt.

Housing presented a similar issue; he could now probably try to get out of the slum coffin somehow, but that would mean bribes and deals. Not that he couldn't do it, but this again would mean attracting attention to himself.

He felt that he was not making use of the situation for the benefit of his family as he should, given that he was allowing himself to be humiliated in such a way.

The Monster was also worrying him:

He had restricted his masochistic requests a great deal recently, that was true (Zderad was to discover why only much later), but He had begun to be generally careless and demanding.

He had expressed the desire to watch Zderad during intercourse with a woman and insisted that He would bring a prostitute to the tomb.

That would not have been a problem really, not now; but when Zderad pointed out that this could be dangerous, could lead to blackmail and so on, He smiled strangely and proclaimed that he knew ways of silencing a little bird like that.

That smacked of God-knows-what, and seriously scared Zderad once again, after a time.

Naturally, he immediately remembered that once the Monster had had enough of him, He could do the same with him (whatever that may be) and, to cap it all, it occurred to him that something similar might have happened to his sister, who had vanished completely.

The Monster then tried another tack and hinted that perhaps Zderad could come to an arrangement with Sylva.

She surely hadn't the slightest intention of losing her husband – and the Ode to Stalin was still in the Monster's possession. Don't forget!

Zderad had managed to appease the Monster, but for how long remained an open question.

The problem of breaking away from the repulsive blackmailer had become more pressing once again.

Zderad had never dared to tell the freak that he knew of Brva's suicide, and, at least roughly, how the Monster had got hold of the Ode to Stalin, because he was afraid that the ghoul would perhaps destroy him immediately, as a precaution.

Zderad was helpless.

Just as he was getting used to it all, new things came up…

Give the Devil an inch –

———

— *"In olden days the muzhik bowed down before the Czar, he went to the dung heap.*
— *Now – behold – progress.*
— *The Czar we have overthrown, toilets we now have, comrades, new*

104

ones, flushing ones.

— Even paper there is."

Zderad was muttering this quasi-Russian rhetoric to himself. Drunk and in good humour, he stumbled across the yard of the pub in X, making for the pissoir on the other side.

At the same time he was contemplating the ability of the Czech language to evoke the idea of Russian simply by means of a minute change of word order.

This method had formerly been regularly used to translate from Russian.

"And you, Ivan Ivanovich, well – what?" But some wise-guys have rejected this approach and now translate stupidly and prosaically: *"And what about you, Ivan Ivanovich?"*

It's stupid.

The first way is a lot richer.

Anyway, the so-called bad translations have a charm of their own, even when they are from other languages.

After all, there is quite a difference whether the translator of the detective story says that: "the serpent raised his diamond-shaped head" as opposed to the know-all innovator with the state diploma in English prosaically blurting out that: "the snake lifted its rhomboid head".

While the first snake is a fairytale serpent, mysterious and worthy of biting Lady Beryl, the second, correctly translated creature, is absolutely ordinary and boring.

So much is obvious.

The celebrations of the church consecration in X proved to be a very successful occasion. For the two whole days that the "young ladies and gentlemen from the City" were guests at the parsonage, no one was sober for a moment.

There were also unbelievable mountains of food, as the Parson's sister was surpassing herself.

This religiously-materialistic festivity was incredible, given the socio-political climate of the day, and yet, it was real nevertheless.[*]

---

[*] The festivities in X are, of course, made up, but are faithfully modelled on true-life events in the fifties, which the author had the pleasure of attending.

Obviously the could not have laid it on out of his miserable monthly salary from the Bureau for Church Affairs.

The devout parishioners must have made a substantial contribution.

Progressive thinkers must have been a feeble minority in X, and the few that existed must have had considerably 'human faces' thus overtaking developments by about sixteen years.[20]

The Parson did have some kind of observer, complete with family, installed in one wing of the huge parsonage, to monitor the effects of the superstitious opium of the people, but he'd dealt with the snoop with typical Jesuitical-rustic cunning.

During the evening of the vigil of the Assassination of the Blessed Martyr he knocked on the comrade's door, and lifting high a well-rounded barrel of his best mead with a struggle, he wished the comrade a happy holiday.

He thus neutralised the vigilant eye of the people for the whole duration of the festivities relatively cheaply (because the source of the mead were the cooperative bees.)

The church was packed for High Mass and the six part Palestrina soared with considerable splendour.

At the end, somewhat out of place, came "The Prayer of Jeremiah".

In the climate of the moment, however, it suddenly seemed that the Prophet was grossly exaggerating.

The Parson's sermon was of a patriotic, though slightly compromising character as appropriate to the Saint. Nevertheless, this must not be overdone, like that Moravec.[21]

The Parson also emphasised his thesis, that, in the final analysis, joining the collective need not be such a bad thing, if it is done right.

After a very substantial lunch at the parsonage, which consisted of several traditional geese, among other things, the Blessing with the Most Holy Sacrament took place in the afternoon. They sang several St. Wenceslas motets, amongst others: "Náš milý svatý Václave,"* ascribed

---

* According to legend, St. Wenceslas and his army lie sleeping deep within Blanik Mountain, ready to emerge and drive off the adversary when the nations 'darkest hour' comes. Wake up!

to the mysterious Gontrášek, from the 15th century.

This was performed by six selected polyphonists, which included Zderad.

In the evening the Parson and the students took off for the pub where the farm co-operative was holding festivities.

After agreement with the co-operative chairman none of the students had to pay for food and drink here either.

An unusual, and anachronistic feature, however, was the Parson's request that perhaps the young gentlemen would sing some folk and patriotic songs, for which he himself produced the manuscripts, some dating far back into the 19th century.

As it was not really possible to get it together with the amateurs, the gravelarks took it on with the comrade conductor in the role of first bass.

They had considerable success.

Then the drinking began in earnest, as well as dancing to the sound of the brass band.

Zderad was not much of a dancer, but nevertheless he took a turn with some of the local girls, as well as some of the female 'amphibians'.[22]

Regretfully, however, no sexual adventure took place and anyway it would not have been right somehow in the presence of Parson Plicka.

As for the others though, I wouldn't like to say.

The festivities appeared to be going well.

In the pub it suddenly seemed that the whole business with the Asiatic colonialism was just a bit of fun, with no horrendous or tragic elements.

Zderad's own problems and the Monster seemed equally remote to him in his lightly inebriated state.

This was the mood he was expressing as he conversed with himself, when we last left him – staggering to the urinal; while we went off to report on the St. Wenceslas' opiate.

———

"Strangely enough, the pub's toilet was empty ..."

Strangely enough, the pub's toilet was empty at that moment.

This fact meant that another aspect of our narrative could develop.

As soon as our friend had completed his libation, thus relieving his over-taxed urological apparatus, the equally inebriated bassist Krůta staggered into the toilet. His eyes were gleaming and his skinny and bony figure was gyrating like a windmill.

He was humming some sort of song in his deep bass so that the closet vibrated with hollow resonance to some of the notes.

Quite unexpectedly, he went up to Zderad, embraced his shoulders with one arm and attempted to kiss him.

Simultaneously he went for Zderad's groin with his other hand.

Our protagonist got mad and pushed Krůta fiercely away, indicating at the same time that he was ready to sock him one.

One queer's attention was quite enough!

There had been rumours about Krůta but Zderad had never believed them, for there was nothing effeminate about Krůta and on top of that he commanded a voice which was not only definitely masculine, but in fact of a kind of superman depth.[*]

Krůta was as tough as old boots and his hands were like shovels, so that if he'd really wanted a fight Zderad would not have had a chance – nevertheless, after a short struggle the bassist retreated in a cowardly manner.

He was looking at Zderad with idiotic surprise.

"But, my dear Zderad, I always thought you were one of us," he mumbled appeasingly.

"How come?" Zderad cut in angrily.

"Well, I – I've seen you a few times with – with that professor."

This was a new and surprising turn of events.

The first thing that came to Zderad's mind was that all the Monster's caution and his own was obviously no use, if even Krůta knew something about it.

---

[*] Zderad evidently shared the commonly held but mistaken view on the nature of homosexuality.

Secondly the problem of finding out the Monster's identity was probably not so difficult and it was becoming clear that Zderad had in fact handled the situation with great ineptitude.

"How come …" he asked in surprise, " … you know him?"

"I do, I do, why shouldn't I? We all know one another. He's a rimmer." (Zderad blushed.)

"Well, who is he then?"

"Whaat, you don't know?"

"No, out with it!"

"OK, but, I'm afraid, you know.

Look out," he whispered suddenly, "not another word!" as a few smallholder *farmers of medium wealth*, who, as we know, are an unstable element,* rushed into the urinal.

Zderad felt as if he had been hit over the head with a sack of potatoes.

He did carry on drinking, he even danced a little, but his earlier mood had vanished.

Going back the next day in a hired coach (even that was possible then, believe it or not!), he tried to approach Krůta several times to find out more, but someone always got in the way and nothing came of it.

He could not help wondering about the prophetic side of his dream with the transmuted camels because the key to the Monster's identity was, in X – Brva's former habitat – after all.

But a wretched outcome, anyway.

Oh, God, oh God, how to get out of this!

---

* A Marxist dogma: 'The farmer of medium wealth is an unstable element' – i.e. regarding his allegiance to the Working Class – here of course, they were also unstable because of drink.

XI

The tram spat Zderad out on the outskirts of the City, where the fields begin and the crested lark sips from the rail grooves.

Today, miniature high-rises of collective construction jut up in the same location – but the author, in his capacity as émigré, is not aware of any other details.

Luckily? Regrettably? Who knows?

Zderad anxiously scans the surroundings.

The place is alien to him. He has not been here for at least ten years.

Standing, or rather squatting to one side are the small villas of clerks, acquired using their life savings in the days of private initiative.

Below, in the distance, we see a pond, next to which stands an ancient little church.

Zderad descends, walks along its bank between the bare fields, right up to some kind of walled park or garden, and then crosses the bridge across the stream, which is to blame for the muddy existence of the aforementioned pond.

Here he finds himself among semi-rustic cottages and various wooden sheds with old pots adorning the planks of rotting fences.

A small child in gumboots is grazing a white hornless goat on the bank.

There is also an inn, which used to be for passing coachmen and is much more substantial than the shacks of the semi-rustic paupers.

It is hereabouts that we may find Krůta's vegetating, marginal existence.

Zderad has come here to see him to find out the identity of his Monster, once and for all, damn it.

He tells himself that he is ready for anything, but in reality he is feeling very small.

He feels peculiarly bare and exposed to danger, like a beetle in a hollow when the stone has been rolled to one side.

And just like the beetle which has suddenly been deprived of its cover, Zderad's soul is also rushing around in confusion and panic.

Krůta's revelation in the gents in X is the magic force which has blithely lifted the lid-stone of supposed secrecy.

— It's not just Krůta though.

— He's in the same boat and will, or rather must, keep quiet.

— But if Krůta knows, others might know too.

— "They" might know, perhaps already do know and are doing nothing because they are covering up for the Monster, or they are afraid of Him for the moment, or something.

— Party and government Capos will keep rolling forever.

— If the Monster falls, Zderad may fall with Him, even though he can't sink much lower: To a jail, or to a concentration camp, most likely.

— Or, if they don't know, they have "ways" (eugh! better not think about it) of finding out from those who do.

— Maybe from Krůta.

Zderad's mind is in turmoil in other respects. Sylva is always out somewhere at her meetings. Of course, he can't confide in her, but at least her physical presence calms him down a little. And now there's very little of it.

— From the "purely marital point of view" as they call it, he can't complain, on the contrary – but he feels that Sylva is somehow slipping away from him.

— Záviš, as can be seen on Saturdays and Sundays, is timid and weepy again.

— Sylva is often out and Zderad doesn't know what to do with his son. He doesn't understand him, somehow. The child seems emotionally backward.

— Everything seems somehow makeshift, exposed, and insecure.

— And the Monster!

— The Monster is getting more intrusive in His strange clammy way.

— Nothing much has changed in their very peculiar liaison, but the creep seems to be trying to establish a closer emotional relationship.

— It seems He is getting more and more used to Zderad, that He loves him (eugh!) Take last time!

The Monster brought him a special present:

A little book, bound in black leather, written in a formal calligraphic script, on parchment.

— It appears that these are the Monster's own poems, a kind of litany (eugh, disgusting!) about Zderad.

— It isn't exactly bad, as poetry; it reminds one, sort of blasphemously, of old Czech baroque poems.

For example:

> Oh, you strange pelican,
> Avis infernalis,
> Underground hurricane,
> Stella borealis.
>
> Silver pallid Moon,
> Shining bait,
> In final doom to swoon
> At your gate.
> etc., etc.

— Of course, it's not exactly socialist realism, and even without some of the more explicit verses, these days it might be enough to send one on a 'pleasure cruise' to that Archipelago.[23]

— Yet, the devil knows, it's not as bad here as it was, or perhaps still is, in the 'you-SS-are'.*

— The Monster doesn't seem to worry about it.

— Why should he, he has worse things to hide.

— If he needs to, of course. THEY are allowed to do anything.

— The Monster is a decadent intellectual all right, but that was clear from the start. That doesn't surprise anyone.

— But who wrote it out and bound it so nicely for Him?

— Or did He do it personally?

Zderad remembers hearing about similar things being done for SS-men in Nazi concentration camps by various artists and artisans.

— So – that's the most likely explanation, and it's even clearer from

---

* Many poets, of whom Osip Mandelstamm is probably the best known, have been sent to labour camps just because they wrote in a style not approved of by the Party. Some crackpots in the West, however, see this as a positive feature – proof of great regard for poetry in the *Country where Yesterday means Tomorrow* (whichever way you look at it). Some people are simply too odd to be true.

this that He must be one of Them.

— Of course, that was always obvious, especially after that Hamouz business.

— And if that is the case – the parallels between the previous and the present Joyful Reality are almost flawless – what must that parchment be made of … and the binding? (Eugh!)

— (Oh, surely not?)

— What do you know about it, twit!

Zderad is literally afraid of the little book.

And afraid to burn it.

Now it's at the bottom of the literary trunk.

— Rest in peace!

But this business with the book and of course the Monster's other tendencies – the Monster mentioned again that He wants to watch Zderad doing the normal thing – cause such a panic inside Zderad that he feels he has to discover His identity whatever happens.

It has to be the first step.

— Otherwise he will leap out of his own skin.

— (Skin? – Eugh!)

He hasn't been able to get Krůta alone.

He either slips away or someone else turns up, and now, having sobered up, Krůta obviously doesn't want to talk.

So Zderad resolved to find him at home, and to get the information out of him at all costs.

That's why he is so tense and nervous now.

Meanwhile, autumn has progressed, the bulky-headed willows by the stream look like witches, and the human-headed guard stone by Bartolomějská and Národní as well as the genitalia of the wooden giants are now entirely bare.[24]

The sky is covered with a grey screen, foretelling rain.

Inclement weather.

So, Krůta lives somewhere here.

Here it is.

Zderad is taken aback to see the house number close at hand.

— No more excuses that he couldn't find the house, or something. He has to get on with it. He has to.

The curved slope of a slight incline, covered in rust-coloured grass and stunted fruit trees, has been hollowed out to form a kind of platform, and on it stands a cute little cottage with a few plank sheds.

There is also a dung heap.

On the bank above the cottage graze a number of goats, presumably Krůta's.

We also note the presence of rabbits and chickens.

Zderad opens the creaking gate.

There is yet the hope that Krůta may not be in – but no, here he comes, in blue overalls, out of one of the sheds (most likely a workshop), smiles in his downtrodden way and wipes his enormous hand on his trousers to offer it to Zderad.

"Hello, Zderad, what brings you here! Well, come on in."

Once inside, Zderad tries to get straight to the point but Krůta is being evasive.

What's the rush, let's have a drink.

He disappears behind a curtain and emerges carrying a bottle and two short glasses, and some sort of tattered book.

He slips the book under the couch (why?) and stands the bottle on the table.

The bottle contains a cheap kind of schnapps which goes by the name of 'Firefly' probably because it glows a yellowish green. It tastes pretty revolting.

Krůta pours, and blabs about everything and nothing.

"Your health!"

Zderad is slowly calming down.

He can see that Krůta is encouraging him to drink without having anything much himself, but he's knocking it back without objections.

He knows he can take it and anyway – it's Dutch courage.

The little cast-iron stove radiates pleasantly and an intimate, comfortably sleepy atmosphere is hatching, like a good natured little furry dragon.

They drink.

Outside it is fast getting dark.

Krůta flicks the switch and draws a flowery curtain over the window. Coincidentally, pictures of various Catholic fetishes, uncommonly on display in the window and the recess, are thus also hidden from view.

Zderad is drinking and Krůta is blabbering: about mutual acquaintances, organ players, carcassingers, priests, organs, a little about "circumstances".

It seems he trusts Zderad, and why not.

After a while, presuming that Zderad must have had enough by now, Krůta pulls out his tattered publication from under the couch.

It turns out that it is a collection of inept pornography with crude illustrations.

They are looking through them, Krůta now sat next to Zderad.

Zderad find the crude stupidity of the drawings as evident as Krůta's tactics, nevertheless the respective physiological reaction is slowly setting in.

This does not escape Krůta who is watching him like a hawk.

Zderad slips his hand into his pocket.

Krůta interprets this movement quite wrongly and thinks his time has come.

Slowly he stretches his shaking hand in the relevant direction.

Zderad lets him for a moment.

Then, as Krůta leans forward to have a better view of the fly buttons and the expected apparition, Zderad sets the razor to his throat.

"Right, that's enough 'cock-a-dawdling' – and now be a good boy, and tell me who that bloke is.

Or I'll cut your throat right here, and then my own. It's all the same to me now! You wouldn't say when asked – so!"

Krůta turns yellow like Chairman Mao himself (I think still a good guy in those days) and his deviant lust leaves him immediately.

He begs Zderad to put the razor away, that he will tell him everything.

But Zderad wasn't born yesterday.

If he agreed, Krůta could raise the alarm (the neighbouring cottages are quite close) or even attack him in desperate self-defence.

— His hands are as big as shovels. No way!

———

Some quarter of an hour later, a nimble figure descends the steps down the slope from the cottage.

Inside, the shattered Krůta is just beginning to shake like a jelly.

— Let's hope his heart is OK.

— Otherwise, Zderad could be in big trouble.

— But, don't be surprised at him. Under the circumstances –

— Right! Now, what next?

————

Kukula is celebrating the christening of his *n*-th child, by which he has 'blissed' his lawful, and surprisingly still pretty, obedient wife within the framework of the contra-contraceptive policy of the Holy Church.

His tiny flat is packed full.

Some of the young 'amphibians' of both sexes are here, as well as a kind of washed-out-looking old man of a very churchy type (perhaps the godfather), a few neighbours and other acquaintances.

Zderad is sitting humbly in the corner, screened by the circulating guests, gulping down salted peanuts and drinking "Blue Portugal" which is, as we know, the poor man's Chianti.

He looks at his watch every minute and is once again ready to jump out of his skin.

In less than an hour he has an appointment with a swarthy gentleman by the name of "Bašno Pál," a.k.a. "Paulos o Bašno" to discuss the details of a certain initiative, which is shortly to take place, and to do some additional reconnaissance of the terrain.

We cannot miss the opportunity to point out a little, quite accidental, piquanterie. 'Bašno', comrades, means "rooster" or "cockerel" in Gypsy, and 'Pál' is the Hungarian form of Paul. This is even more obvious from the alternative, entirely Gypsy form of his name, 'Paulos', which happens to be the same as in the original Greek version of "The Acts of Apostles". However, Bašno Pál is an entirely honest crook, and has nothing in common with the successfully converted Stalinist nightingale of Universal Dancing.[*]

————

[*] The passage commemorates Pavel (Paul) Kohout (Rooster or Cockerel), a Stalinist poet later turned dissident and a great favourite with many prominent Western

Anyway, Bašno Pál's tattered identity booklet contains completely different names.

In this connection, let us remind more literary-minded readers of old Ring Lardner and his New York gangsters.

Paulos o Bašno – Paul the Rooster, see?

It was Bašno who inadvertently inspired Zderad, as to the form of pressure to put on poor old Krůta.

That night, when he was fleeing from Hamouz and met up in the pub with the dustman Döme, and later his mates, he listened, unbeknown, to the Rooster's praise of the razor, among other things.

There are various personal weapons, explained o Bašno in his throaty language described by the people as "čogora-mogora paytáš". For example *'i čurri'* (knife), or *'i šprincengeri'* (sprayer or gun), but the razor is best.

"I muradi hi najfedér."

Not only does it cause the greatest havoc when applied and *'na kérel vika'* (it makes no rumpus – is silent), but it is not a crime to carry it. You can also have *'jek kotér sapún'* (a piece of soap) and *'muradáno šuládo'* (a shaving brush) in your pocket, so that if *'o šelengéro'* (the bounder or fetterer, i.e. policeman) searches you, you can always say that you carry it around for shaving and you are *'caklúno'* (glass, i.e. clear as glass).

"I muradi hi sakovestár najfedér" – the razor is the best of all – he repeated.

———

Then, about a month ago, a partial revelation of the mystery had taken place in Krůta's cottage.

Yes, Krůta does know the Man. He used to come to one of 'our' locals before the war. He's about the same age as Krůta.

"His name? Julius Skomelný. Dr. Julius Skomelný.

---

intellectuals like Louis Aragon, who once called him the Czech intellectual "numéro un". He once wrote the text to a song which meant: "Tomorrow people everywhere will be dancing, after our victorious red flags have flown up the masts of the world." The song was being played everywhere and was very annoying, because at that time there was a lot of arrests, torture, bullying and terror in general. In contrast, the Gypsy Bašno Pál is only a small time crook without much intelligence and versatility.

He used to be a priest but then He was defrocked by the Consistory. Now? Well, He's at the University.

He's an educated man., knows lots of languages, like you, but – He's a real bastard. He plays the piano and organ really well, too.

He should have stuck to music –

Nobody wanted to have anything to do with Him, after a while.

He's a rimmer, and he likes to be beaten.

He doesn't like much else, really.

But, they say that He likes it both ways.

They say He had girls as well, and those He flogged and tortured. Strange, isn't it. I wouldn't hurt a fly, myself, and as far as I'm concerned, girls needn't exist at all.

What is He doing now? Like I've told you, something at the University. I think He was with the Seminary for a while as a cadre officer or maybe a Marxism tutor.

It seems He abused the students there, as well. There was some kind of scandal, the Dean complained to the Party, so they put Him somewhere else. But nothing happened to Him."

(So that was it – poor old Brva! That's why there was the Mary of Egypt – entering the Holy Land via prostitution. He would probably have ruined him through his cadre profile or failed him at exams.*)

"He's involved in the Battle against the Church, he broadcasts on the radio sometimes." (Zderad did not have a radio, otherwise the poor fool would not have had to threaten a friend's life – but a radio distorts the voice and there was practically no television in those days: it was only just starting.)

"They say, but Zderad please don't tell anyone – they say that He was mixed up in the Číhošť Miracle business.† No one knows for sure,

---

* Very surprisingly, the communists in Czechoslovakia did not abolish theological seminaries, but simply shaped them according to their own image. So, to be admitted you had to be politically reliable, they taught you Marxism, including that there is no God etc. It seemed bizarre and stupid, until two decades later this blend of Catholicism and communism has come into its own in Latin America.

† A fraudulent miracle staged by the police themselves. They accused a priest who refused to confess to the crime and eventually died under torture. A film featuring the priest's confession was shot anyway, using an actor who was then recognised as a fraud by the priest's parishioners and the news spread very quickly, so that the whole action failed to produce the planned psychological effect of discrediting the clergy. The

though. But it would be just like Him.

They say He was with the Nazis as well – and He speaks Hebrew, you know.

That Baldur von Schirach[*] bloke – he was one of our boys, too. But of course They will know all that about Him. They know everything, after all.

And the business with the Seminary and –

Well you know, They probably don't care as long as He's doing it for Them.

Just like the Germans.

What – in the Party? People like Him don't even have to be, do they.

Listen, it's like with Archives, they all come under the Interior Ministry now.

And they don't bother the archivists with Party membership or make them join the Union, because the swine themselves don't have to be in it, do they?! In the GDR they even have former Gestapo men in the force, they say.

But, Zderad, please! …

Oh no, no – I just saw Him a couple of times when we were singing, He was watching you. Other than that, I don't know anything and I don't want to know. …

Well – I – I could be persuaded, you know. …

Ouch! Zderad!

Well you know, we're not all like that. …That's not true. And we're all unhappy, you know, even that Julie. Lord knows!

I wanted to get cured of it. It cost me a fortune with a Jewish guy and nothing came of it." …

—— "Oh, come on Krůta, stop crying.

Look, you wouldn't come out with it, so I – don't blame me.

All right then.

But no nonsense, and start talking!"

Miracle of Číhošť was the signal for a major persecution of the clergy. Czech Catholics believe that a miracle did in fact take place and the secret police were attempting to discredit it by producing a fake one.

[*] Baldour von Schirach – leader of the Hitlerjugend movement in Nazi Germany.

"You know, I was just scared. We're all scared of Him, you just don't know what He can dig up against you, someone like Him. –

No, I don't know that.

But probably, obviously not around here or where you are.

He must be making a packet out of that religious stuff.

And His family were well off too. But they were all odd, that lot.

That's not something They care about, either.

One priest was telling me that Lenin was a big landowner's son.

And Engels owned a factory.

No, don't worry, I can see why you want to know.

Still, I don't know why it bothers you so much – we're all poor bastards anyway, my God.

Yes – but still – if anyone found out I know him so well, they'd know straight off what kind of a guy I am, and I'm not Him, I wouldn't get away with it, would I.

(Excessive caution could well have cost Krůta his life, though.)

No, I swear to you – not a single word."

———

Well, well, thought Zderad, walking briskly to the tram stop: Doctor Julius Skomelný.

As soon as we know the spectre's name we feel his power has diminished. This is an old archetypal experience.

— The name fits. Skomelný then. Like "zkomolený," garbled, mixed up, warped. Mystically ghoulish, evocative of some dark arts. Skomelný! There's a Lake Skomelno by Rokycany, that is itself kind of ghastly.

— Like white rocks by the light of the full moon, or some such. Something white, monstrously large, smooth and stifling, rolling right over you.

— And Julius.

— That smacks of the upper classes. I bet He went around in a cute little sailor's outfit as a little boy.

— That figures.

— And, both ways; bi–

— Gaius Julius Caesar.

— Omnibus ille viris mulier mas ille puellis.*
— But He's a total sadomasochist, so Krůta said.
— Jeez!
— Julius –
— I can't recall whether Nero had that among his names.
— And what about Tiberius?
— Even as "Julius" it sounds like a diminutive sobriquet.
— *"Julie is a bastard"* Krůta had said.
— Chewlius – ?!
— Whatever. I think I am really in trouble.
— Mas ille puellis – Sylva!
— I guessed right. So that's why.
— God, oh God, oh God, if you're out there, have mercy!
— He's the high priest of these vulturavens.[25]
— When He's had enough of me – that'll be it!
— But I can't get to him!
— Of course they know all about Him, if even that idiot Krůta knows.
— I bet Parson Plicka knew. Did he?
— Well, well, a "doctor".
— The Devil is often represented as an intellectual, a doctor.
— Doctor logicus. Viz Anatole France, *par exemple, n'est-ce pas*?
— Oh, God, oh, God, there's no way out of this one.
— Even so, I must keep trying. I must!
— It would be so stifling otherwise.

———

A rehearsal with the academic amphibians.

A break.

A cigarette on the church balcony, outside the organ loft – outside the canonical space.

"Hey, listen. You're doing philosophy aren't you? Have you got a Skomelný at the faculty? Professor, should I say?"

"No, not yet, he's still a Reader. Don't you listen to the radio?

Yes, philosophy. He could teach anything. He knows – but –

---

* "A woman to all men and a man to all girls". A characteristic of Gaius Julius Caesar as described in a contemporary poem, purportedly written by the oracle, Sybil.

Well – I'd better – and why are you so interested? Aha, so you heard him speak.

No, he lives here, in the City.

Well, I dunno – a lot of people are flying high now – "

"Right, OK, I won't keep you.

I need to catch up over there – with Joe."

———

"Toil be praised, comrade, excuse me but is comrade Dr. Skomelný in today?"

— (Of course he isn't, Zderad made very sure of that beforehand.)

"Oh – look, I really have to speak to him very urgently, it's about my term-credits. You – couldn't give me his home address, could you?

I know you're not allowed to. But comrade please, it's terribly important. The credits – I missed some dates – I'm a bit scared of him you see – but maybe I could work something out with him – but I don't know. If I don't do it by the end of November I won't be able to sign on for next year. Please, couldn't you – ?!?!???!"

The girl blushes, hesitates, then quickly types out a card.

"Here, but don't tell anyone! And don't say it was me!"

"Thanks comrade, you're a darling."

Zderad's sex appeal worked in the normal direction this time.

— Right, let's get out of here quick, before someone finds out. –

———

Over a railway crossing.

The first sprinkling of snow.

The posh quarter, where the vulturavens nest.

Perhaps He has special security, as the important jerk that He is – but onward!

A beautiful villa with a large garden.

— The garden's well kept.

— It looks like the villa is hidden from view in the summer by the trees. Discretion assured.

— So this is how the bastards live!

— Let's just hope – well, once more unto the breach dear friends!

— A discreet name plate: Dr. J. Skomelný.

— So it's true. I almost thought he just kind of materialised straight from hell every time.

— And then, which way? We'll sort that out later.

The sound of a motor and wheels on gravel.

A Fiat.

A well turned-out blonde with two well-behaved kiddies getting out.

The older one has a pioneer neck-scarf.

— Of course, school's over.

"Excuse me, madam comrade, does Comrade Major Pišvejc live here?"

"No, you've made a mistake."

"Thank you, I can't find his house here."

— Right, that's that.

— (Pišvejc, you idiot, why Pišvejc? Your sense of the absurd could give you away. You should have said someone ordinary.)

———

At that moment Zderad's mental projection stopped abruptly, for Venca of St. Nicholas entered the Kukula abode.

Plastered, as he usually was these days.

Not so much as a hello.

He sat down, rather heavily, at the piano, and started extemporizing a bit.

His technique was pretty bad, but the things he played made sense. Venca was talented, no denying that, if only …

The sophisticated amphibians began gathering round. Venca, an interesting persona with his full black beard, which, as some of you may remember, was very eccentric in those days, now progressed to a different key and started something which sounded like an introduction to a song.

Then he started singing.

He had a reasonable voice, baritone, which we happen to know already.

He was singing something about a pair of quails in clover.

— Not bad.

"Venca, that's quite good, even from you!"

Venca is showing his yellow stained smoker's teeth between the black bristles.

"That's not mine," he says in a significant and ironic way. "That's Míťa Nerad."

"Oh yes, the words, we know."

"No, no, the music as well, my little comrades."

"How come?"

"Simple, words and music by Míťa Nerad."

"Venca" – chimed in Zderad in an ironically mournful way. "Give over. You're not fooling anyone. We're all musicians here – and we've all heard you improvising at the old Nicholas?

That's your style."

Zderad struck a few chords which had come from Venca's fingers a short while ago.

"It's Míťa Nerad," grins Venca in defiance.

"He's also a composer, is he not. *'The universal genius of all Czech Lands and affiliated parishes.'*

You all know he also writes musicals. 'The Hiding Place Under the Ladder',²⁶ and so on, as well as songs.

The State Publishing House of Art and Culture is at this moment preparing it for print.

Toil hail, I'm off!"

He went out, as he had come in.

Vociferous debate broke out among the assembled company:

" – But that 'Hiding Place' thing, that was already being played during the First Republic* – "

"Well, I don't know, maybe he's polished it up for him – "

"You know Venca, anything for a drink – eh? – "

"But Nerad doesn't need it."

"No, he doesn't, really, but why not? It's being done in the West, ghosting. He can afford it."

"Hey, look, don't be such bastards. Nerad's no Foltýn,† – he has

---

* 1918–1938 – the first or "bourgeois democratic" Czechoslovak Republic.

† Foltýn: a character from a book by Karel Čapek (1890–1938). An incompetent composer who had an entire opera composed by various "ghosts".

plenty of talent no matter what else he's like, why not for music?"

"Sure he's no Foltýn. Foltýn was skinny."

"So what about that 'Song of Liberation' – don't tell me he was really that naive. ..."

"Hey, come on, have a drink instead. Pass more water under the bridge. ..."

"Maybe Venca was just bragging, making himself out to be someone. Yeah, I wouldn't put it past him."

"But the style was his, for sure."

"And it was good music."

"Wasted, that Venca."

———

We're all whores, thought Zderad as he was leaving Kukula's place. One way or the other.

— At least mine's not the worst variety.

— (Isn't it?)

— Well, at least it's obvious, brutal. Up front.

— Oh, God, oh, God, oh, God, if there is some kind of God, have mercy on me!

XII

— Whiteness.

— Crows.

— Rooks, actually.

— Crows don't have that white bit around the beak. And they have a different profile.

— Their beaks continue smoothly into the forehead, just like those of some citizens.

— A train.

— Heaviness.

— Lighting up time.

— Soon the blue will descend, even the snow will turn blue and glow with a kind of spectral phosphorescence. And then there will be darkness.

— Soon.

— It is December already.

— And he still knows nothing.

— It could have been her – or maybe not.

— That silent wreck.

— People do resemble one another.

— And she didn't speak.

— They told him she wouldn't.

— And if it was her?

— Wouldn't it be a thousand times worse?

— Better that it isn't her. Please God don't let it be her.

— Why did he have to stick his nose in?

— He didn't have to listen to that know-all bragging in front of the girls. It's his own fault. Those who ask too much find out too much.

———

"Crows. Rooks, actually ..."

It happened like this:

On one occasion, when helping out with the academic amphibians (Zderad was attracted to them although this meant he was once again a pariah) he overheard a medical student telling the girls about his vacation experiences in a provincial mental hospital.

He was bragging and cynical, and the girls were in awe.

He was telling them how they conducted an experiment with some kind of potion (as far as Zderad remembered he said it made urine blue) with which you can wake up chronic autistic schizophrenics for a moment, and how he experimented with it as the consultant's research assistant. He talked about a chronic catatonic female (what is that?) who just lies on her bed. She's about thirty but looks at least fifty.

"According to her papers, she is an orphan, the daughter of a crofter. She has scars from automutilation.

You know, they hurt themselves deliberately in the hyperkinetic stage.

Oh, there's no need to be scared, silly girl.

When they gave her the drug it woke her for about an hour, but it does not remove their delusions, unfortunately.

She spoke to them, but still in that kind of dead voice, and told them that she was the daughter of a higher ranking civil servant from the City (megalomanic delusion, said the student), that they locked her up, and tortured and abused her. She spoke about a Devil with white eyes, who used to take her into a tomb. He tortured her there with another man. That was after the interrogations. They had let her go but the Devil found her and kept her in a cottage somewhere. And he used to drive her to a castle, to the tomb. And what she said they did to her – well I'm not going to tell you that, girls. Well – delusions. She said she had a baby and the Devil killed it and made her drink its blood.

Terrible delusions, how could this happen to a human mind?

Naturally, this proves that the method is no good. Apart from the fact that the effect is not permanent we also found that it doesn't remove delusions and hallucinations.

So we wrote it all down for the consultant and packed it in.

The girl was always feeble-minded anyway, she didn't get much education, well, you know, a crofter's daughter from the mountains.

What, do I enjoy it? Of course I do, and you haven't heard anything yet. They also have dangerous madmen there, etc, etc."

The whole thing stuck in Zderad's mind like a knife.

He forgot about it a bit, because of other events, which have already been partially described, but it kept coming back to him.

The possibility was obvious.

Jenůfka (Zderad's parents obviously delighted in strange names, his father for instance was also called Záviš, so Zderad's son was named after his grandfather) had disappeared without trace, as we have already mentioned.

And then the other things – *"the devil with white eyes"* and the tomb – but no, it couldn't be, not even these days, here –

(And yet, what about Haarmann in the decent Weimar republic?).

Meanwhile the autumn turned into winter and Zderad's speculations were submerged by other events.

Now, however, he had the time.

He was one of those people who are spurred into action by uncertainty.

Sylva was at home in Mlno with Záviš for the Christmas holidays.

Zderad will be visiting them for Christmas itself. At the moment he is still working. (If only she knew!)

As far as further investigation of his "monstrous" affair was concerned, Bašno Pál had decided that they would wait for Skomelný to take his family away for the holidays, which was expected to happen soon.

Bašno made progress in a very professional way and it appeared he was very skilful in finding out all the relevant details.

Apart from that, the Monster had restricted his attentions considerably, possibly because of pressures of work or perhaps because of the cold, and he also informed Zderad that they would not be seeing one another until the end of January.

Zderad already knew why, from Bašno.

He did, however, bring him a "Christmas present" which consisted of a set of whips and truncheons which made Zderad's stomach heave and which they deposited in the tomb. He also gave him a considerable sum of money.

This money enabled Zderad to make the trip from which he was just returning.

Heavy-hearted.

———

The details of how the trip was organised would bore you.

A key role was played by Zderad's former colleague, who did complete his studies and who had the unrewarding role of a poorly paid clinical psychologist in the said mental hospital.

At that time it did not even pay much in the prosperous West and in Czechoslovakia earnings were minimal, because, comrades, our friends have nothing like that in their most progressive country (see "Ответ физиолога психологам" by I.P. Pavlov*).

But it was quiet and hidden away, almost like funerary singing. A marginal, proletarian-intellectual existence for "internal émigrés".

———

The whiteness was on the way there, too.

His colleague was waiting for him at the station with an old, rusty, disused ambulance, which he could use for personal transport.

On his head he wore a Russian style fur hat, but his body was wrapped in a thin coat.

Even so, he made a very Soviet impression, standing there in the snow.

Perhaps it was because there were birch trees around the station.

It was very dreamlike.

His colleague was driving him along the almost completely white fields.

In an ambulance.

There were so many rooks on one of the fields, it looked like a

---

* Pavlov was actually a behaviourist but he called himself a physiologist rather than a psychologist. Once upon a time he wrote the article "A physiologist's answer to psychologists," where he argued along the same lines as an American behaviourist calling himself a psychologist might have done in reply to "mentalistic" psychologists. Unfortunately, because of the terminology used, he made it very difficult for any psychologist of whatever persuasion to later survive in the newly established Soviet satellite states. In the incomparably more advanced and westernised Czechoslovakia, the Russians only succeeded in forcing psychologists to adopt a very low profile, akin to going underground, for some ten or fifteen years, until they finally realised what the situation actually was, and relented.

surrealist painting.

Crunching in the snow, he was led through the huge complex of buildings, pavilions and snow-covered little fields and groves.

And towers.

Strange towers, where the provincial fin-du-siécle architect let himself go, because it was all for madmen and he didn't have to take conventional tastes into account.

One was the water tower, in which his colleague said he had once almost drowned. He was proud of the fact that he must be one of the few people, or perhaps the only one, who had ever been drowning up a tower. He had climbed up there and the rotten planks had given way under him.

In another turret, he said, a famous Jewish professor of psychiatry had lived, while he was still a provincial intern.

That one was older.

Then he took Zderad to her.

A skinny figure lay motionless in a white ward, in a white nightgown, on a white bed, in white sheets.

And outside, whiteness.

A yellow face and glassy eyes.

— But it could have been her. Perhaps.

— But she was skinny, yellow, old and withdrawn.

— Hair almost completely grey.

— A bit like an Icon.

— Or a gothic statue.

Zderad sat beside her for a long time, holding her by her yellow little hand, trying to speak to her, recalling little family jokes from their joint childhood which no one else would understand.

"Jenůfka?"

Nothing.

His friend has left him by then and a fat stupid-looking nurse eyed him with suspicion.

Still nothing.

It grew dark, the lights were turned on.

The yellow face now looked even more holy as the bulb shone

through the thin, uncombed hair.
  Nothing.

"A skinny figure …"

He then went through her case notes, with his colleague's assistance – who had introduced him as a psychologist from the City – and notes of the student, written up during the drug experiment.

The case notes were about a stranger, just as the student had described them.

The research notes had some suspect features.

Zderad bitterly regretted having read them.

Dear reader, we will not quote from them either.

Our story is strange and sad enough as it is.

———

Then they had some kind of disgusting mash in the staff canteen, followed by tea and a game of chess in his friend's bachelor quarters.

He really did have reproductions of surrealist paintings on the walls, but the surroundings would have been surreal even without that.

A restless sleep on a couch in the alcove.

And the next day, going back.

In the afternoon.

In the morning he made another futile attempt.

Zderad was not given to tearful misery as we have already seen. He was a pretty tough customer. It was a good thing.

That way he did not make a spectacle of himself for the other passengers on the train.

XIII

"New Year's Eve night of glass and firework spark, as old men squat in hell-wine-cellars dark, confide in waiters with a knowing smile, resembling poets for a little while" ... etc. writes the poet Míťa Nerad. Oh! – I beg your pardon.

But why be a hypocrite.

It's clear from Chapter XI, in spite of *de mortuis nil nisi bene,*[*] and even Venca of St. Nicholas has not been camouflaged with all due care, because he isn't doing anything wrong.

Ghosting is work like any other and even prominent representatives of the People like their drink.

If he's still alive somewhere, you can ask him about that National Artist's music.

I can't imagine that Venca would want to sue anyone anyway, he would consider it below his dignity – unless he has changed beyond all recognition.

But should you ask him about the identity of Zderad, then you ought to know that he truly is a concoction of numerous personalities and did not exist in reality at the time described.

––––––––

All right then, New Year's Eve.

And as for the operation, call it this or that, as you wish.

After Christmas Day in Mlno, Zderad returned to the City under some pretext.

The Monster, alias Dr. Skomelný, is away with his orderly, cover-up family.

In the Crimea? Or just in the Špindl?[†]

––––––––––

[*] 'Speak nought but well of the dead.'

[†] Špindlerův Mlýn — a skiing resort in the Krkonoše mountains, usually patronised by the better off of any period.

I don't know.

The span of one's own experience is considerably limited in this respect as a result of one's rather featureless cadre profile, and we have no idea where prominent intellectual comrades do spend their well-earned holidays in the early fifties.

Why don't you ask one of them yourself? After all there are plenty of them in the West now and they still "represent" us in the media, because after all, anyone with a Name wants to associate with his own kind. Does it not even occur to those of their kind in the West how their Eastern Block counterparts came to fame, or how artificially fame and obscurity can be created?

New Year's Eve had been selected by Bašno Pál and the other experts as the most suitable for the event.

It is true that it is not one of the quietest nights and that people are up. Such people, however, are sozzled, and therefore in good humour and rather unobservant.

Apart from this, lights and noise and similar are generally ascribed to merrymaking.

It is also likely that the vigilance and awareness of the National Security Man may be somewhat reduced.

All in all, the date selected has more advantages than disadvantages.

———

No doubt it is clear by now what is going on:

Zderad has decided that with the help of the Gypsies, originally organised by the dustman, he will break into the Monster's villa and, if possible, take possession of the Ode to Stalin.

He could not think of anything more intelligent to do, and even though he was otherwise quite bright, he even overlooked the fact that, once caught, he could stay held, under any pretext.

Indeed, that could have been the case from the beginning.

But – and this is a manifestation of the intelligence of the comrade doctor – it was simpler to tie him down with something more concrete and tangible.

Zderad, as an uninitiated citizen, could still be of the naive opinion that if he hadn't done anything, nothing could happen to him and therefore he could not be blackmailed.

This view is of course grossly erroneous. However, to convince 'the patient' to see it otherwise requires time and effort, which is a feat arduous, if not necessarily unpleasant, for the 'therapists' in question.

In our case, however – and let us keep in mind the objective of the event – the persuasive techniques could not be easily applied. Initial protestations would attract too much attention from persons who were not directly involved.

The Monster therefore chose the path of least resistance. Having observed Zderad's stately figure, he could not contain himself, etc. He therefore made His catch with a genuine hook.

So, Zderad, using the dustman as intermediary, arranged for experts to be found, who, for a remuneration of 1000 crowns for the leader and 500 for the three assistants, would burgle Skomelný's villa and if possible take possession of the fatal Opus.

There was certain pleasure in the fact that the event was being financed by the Monster himself.

As additional compensation, they were to keep anything else they found and chose to take.

It was however necessary for Zderad to take part in the expedition, as one could not expect illiterate, or at best semiliterate Gypsies to be able to safely identify the corpus delicti.

He was also hoping that he would be able to ensure that no undue excesses took place.

And finally – let's admit it – Zderad was in fact looking forward to the burglary!

On the day, he bought himself a bottle of good wine with his whoring money, for the purposes of celebrating New Year's Eve and his mood was generally exalted and festive. The feeling of danger added a little spice to it.

Prominent philosophers and men of letters have emphasised many times that every human being corrals a whole herd of very different personalities.

Some of these are always ready to spring into action and do so as soon as the opportunity presents itself.

Others are buried somewhere deep inside and emerge perhaps once in a lifetime, if at all, in which case, of course, it is impossible to prove their existence.

Zderad carried within him a clearly violent and semi-criminal element as we have seen on at least two occasions already.

His bourgeois childhood and early youth did not allow it to develop fully.

His teachers and pedagogues were often surprised, however, that this, on the whole decent pupil and later student with intellectual interests, could occasionally be capable of passionate brutalities.

As a boy, for example, Zderad used to brawl with dedication and success.

The middle-class residential area in which he spent his proper childhood was on the other side of a park, whose far side bordered on precisely the slums in which he now regrettably had to dwell.

The proletarian kids used to organise raids on the park, in order to terrorise the little goodie-goodies and steal their toys.

The marauders also attacked Zderad a few times, misled by his bourgeois outfits, but they never got much enjoyment out of it, in fact just the opposite.

While still at grammar school, Zderad once got a very low grade for "moral conduct" on his report, because he punched a decent, slightly older schoolmate, and knocked him down into the urinal gutter in the lavatory, thus giving him a black eye.

Later he would recall this event with joy and pride, because the said model schoolboy developed into a prize specimen of a Comrade, ascending as high as the Presidium of the government. (Naturally, not yet during the time of our narrative, as high posts in governments of communist countries require compulsory senility.)

This satisfaction was in reality quite useless, of course, since, in contrast to his victim, Zderad was moving equally rapidly on the social scale, except downward.

The latter undeserved social slide was, however, favourable and conducive to the further development of Zderad's more or less latent characteristics.

As we have already seen, Zderad was catching up in leaps and bounds on those things which bourgeois society had deprived him of and via prostitution and associating with the 'wrong sort' was about to attain the common burglary level

———

The "H-hour" had been set by Bašno Pál for two a.m.

Dear hypothetical reader –

Hold it! quoth the hypothetical reader, twitching his or her hypercritical snout.

It seems the author's confabulatory ability is somewhat feeble: Sexual blackmail under communism, due to anti-state literature – I seem to have come across that before, though it was just an episode and in a more acceptable rococo form.

And to resolve the matter by housebreaking, that's been done too.

And in a roundabout way, the role of the policeman or spy or whatever combined with an unrequited erotomaniac – that's been done too, elsewhere, but next along the bookshelf almost.

All we need now is for the slum balcony to collapse. – [27]

Dear hypercritical reader then:

We can, I'm sure, agree that there is a resemblance, but of a sufficiently distant kind, such as between a man and a horse in the sense that they each have a head.

I do realise that you find such far-fetched literary comparisons being drawn all too often, but let's be reasonable.

Take, for instance, the fact that practically every novel involves some sort of cohabitation, described more or less explicitly.

It happens in life, authors enjoy describing it and readers like to read about it.

Nobody would regard that as plagiarism.

More to the point: Every proper "Western" involves guns, horse-riding and the odd bit of cattle-ranching. There are bribed sheriffs and unbribable heroes etc… That's part of the genre.

Likewise in the case of "Easterns," a genre in the making, there just have to be secret policemen, blackmailers, whores and other typical characters.

The originality of the author shapes the developments within these bounds.

Our little tale, coming as it does from much the same background as other stories, will have the same generalised features.

Be patient. We'll soon see how the plot thickens.

———

So, the "H-hour" had been set for two in the morning.

Zderad, having welcomed in the New Year with his bottle, got up at around one a.m.

He pushed a few props connected with his forthcoming amateur production into his pockets.

There were cotton gloves, which prevent fingerprints while not impeding the mobility of the fingers, and, just in case *'i muradi'*, a razor.

He felt a need to be armed.

For a moment he considered whether he should take along the recommended brush and soap but then decided against it. Why carry around unnecessary junk.

He put on his old, pre-prostitution coat. For one thing he didn't want to ruin his new one, and also, he thought that since the new one was so obviously new, it could prove to be a means of identification.

On his head he put a black ski hat, one of several to cover his head with in cold weather, whichever one first came to hand.

As some people may remember, brimmed hats were not very popular at that time as they were vaguely associated with the West and the bourgeoisie.

Only high ranking comrades and old people wore them unashamedly.

Perhaps some of you will wonder at the petty details that were vaguely dangerous at the time, but it's true. Just ask those who lived through it.

The ski hat Zderad put on was of a type locally called a "pochválem,"[28] though the etymology of the word is unclear. It seems this form of headgear was akin to the old "soli Deo" skullcap – but even so, we have little to go on.

The pochválem was made of such thin weave that when it was pulled over the face one could see right through it even in conditions of reduced visibility, as Zderad had tested before departure. When pulled back up it became a completely inconspicuous form of headgear.

Zderad was gripped by a pleasant frisson of adventure.

He left the building, which was not even locked for the night, (a good sign, indicative of that night's general level of vigilance) and strolled through the streets, occasionally passing little drunken groups of merrymakers.

On one little square he was overtaken by a Communal Services van which stopped in front of him.

"Dzerad? *Chuť andro!*" (Hop in).

The driver was Góno o Graj (Frankie the Horse) in civvy-street a tractor driver and thus an example of the success of the civilising endeavours of the Party and government, as far as the Gypsies were concerned.

The communal van had been organised by the dustman, who was not otherwise participating physically.

"I fat man, *kamarát*, I do no run."

Döme, the de-gypsified Rom, was also probably too civilised for the operation, which could not be said about Zderad.

He had apparent organisational abilities, as we shall see.

A little later they picked up another two lads. One was called Pír, meaning Foot, but his first name was Jura, rather than Michael.

The second one had a wild, romantic-sounding name. He was called Pinkášiš o Ruv (Leo the Wolf).

They had to pop into the van, which could have seemed somewhat conspicuous, but everything went smoothly.

Before long, they arrived at the railway crossing, which, perhaps unintentionally, separates the comrades off from the dwellings of ordinary mortals. They passed over it without incident.

Then they continued in the direction of the Monster's residence.

Góno slowed down and they proceeded at walking pace.

Bašno appeared silently like a ghost by the driver's window:

"*Cit*" – he whispered "*the andr'i bar. Me už pchárďom e vúdar.*" (Ssh – and into the garden – I've opened the gate.)

The van slipped inside and Bašno closed the gate, but he didn't lock it. Everything was perfectly planned so the burglars used a key to get in.

Pinkášiš o Ruv was in charge of the keys, being a trained *'šlosengero'*, or locksmith.

Either it was not usual at the time or the Monster had not yet got round to it, but there was no alarm in the building.

That had also been checked out beforehand.

A whispered debate then followed as to whether they should turn on the lights or work *'tykňa dudeskrentsa,'* i.e. by torchlight.

Because there were still some lights on in some other villas, Bašno Pál decided that they would turn on the lights but draw the curtains.

Which they did.

The eyes of the lumpenproletariat[*] now beheld a miniature stately home.[†]

Several doors led off from a fairly nondescript little hallway.

One door opened into a very well equipped smallish kitchen, with a large electric fridge, which was switched off at the moment, for the holidays.

Jura made for it, but Bašno stopped him.

Another door led into a sort of passage with another three doors in it.

Two little rooms were clearly for the children, full of toys, school-books and various Lenins, Stalins and Kalinins.

The third, larger room, was by all accounts the master bedroom.

The beds were separated by a bedside table, like in America.

There was no hint of the fact that the master of the house was an incredible pervert.

It was only on closer inspection that Zderad noticed, hanging above one of the beds, a reproduction of a Michelangelo drawing – a male nude from behind, and a little below.

This picture, it flashed through his mind, is a help to the Monster when performing his socialist marital duties. He probably looks at it while doing it and imagines he is rimming.

The Gypsies were staring at everything and touching this and that.

But Bašno didn't let them:

---

[*] Lumpenproletariat – "proletariate in rags" – a Marxist term describing deprived people such as vagabonds and Gypsies as opposed to the actual working class.

[†] The author has seen such a residence in Prague with his own eyes. So this is no mere flight of fancy.

"Dureder, dureder, amen našti adarde sam tarde savóra raťaha!"
(Come on, come on, we can't stand here all night.)
"Le! Dykas, so ehi andr'e avre štúbe."
(Right, let's see what's in the other rooms.)
Bašno was obviously reasonable and in command of the situation. Zderad was glad he didn't have to interfere.

The other area of the house exceeded all expectations. *"Daj devleske – odoj ehi jek dyz"* (Mother of God, this is a castle) said Jura in admiration.

The living area was divided into two large rooms.

The room closest to the kitchen and bedrooms had an alcove and was furnished as a lounge with armchairs and sofas and a round glass-topped little table. It was pretty decent but still ordinary.

It was the second room which took our proletariat's breath away.

Someone, whether the Monster himself, or the capitalist from whom he had confiscated the house, had had the upper floor removed, so that the result was a kind of stately hall.

The windows were in two layers, one above the other.

The furniture was very grand, probably stolen from various monasteries and the like.

Along the whole length of it stretched massive oak refectory tables, with matching medieval-looking dining armchairs.

This is where the Monster gives feasts for the other prominent comrade vulturavens no doubt.

It had become clear ages ago that he simply could not afford to own all this, or even to maintain it, on his standard salary, of a University Reader.

On the facing wall hung a gigantic church painting in a massive baroque carved frame – obviously a Škréta[29] or something.
— How come they let him keep it?
— What about the National Gallery?
— Under the painting was a massive writing desk.
— And along the whole wall a bookcase. Baroque. Twisting pillars and so on. Probably stolen as well, or what.
— A hoard of grand furniture, paintings, statuettes, vases.
— And that library!

It was obvious that there was no chance of finding one single sheet of paper in that amount of literature, in the short space of time remaining until morning. Who knows, it could be anywhere.

Zderad only now became fully aware of the absurdity of his plan, but he nevertheless attempted a brief exploration of the bookcase.

— He would be much more likely to find the proverbial needle in a haystack.

— There must be a safe here somewhere, behind a painting, but where? Or there could be secret drawers, there are always some in old furniture.

— No time to look for them. Daft, daft from the word go.

— Anyway, the Monster probably keeps all important material somewhere else. There's nothing in here, either, to suggest that the master of the house is a sexual beast.

— Not even any base literature; rather, antiquarian editions of Greek and Roman authors in grand bindings, commentaries on Aristotle, Summa Theologiae in *n*-volumes – masses and masses of books in every possible language.

— No chance!

The only books which Zderad glanced at and which gave a distant hint on any kind of perversity or infernality were:

Rassmussen: "La folie de Jésus".

– (A book arguing that Christ was insane.)

Minkowski: "L'art profanne de l'église".

– (A book on pornographic sculptures in gothic cathedrals.)

And from a small revolving bookcase Zderad by chance pulled out a copy of "Les chants de Maldoror," illustrations by Dalí.

— Well, and that would seem to be that, on cursory inspection.

There were also a few copies of the comrade's 'history of philosophy' lecture notes, and Zderad flicked through with interest.

It was written in the usual simplified, stupid Party style, as if for complete idiots, which immediately made everything into a lie.

Zderad finds it amazing that the intelligent, educated Monster could sink to writing such crap.

Then he realises that He must be doing it out of sado-masochism, and that he gets pleasure from this degradation of himself and of the philosophers.

— Otherwise he would have to throw up a thousand times before he'd finished it!

— Which — is the only clue – however indirect and subtle.

— No chance!

— What must Zderad have been thinking?

— The Monster wasn't born yesterday.

— But – His pad shows that He must be a much bigger fish than Zderad first though. Now you know who you're up against.

— If that's the case, then at least we'll clean him out good and proper!

Various silver candelabra and precious goblets, probably for mass, are disappearing into the Gypsy sacks.

— The surprising thing is that He doesn't take better care of it, at least when going away – perhaps He's got so much money that this is nothing to him. Or perhaps He is cultivating the philosophical contempt for worldly goods.

— Easy come, easy go.

Out of the sideboard comes noble silver, probably from a monastery or bishop's residence. There is also porcelain and cut glass, but the Gypsies will probably smash that.

"Bašneja, hár oda khámes te bikenes? E šelengére oda džánena." (Rooster, where do you think you'll sell this. The cops will trace it.)

"Náne dar, more, náne dar. Andr'o cizo them prek'e bergi." (No fear, mate, no fear, in a foreign country, over the hills.)

— How the — ????

— Well, if you say so, let's get on with it. They probably sell it on to some antique dealers. Zderad has heard about art being smuggled out of the country.

— Before the comrades could catch their breath, loads of things had gone.

— It's better than ruining it by neglect or wilful damage.

Zderad knew of a case when a man transported a whole church organ out of the evacuated border region, bit by bit, to his house, including the 32 foot sub-bass pipe, all made of tin, and put it all together again in his yard in a shed he built specially for it. Originally he'd intended to remove the upper floor of his house but it wouldn't fit in widthways either.

— But – why not?

— Should the Monster have it? Considering They will be here for ever and ever, amen – in any case, now.

— That's obvious.

Whoosh, moosh, the sacks are filling and into the van with them. There and back.

There are still some large baroque statues.

"Tu, Dzeradeja. Tu hal jek goďaver rom. Tu džavas andr'e rašajeske ráklolengeri.

So ode kaštúne paňári? Te san dragi? Te jek šte lel te bikenel?" (Hey, Zderad, you are a wise man. You went to those schools. What about those wooden dummies? Are they expensive? Do they sell?"

Zderad is pleased that Bašno addressed him as 'rom' meaning not only "man" but mainly "gypsy". So he considers him as one of their own. But we've been here a damn long time and transporting those heavy bastards …

"Well, if you can get them out of the country as you say, then yes. But I don't know. They're bloody heavy things," Zderad is too nervous to speak in Gypsy.

"Náne dar, more, náne dar."

— It's coming up to five o'clock.

— People will be sleeping late on New Year, but still.

— Things seem to be going smoothly so far.

— Apart from the main point of the event, however.

— But that was just clutching at straws anyway.

— At least we've done some damage here.

Meanwhile, everything is vanishing into the van.

— Where are they intending to take it all?

— The Gypsies have got hold of an angel of sorts with gilded wings. He is stuck in the doorway. Oh Gawd! But the angel is out at last.

— Now they have a younger looking saint with a beard.

— Zderad lends a hand. The sooner they are out of here the better.

— They are primitives, just the same!

— Góno has got hold of a bottle of cognac from somewhere. That's great, he's the driver!

— Damn.

Some rather late merrymakers have stopped at the gate and are looking in to see what's going on.

The van is clearly lit up by the light streaming from the doorway.

They are not wearing masks, they didn't seem to need them until now.

— Everything was going too well so now we're for it!

Zderad is trying to make a decision. Perhaps it would be better to do nothing and rely on the drunkenness of the nosey parkers, but –

— Quick, off with his coat and over the statue.

The saint is transformed into a regular member of the party.

Góno has got that bottle.

Zderad pulls it from his hand, lifts it above his head and sings out in Russian: *"Прощай любимый город!"* Proščáj, ljubýmiy górod, Farewell, favourite city.

— There you go, the Advisors are having a good time.

— Quick, go home so that you don't get involved in anything. Even if They are obviously stealing,

— They are allowed to – after all, They rule here.

The little group quickly disperses.

— It worked.

— Thank God!

— Right, now a quick look to see if anything smaller is still worth taking and that we haven't left anything of ours behind, then straighten things, turn out the lights, lock the door – and off.

Pinkášiš o Ruv is squatting in the corner in a peculiar position.

"So khéres, dyliná?"

"Činav. Mek amen na chuden."

(What are you doing, you fool? –

Shitting. So they don't catch us.)

— Folk legend has the upper hand. Burglars often need to relieve themselves, from the nerves, and to explain it away they assert that it's magic, against being caught. Operation this-or-that went smoothly and successfully – apart from its original objective – and no one has had to shit his pants – but – with due respect to tradition! Anyway it's a good manifestation of our true devotion to the dear comrade doctor…

— Let's get out of here!

The streets are beautifully empty and of course it's still dark.

The idea of the communal van was great. Maybe there was some communal machinery breakdown and they were called out on an emergency or something.

Zderad hops out on the other side of the bridge. But before that Bašno gives him back his thousand crowns:

"Le, more. Me jon na štendrvav. Andral oda kerdom doha, more." (Here mate, I don't need it. I've made enough out of this one, mate.)

Still, it has to be said that the Gypsies behaved in an exemplary, sober and intelligent way. They didn't break anything, they took just that one bottle of cognac from the booze cupboard, and Wolf's little act was just a magic rite.

The burglary was done in a very neutral way, without the characteristic indicators. They didn't leave anything behind either. There is hope that they won't be caught.

Nevertheless the visit to the Monster's chateau did not fulfil the original intention.

And even if it had, it would not have helped anyway, as we shall see. The Monster is no little histrionic prima donna and the whole affair is somewhat different than it seems.

— But – hell and damnation – our main character curses himself as he walks through the lifeless City.

— We're idiots!

— It's obvious: the upper floor was missing over that great hall, but what about over the kitchen and bedrooms? And above that first lounge? There must be a top floor there. And there was no sign of any staircase.

— Well, well, who knows! Maybe if we had got up there we could have gone off with some compromising material, some kind of antidote to the Stalin thing, or even find the poem.

— Why didn't we think of it, even that Bašno, who's seen it all! Who knows what's in there!

— But at least we've done him some harm.

XIV

— "Mrs. Hamouz, you really ought to keep a better eye on Nadia. I don't know what that girl's coming to."

"How do you mean, Mr. Zderad?"

"Well, she's getting a bit fresh. She tried it on me, but I sent her packing!"

Mrs. Hamouz, or rather Hamouz's common law wife, a tiny, grotesque individual, giggles repulsively.

Zderad's moral intervention is obviously missing the mark.

You see, it's like this:

Since last summer, when Zderad attacked Hamouz and restored some kind of order (perhaps with the Monster's aid, but we don't know that), Nadia sees him as some kind of hero.

She also comes crawling to him to help her with her Russian and Maths, which flatters Zderad.

It makes him feel that his unfinished education was not entirely wasted.

He can sometimes ask her to look after little Záviš when he's home from school at the weekend or when he has to stay at home, so that the others don't catch his cold.

Albeit the Zderads, middle-class at heart, don't like to see her taking him outside to mix with the riffraff.

'We ought to try and move elsewhere' they've been saying to each other.

It doesn't seem a realistic possibility at the moment.

Unfortunately, Nadia appears to be manifesting rapid and premature signs of puberty, both physically and psychologically.

She's only about eight years old (how old exactly?), but she seems to be one of those girls who mature at around nine.

It's quite common in southern Europe, though not around here.

She'll probably be tiny like her mother. But she's beginning to be cheeky, and on top of it, in an unpleasantly worldly-wise, proletarian way.

Like last time, when the conversation turned to Hamouz flogging her (he doesn't do it anymore), she offered to show Zderad her weals, and started to do it, surely not out of genuine naivety.

Zderad found the idea provocative, and so he quickly threw her out.

He decided that he would only let her visit him when Sylva was at home.

Little girls like that are inclined to make things up, he knew that very well.

— Nadia is becoming a revolting brat.

— Maybe Hamouz had reason to beat her, even if too much.

— Oh God, the rabble we have to live with around here! And actually I belong here – I'm no better.

Zderad was bitterly aware of his overall downward slide.

His occasional contacts with the amphibian intelligentsia only emphasised it.

As for Sylva, she was pretty much always at meetings.

But the worst thing was that he knew that there was no way out of his situation.

Somehow he was losing touch with the normal world, even with Sylva.

She was now somehow better dressed, more self-assured and dignified.

A teacher.

She was drifting away from him.

When Zderad tried to match up to her, the only result was a kind of proletarian impertinence.

— What do you expect.

— A whore, Gypsies' crony and now a burglar even.

— The pits.

— Mud.

— No light at the end of the tunnel.

———

The Monster made no comment about the break-in at his home during his meetings with Zderad. That was to be expected. He still thought that, for Zderad, He remained a mysterious phantom without trace, history or identity.

Zderad would have liked to know if he was under suspicion, but it was not likely. His papers had not been touched, and Zderad didn't look the type to steal chalices and statues. Most likely He doesn't know anything.

Just for safety, Zderad restricted his visits to the Gypsy local (Those bastards have eyes everywhere), but there was little danger in that.

The burglary of the Monster's villa was done in quite a civilised way, uncharacteristic of Gypsies. The respective authorities were probably not even aware that by forcing settlement and training in various crafts and trades, they had weaned a more refined criminal group than that traditionally associated with Gypsies.

Döme told Zderad, just by the way, that everything turned out fine, that the antiques had been transported "out" and successfully sold, and that no one seems to know anything. He also offered a share, but Zderad turned it down.

Why? He didn't know, really.

Maybe he didn't want to be reminded of his part in it.

———

Life dragged by, miserable and not even sweet and post mortally dreamy anymore.

It was a kind of mental prison.

Even the meetings and drinking with the quartet didn't calm him down.

Krůta was there, and to a certain extent shared at least a part of his revolting secret.

He looked amicable and as if nothing had happened, (Zderad had given him a considerable sum of money as damages for his fright and the greedy crofter pocketed it without a word) but the very thought of their meeting in the cottage continued to embarrass Zderad.

Anyway, Krůta must have wondered where he came by the money and it wouldn't take much to put two and two together.

He wasn't born yesterday, and he had the proverbial crofter's cunning.

Everything was somehow wretched now.

Even all that initial energetic operation which involved Krůta was a waste of time.

Zderad knew now that it would have been futile even if he had found the Greek poem.

It had all been just a kind of convulsive gesture.

The Monster came back at the beginning of February, and was even more disgusting than before. He had a raging appetite.

After a month with his orderly little family, he clearly wanted to make up for it.

He didn't demand to be flogged so much – and Zderad knew why: While his wife wasn't safely ensconced somewhere out of visiting range, he couldn't afford to have weals and bruises – but he made up for that in different and even more disgusting ways.

Let's not go into details.

It is sufficient that you know of his basic turpitudes, for we are writing a fundamentally decent narrative.

Another Victorious February – anniversary of the communist takeover in 1948 – with all its celebrations and corresponding rites of the fifties was looming on the horizon, and this made cultivating 'internal emigration' difficult.

As agreed with Sylva, Zderad stuck onto their windowpane the perfunctory National and Soviet flags, and a scruffy looking pigeon picture referred to as Picasso's dove of peace. Whenever he came home, he had to look at it.

It was not advisable to leave your window bare.

Old timers will vouch for that.

The only advantage in Zderad's present line of work was the absence of political meetings and processions.

As we've said at the beginning, the funereal industry is so incompatible with such things, that nobody could imagine even suggesting the participation of such funereal human dregs, at least not seriously.

Besides, people don't stop dying and being buried in February, Victorious or otherwise.

It is equally inconceivable to glorify the Revolution with funeral attendants marching side by side in close formation. That much is plain.

But Sylva had to look busy, partly for the sake of Mr. Burda. He appeared personally outside Zderad's coffin-dwelling a few times, with organisational matters to discuss, instructions to impart, and whatnot.

Zderad felt humiliated by having this communist twit prying into their impoverished lifestyle.

Then there was the deathly cold winter weather, the whiteness, the black crows, insistently reminding Zderad of his absurd visit to the asylum and the questions and emotions thus provoked.

The freezing cold smacks of bitterness in a number of languages, and it was, indeed, bitterly cold…

———

In this frame of mind, Zderad turned to music.

We've spoken earlier of his untrained, natural talent for arranging song parts.

Now, when he had, by his own estimation, reached the nadir of moral worth (how wrong he could be), it was as if secret doors had swung open somewhere within. From these outpoured unheard of, formless and healing sounds.

It's a known fact that you can see stars from inside a very deep well even in broad daylight, and the allegorical interpretation seems beautifully and subtly fitting.

And so it was as he lay alone one day, all alone, on his poor man's bed in his cold and putrid coffin-dwelling, that there arose within him a strange and hitherto unknown feeling. As many times before, he was absorbed in the projection of his miserably crippled life before his inner eye, becoming more crippled with each new day.

He saw it as if detached, from a distance, and a height.

This much had happened before, and often.

He wondered at it all, where it was leading, why, and who he might be anyway, this Zderad, the one who has to put up with it and live through it.

Then, suddenly, he felt as if he was not alone.

Some kind of vast, lofty, wise and all encompassing Consciousness seemed to be watching him; separate, yet benignly and unfathomably empathetic.

Zderad had often felt sorry for himself, but this kind of pleasant and lasting fellow-feeling had a different, un-personified and incredibly calming flavour.

This state of mind cannot be pictured or represented visually. It could nevertheless be likened to a vast, cosmic, gentle-featured and benign face, looking at him from the detached heights of vertigo, nonhuman, superhuman, but benevolently on his side.

It seemed that this gigantic, placid and impenetrably wise Being had lifted him up before its gaze on an outstretched palm.

It seemed to be telling him with Its clear mind, clear as running water, that It knew, It knew everything, including things he didn't know about himself.

It seemed to be saying: "I know, you're suffering, but believe me, it's all right, it has to be so, and look, I'm with you, nothing bad can happen to you."

Of course, dear reader, these are just words and images. Seldom is a writer so far short of expressing what he is trying to get at.

You can't rightly say that the state of mind was reassuring, or calming.

The face, though there was none, was mute, and only seemed to be looking on, but – what am I saying, even that's all wrong.

It simply defies language.

Zderad was looking back at this Being, if you could call It such. Then, inconspicuously, dispassionately and cosmically the perspective changed.

Whereas before Zderad had looked, as it were, up, and the Consciousness down at him, they had somehow swapped places.

It dawned on him with a certain calm, spiritual dread that the "face," the Being, the Consciousness, was he himself.

It was he himself who looked down at this wretched, impermanent, stinking worm called Zderad.

He understood him deeply and completely.

He was like the mathematician, picking over some figment of his discipline, suddenly seeing it with his holistic soul, without speculation, in its mathematical essence.

It was with that same all-exhausting and instantaneous vision that the eternal Zderad observed the temporal one.

We can't say how long this went on.

When he had finally returned to his body and his ignorance, he was left with an aftertaste, a dim recollection of this strange state of mind.

It may have saved him, for he had been considering how to end it all, dramatically even, by hanging himself one night on a tree outside the Monster's bedroom.

———

There are many who might say, cynically, that Zderad was cracking up after all the goings on.

They could point out that similar states are produced artificially by various drugs, and cannot therefore be ascribed any metaphysical meaning.

The rigid Catholic theologians of the fifties would argue that mystical states do not come to those engaged in mortal sin (whereas nowadays each one would argue it differently, depending on how he felt), and Zderad was certainly a sinner, even by the most liberal interpretation.

Therefore, this cosmic visitation cannot have been a positive phenomenon, such as an angel, not to mention God.

Also, the change of viewpoint which Zderad experienced smacks of pantheistic heresy, and so on and so forth.

Therefore, if this were not a natural, though pathological state, then this Consciousness was Lord knows what! Lucifer, the fallen angel of light, etc.

These, and other objections were clear to Zderad, once he had retracted within his spatiotemporally limited reach.

He also recalled having read of the principle of अवलोकितेश्वर –

"Avalokiteśvara," which the well-enough-read will know means "He who looks down," the cosmic Bódhisattva, or principle of universal compassion in Mahayana Buddhism. He also remembered statues of Buddha he had seen, holding on their laps smaller statues of Buddha or other meditating ascetics, watching over them with detachment, but benign empathy.

This seemed the closest visual representation of his experience.

He still had no idea what to make of it.

His active mind began to speculate, and the bare event became lost in a thorn-bush of interpretation.

We're none too sure what to make of it either, dear consumer.

That is why we have only described it, if that, or rather, failed.

———

In his more normal, less ethereal states Zderad started hearing music. That's not to say he heard it through his ears.

He was aware of it, as he was of mathematical sets and relationships. And, without anyone knowing, he began to write it down.

He found that while the flow lasted, he could channel, direct and modify it, as a child plays with a stream, channelling it through dams and waterwheels.

The trouble was, the flow often stopped as soon as he picked up his manuscript paper, leaving an impression or aftertaste, insufficient for any useful purpose.

A good composer must surely be able to keep the flow going.

Even so, he managed to catch a few drops now and again.

For instance, there was the Motet for Lent, from Isiah or somewhere.

The text was taken from other musical settings.

It seemed most appropriate to his own and the national scabies, on the occasion of Victorious Februarium especially.

TRADIDERUNT ME IN MANUS IMPIORUM –

They have put me into the hands of the ungodly and cast me among criminals.

And they spared not my soul.

Strong men joined forces against me and towered like giants.

Foreigners rose up against me and the powerful sought my soul.

And they rose up before me like giants.

Fine, the motet proper for four mixed voices is a decent composition, but it's nothing to write home about.

Even if the monstrosity of the giants is so well expressed by the bass part.

But when Zderad got to the "Versus" about the foreigners (ALIENI INSURREXERUNT ADVERSUS ME) the mysterious dark vault of his musical mind burst open and the Flow came clear and distinct.

In an instant he heard through his disembodied inner ear a trio of female voices:

Two sopranos were imitating each other in prime or unison, whilst an alto hooted in the lower octave like an unfettered augmenting mirror.

After one or two unsuccessful attempts, Zderad managed some sort of encapsulation of the apparition, and when he came back to it later, he knew it for what it was – a damn good piece.

Granted, it had seemed better in the original, but even the faint reflection he was left with was worthwhile.

This kind of phenomenon seems common enough.

Fortuna, like an insect, can land on any mule, and though inclined to stir the waters of Lake Bethesda, the Spirit can do the same for a duck pond on an obscure village green.

The successful little piece gratified Zderad immensely for several days.

He was not brave enough to show it off, although he was sure it was good, and the "Alieni" even excellent.

At last he showed it to Venca of St. Nicholas, who was full of praise. He wanted to include it in some programme with his amphibians.

Zderad was pleased.

He wanted it performed, but not under his own name:

Oversensitive, or stupid – maybe.

———

If anyone should want to make sure that the Trio is indeed as good as we make out, he'll have to search through the respective archives, which for some researchers means revoking their émigré criminality first.

The score is probably lost by now.

And, if found, it might be described as too traditional, or conservative, or too far from the modern emphasis on rusty hinges creaking in a crosswind.

That doesn't matter. It's a good piece. For sure.

If you're interested, look for it.

———

— Joy, joy of joys!

Νῦν χρὴ μεθύσθην καί τινα πρὸς βίος
πώνην, ἐπειδὴ κάφανε Μύρσιλος

"Now it is time to get drunk, let each man drink his plenty, old Myrsilos (tyrant) is dead."

The great Stalin has kicked the bucket, and Zderad is drunk, as called upon to do by Alkaios, the ancient poet.

At home, of course. The pubs might even be closed.

Street radio plays sombre music, and surprisingly enough, of the Catholic churchy variety.

— And the commies, the cretins, are crying. Honestly!

— They're just kidding, aren't they?

Burda came to see Sylva with reddened eyes and shook her hand mournfully. It's surprising he didn't fall sobbing around her neck.

— The main thing is, no one must see how happy we are really.

— Shh.

— Kick yourself.

— The chances are, nothing much will change, but the fact he's dead is enough in itself. The main difference is –

— Wait, wait a second.

— It probably makes no difference, damn it all to Hell! "Comrades, let us not besmirch the bright and sacred Memory!"

— After all, take Mohammed for instance. He's been dead hundreds of years, but just you try going to Baghdad or someplace and calling him names! And others.

— It might even get worse, the comrades might try to get the grief out of their system with a 'pogrom' on the blasphemers – a holocaust.

— But we can hope.

There were some grounds for hope, though unbeknown to Zderad and other mere mortals. The deposal of the Godhead was being discussed behind closed doors.

But such hope was short lived, since, as we have seen, Zderad's yoke was not exclusively down to any poem.

Yet, when Zderad set off reluctantly one day for his infernal rendezvous, he found himself waiting in vain.

— Maybe then, after all!

But he rejoiced too soon.

Comrade Skomelný had most likely been detained by important business, or decided to wait and see.

His disappearance was only temporary as we shall discover.

He was to appear again, more disgusting than ever, like a sewer Phoenix reborn from a stinking methane flame.

But all in good time.

———

Soon after the Generalissimus, even his Locum Tenens governor for Czechoslovakia hung up his slippers.*

But that didn't help much, or soon, or Zderad in particular.

———

"Zderad, she's back again," whispers Krůta.

"Who?"

"Julie – she's standing right over there."

Zderad had completely forgotten about "Julie". Not only his affair thereto but also His or rather "Her" (ugh) mere existence.

It was his own red-letter day.

At some Benediction or other, in a smallish church, the amphibians were performing his motet, incognito, under an assumed name.

Zderad took part in the other singsongs, but he slipped away for the motet and went up to the gallery to listen.

— To hear your own composition performed is one of the best feelings on this – by no means worst imaginable – earth.

— It's good, it IS good.

— Something of him shall remain behind.

— Not much, but better than nothing.

— The anonymity adds a pleasantly melancholy dimension.

— I shall perish, but my creation will outlast me.

Admittedly there was precious little to speak of, but let's forgive our

———

* Stalin died on 8th March 1953, Gottwald on 14th March. 1953.

protagonist.

Poor chap, he'd had so few successes in his life.

In fact, nothing but failures.

But in his newfound, dignified and positive frame of mind he was oblivious to the chronic degradation which followed him around.

It attracted his attention now and then like lingering toothache, but still it underpinned his mind with a stubbornly unpleasant tone. He constantly retained a sense of failure. This feeling of worthlessness was now totally absent for a moment, thanks to a humble and covert artistic work.

And since his down-trodden state was so much down to the Monster, it too had gone, with His current disappearance.

His physical re-appearance came abruptly, like a pistol shot.

———

Zderad was walking back toward his slum dwelling quarter, which was still some way off.

He liked walking, as we have mentioned.

He looked round several times, but the Monster was not following.

Just as he breathed a sigh of relief, someone grabbed him by the sleeve.

"I am to speak with you."

A backstreet in the City centre. The street happened to be deserted.

As indicated, and to remind you, it was Sunday, evening, in March.

The massive entrance to some building was barred by a decorative railing, probably dating from the thirties.

The Monster was standing behind the ironwork.

He quickly stepped back into the shadow so as not to be seen.

He beckoned Zderad to follow him, through a gap in the railings, where a bar seemed to have been severed.

It was difficult, but possible to squeeze through.

They went deeper into the archway, hidden from the gaze of potential passers-by.

What could have happened if Zderad had ignored the Monster and carried on?

Despite all that is now about to follow, the answer is, probably, nothing. But there again, had he taken that risk –

To have done so, however, he would have needed a name like Zderadusz, and to have been born a bit further to the northeast.

Czechs used to be manlier men!

The Monster watched Zderad with his deathly eyes.

His soft mouth opened into an aggressive grin, showing yellowing teeth. He seemed tense and vicious.

"Welcome," he said.

Then straight to the point. He never went around the houses, bush-beating.

"Comrade Stalin is dead.

That's nothing much to us though, is it?

We wouldn't want to besmirch his glowing memory.

But there are those who speak of a 'personality cult'.

For the moment it's under control.

The statue will probably come down.*

Nobody is sure yet. But don't think you're free to do a runner – or else."

He passed Zderad a photograph, again.

This time Zderad didn't feel the need to 'be excused'.

He had grown a skin as thick as a shell.

As he looked at the Monster an idea started to hatch in the margin of his mind. He reached into his pocket.

"I muradi his andr'e positi." (The razor was in the pocket.)

He carried it on him all the time nowadays, out of a machismo snobbery, you understand.

He wanted to touch the weapon to gather strength.

The photograph was pornographic.

Not only that, it was perverse.

It showed two naked men, one of whom was Zderad, and the other – Father Plicka!

---

* The biggest of all statues of Stalin in the fifties was in Prague – (the Russians regarded it as too incredible to be sincere, which it may not have been). It was demolished after Stalin's death.

To give the full picture, Plicka was kneeling in front of Zderad –
fellatio penis.

Zderad was more astonished than frightened by it.

"But that's – rubbish!"

Then he noticed that his body wasn't even his own.

He'd never seen the Parson naked, so he couldn't make a comparison.

Apart from a few errors of detail, which we won't go into, the
PseudoZderad was more slightly built than the original.

He had much narrower shoulders – Zderad being, as described,
quite broad – but he was more hirsute.

His bodily proportions were quite different, too.

Relatively longer legs, for instance.

Photographic wizardry of this kind was later exposed to the public,
so we needn't go into the technicalities.

Even Zderad rapidly saw it for what it was.

It could have been a bluff, without official sanction.

Who knows.

It might not even have come from the Interior Ministry's photolab.

What annoyed Zderad was that the heads had most likely been photographed during the St. Wenceslas feast in X.

The Vicar, in good spirits, had been sampling straight out of a bottle
of last year's mead, before he passed it round.

It was clear they'd followed him even there!

The Bastards!

The Vicar's mead-barrel antics had been to no avail.

"That's not me and you know it!"

"It's you if I say so, dearie, you should know that by now, or don't
you?"

"And why Father Plicka?"

"He's too well liked.

And, he encourages collectives. That's inconvenient.

The 'Pastor-Shister' has to be the enemy of the people, right.*

Well, if you're good, cute-arse, we may redo the head.

Or we may leave off the Parson thanks to your – friendly persuasion. There's no rush.

Well – you'd have to be very good – Anyway, we shan't be seeing each other for a while, I'm sorry to say.

Until May."

(He gave a date.)

"Otherwise: *same place same time.*"

(He said the phrase in English, showing off his linguistic prowess, as he often did to Zderad, who could appreciate such things.)

"You'll be bringing darling Sylva, won't you?

You've got nearly two months. To bring her round (!)"

He gave a wild look, with his lower lip protruding slightly.

"Or else – my regrets.

So long then, cute-arse – see you in May."

He climbed through the railings and was gone.

An idea was pecking inside Zderad's head again, but not hatching as yet.

---

* Framing priests as homosexuals was a popular security-forces technique of the fifties. Most often it involved assaulting choirboys. Firstly, because of the much higher legal penalties for assaulting anyone under-age, secondly to save the trouble of how to keep the "victim" out of it. A child could also be more easily persuaded to be a prosecution witness, since it did not have to be persuaded that adults wielded instruments of torture, in view of corporal punishment.

XV

Zderad felt chronically sick.

For some time now the Monster had been chasing him around the spatio-temporal chessboard and now he was getting ready to checkmate.

Knowing Sylva, Zderad was sure there was simply no way he could persuade her.

He couldn't even imagine how he would tell her.

Sylva was absolutely rustically normal, and on top of that there was her evangelical upbringing.

She was a good wife nonetheless, "in every way" as they say, but strictly within the bounds of normality.

— It was simply unimaginable.

— Even if he resorted to Dutch courage and told her everything, she'd be sure to make a scene.

— She's so naive.

— And then, it would most likely be over for all of them.

— Even little Záviš.

— Zderad knew, or had heard, that there were even children in the Joyful Corrective Centres.

— And even if she were to agree to it all, which was of course quite unimaginable, who knows what the Monster really had in mind.

— OMNIBUS ILLE VIRIS MULIER, MAS ILLE PUELLIS.

— "Julie *is* a bastard."

— And think of that mad woman on the white bed, who might have been Jenůfka.

— No way.

The only way out of the woods now clearly had to be a very drastic one. That's how the depressive kills himself and his family (Erweiteter Selbstmord – extended suicide they call it in those fat German psychiatric textbooks), to protect his nearest and dearest from some dreadful fate. Except that, unlike Zderad's case, the dreadful fate exists only in the depressive's mind, a so called depressive delusion.

Zderad had already made up his mind.

The only questions where when, and how.

— When?

— Right at the end. When there is really nothing else left to do.

— They still have well over a month to the deadline, and even then it might not be immediately.

— First, the Monster will come to plead, threaten, whinge.

— He might even back down, like so many times before.

— (But, you can't rely on that.)

— But he'll have to do it before They nick him.

— That could be a problem.

— We'll wait and see.

— Usually no one's in a hurry to die while there are still other options and while the quality of life is the least bit bearable.

— Let them enjoy life a bit longer, poor souls.

Sometimes, when Zderad looked at his wife and son, he came close to tears. He was tough of course, and frankly, not one to cry.

It was curious how he could be touched to tears by music, well, only sometimes, when it was really good, but the rest of the time he was so tough he even surprised himself.

— The next thing is, how?

— Most likely *"i muradi."*

— It'll be bloody, but so be it.

— Nothing will matter by then, will it, and the whole thing is drastic enough in any case. And it'll be quick.

— So how exactly?

— Perhaps once they're asleep.

— Sylva first, that goes without saying.

— If things didn't go smoothly with little Záviš, she'd defend the child like a lioness, and she's damned strong. Almost like a man.

— But he still couldn't see himself killing the boy.

— It must be done! Who knows what He could – he's had enough hints by now.

— Maybe He enjoys torturing children. Or one of His cohorts.

— And finally, himself.

— The razor seems the best thing for that, definitely.

— *I muradi hi sakovestar najfeder.*

— *Čáčes!* (Really.)

———

— But meanwhile – let's enjoy life a little.

Zderad didn't want to be restricted for reasons of secrecy any longer.

There was still the whored-hoard in the bottom of his literary trunk.

Now he could spend the lot, there wasn't much time left, and nobody to save up for.

Sylva kept going to meetings, and he had the evenings largely to himself.

For starters, he did buy the leather jacket, and a leather coat too, like Krůta's.

It was a secret service cast-off – someone had decided it made the lads too conspicuous – and then there were the associations with a bygone régime.

There were two very suspicious breast pockets in the lining – *"per i karibnaskeri"* – obviously for a handgun.

If Sylva were to ask how he came by it, he was prepared to tell her where to go in no uncertain terms. But she didn't ask. Most likely she didn't notice: She was not very feminine, in that respect.

— And if a nosy neighbour were to ask, which she wouldn't, what was likely to happen if he told her?

— *"Well Missus, I got this by whoring.*

— *I have this queer, Dr. Julius Skomelný, from the University, who lives in such and such a posh villa. He has a little wife and two proper little children. Pioneers.*

— *He's engaged in the Battle against the Church and He decides on the strategy and tactics against priests. He also preaches on the radio.*

— *He pays me because I let him lick my arse, and I thrash him. Basically. And a few other things of that kind.*

— *Would you like me to tell you about those too? But, Missus, don't throw up now."*

— What could happen?

It had been quite some time, but Zderad was a free man again.

Nobody could touch him now.

Even if they came for him unexpectedly, he'd still stand a good chance of ending it swiftly and relatively painlessly. They'd hardly object to him blowing his nose, at least not right at the beginning, and the razor could surely be hidden in the handkerchief.

Just himself though, that would be a bit of a snag.

I muradi ehis furt andr'i leskri positi.

(The razor was always in his pocket.)

What Zderad didn't realize was that all this time the Monster had been afraid of just the kind of neighbourly conversation he'd imagined.

Now and again when He woke in his spacious, gracious bedroom, the freak would sweat with fright.

Not that it would finish him, necessarily.

But it might.

Zderad was not clearly aware of one thing:

The vulturavens tore the living guts from one another and constantly had to insure and secure themselves against their apparently closest friends. The pitiful sods.

———

He was living it up.

In a refined way, to a certain extent.

Several times he bought himself concert tickets.

Not in the gallery, or the organ loft, like at times in the past.

With dignity and expense, in the front stalls.

And a suit, to keep decorum.

Sometimes he even went by taxi.

Life could be quite decent, now that the Monster was not in it.

A pity, a thousand-fold pity there was so little of it left.

Zderad would stand on the embankment, watching the river and musing about the likelihood that he would soon not be able to see it.

It didn't even make him feel sad, just kind of unreal.

Reminiscent of when his family and life had vamoosed.

In its own way it was quite agreeable.

———

By that time the sun would make its disappearance behind the cathedral quite swiftly, and the starry fireworks would explode in their turn. The abyss of the nocturnal heavens gaped with monstrous jaws, howling with all the pleasures and pains of all-encompassing Being, which writhed with the cruel ecstasy of existence in an unfathomable universe.

Every conceivable oddity roamed the earth and the angels stood in trepidation above it all, appalled with insane glee.

In the slum jungles, male bedbugs were copulating not only with females but also with their young, thus feeding them on their own semen.

In Father Plicka's beehives, the mysterious and incredible lifecycle of invertebrates was unfolding.

Sucked onto a bee larva, as the bees had already begun laying in early spring, was the female mite *Pediculoides ventricosus Newport*. She had started out very tiny, 0.20 mm long, and mobile.

Now, however, she had swelled tenfold in size and was no longer capable of movement.

Precisely on that evening and at that moment when Zderad was looking down at the nocturnal river under the silent roar of the stars, the mite prepared to give birth.

The first to be born was her only son, a tiny male who immediately burrowed his proboscis into his mother's body near her sexual orifice and started feeding on her blood.

One after another all her teeny daughters emerged from the innards of the Pediculoides female, numbering 299 in all.

Their brother took possession of each one of them and fertilised all 299.

The young females fell away, to lie among the grime on the hive floor, to continue their development, for they were still only larvae.

Their mother now perished, and with her died their brother and husband. When they mature, the females will themselves parasitize bees and their larvae, and the whole bizarre process will be repeated.

Such are the many countless lifestyles that inhabit our planet, each type more weird than the next.

And how many more must there be, lurking in the hidden depths of the universe.

What is man, to rebel against his fate?

And any deity there might be, seems, from our limited perspective, almost deranged.

Because everything, even the wildest thing we can imagine seems to exist, somewhere, somehow, already.

By comparison, our lives are quite orderly and tame, even if they may resemble the lives of the Monster, or of Zderad.

Death is just a pause between the notes of the vast organ pipes of existence and the universe is one ecstatic, existential frenzy.

―――――

But man cannot live by culture alone.

Although Sylva now came home almost always late at night, (what can they possibly have to discuss all the time – she's probably joined the Party as well by now and hasn't the nerve to tell Zderad) surprisingly she didn't complain of tiredness and never rejected him.

Her embraces were now not only passionate, but also loving.

Almost as if she suspected something.

As if she was saying farewell.

Zderad wasn't surprised by it for he felt something similar himself.

Well, dear consumer, let us not pore over the details.

We don't have the right, somehow.

It is their own private business.

The priests call marriage a sacrament and there must be some grounds for the notion.

Let's leave them, delicately close the door – pardon me, I mean the miserable patched-up curtain on rusty curtain-rings – and tiptoe away.

―――――

However, Zderad played even less than before with little Záviš. It tore at his heart too much.

―――――

But the human heart has many chambers.

Zderad was not deprived to any extent, yet his considerable lecherousness did not let him off.

Just the once, at least now, to do something out of the ordinary, to let himself go!

Of course, the Monster does not count, our hero is not that way inclined, but how about a Chinese, or a Black girl, or some young thing, just short of the legal age.

(Evidently, young Nadia had not left his subconscious!).

Or a twisted one, in whichever sense.

To revel, drink, sing, go wild. Until it all comes crashing down.

————

— Because, most likely, there is no God. That other time, that Consciousness, that Avaloketiśvara, who knows where that came from. It's gone now, anyway.

— And if there is a God, merciful and wise, surely not the kind to condemn him for not wanting to allow his family to suffer who-knows-what kind of humiliation and torture.

— And if it is the case that the world is *His* doing, let *Him* keep out of it now!

— Let *Him* see what *He* has caused with *His* irresponsible creativity.

— Why, for example, does the Monster exist?

— After all, that one is the most wretched of wretches if He feels compelled to do what He does!

— No wonder He has become evil, and worse than evil.

— And who is to blame for that, eh?

— This God has no right to be surprised if I don't want any part of it, if I prefer nothingness.

— And if there is a hell, I'd rather go there than expose my wife and child to who-knows-what torture.

— Some doltish philosopher, Aristotle I think, asserts that being is better than not being.

— Hardly.

— Not in all cases.

— Certainly not in mine.

— But first, I want to have some fun.

— Something more out of the ordinary.

— (Isn't the Monster enough for you?)

— Ah – shush!

————

It was under these circumstances that Zderad turned to Kopta.

Turgo, you see, was ill with some kind of senile arthritis or podagra, and even before this he'd been going downhill for some time.

This last year he'd been more morose than before. He knew now that it was all over for him, that life had nothing more to offer.

For him, who had played in a quartet at the age of six!

How screwed up it had all got.

In short – he offed.

He was poorly. What he lived on was a mystery. Savings of some kind, perhaps. And Kopta had taken his place.

Kopta was a little man, getting on for fifty. He had a weird pointy nose, very long and reddened as if from a cold, but more likely from drink; and thick glasses, bifocals I think.

His head was shiny bald, edged with closely cropped hair of an uncertain dirty colour.

His shoulders sloped and his neck emerged from them like the neck of a bottle; and from the waist down he was shaped more like an older woman.

He had a very good voice. A baritone, probably trained, but un-wavering and neat, with a phenomenal range.

He could climb up to first tenor or descend down to second bass, though he lacked the spectacular foot-pedal depths which inverted Krůta would occasionally show off with. (Incidentally, it was he who had taken over the accompanist's role).

Kopta had been a petty clerk in some archives or, wait, let's say with the proanimabus office.[30]

But he lost his crust.

Maybe through drink, but there again, he didn't seem to drink that much.

Or maybe the communists had abolished the proanimabus. But probably not: the proanimabus seems to be just the sort of institution which they could have easily overlooked and missed somehow, due to a lack of Asiatic institutional analogues.

Well, we just don't know.

But he had to make a living by gravelarking.

Why Kopta had failed to make it was just as much a mystery as that of the Turgonis.

In the official higher musical echelons, in the theatres and concert halls, another man, who could have passed for Kopta's twin, was doing very nicely as a soloist. He was just a bit darker.

Even his voice was very similar in timbre and range, and he was often in the papers because of it.

He lived like a king.

Try and explain that, if you can.

Kopta was somehow always idiotically happy and euphoric. He was always nattering and making jokes, even quite wittily sometimes.

He was also sex-mad. He often spoke about women, hookers and everything that goes with it.

He seemed to know what he was talking about.

———

When, for the second time in their history, the Russians 'cut a window through to Europe' as they put it, and climbed inside in their muddy 'sapogi' boots with the blessing of senile Western Powers, it took them some considerable time to acclimatise to the unusually arcane conditions.

For this reason their ideological words of wisdom, respectfully imported by their collaborators in officialdom, long continued to be characterised by an ancient Slav simple-mindedness which did not have much effect on the worldly-wise inhabitants of the City.

So, for instance at the School of Moral Philosophy, an emaciated crackpot with a ha'penny's worth of grey matter, preached that sexual perversions were the product of capitalist economics, and therefore, that they did not and could not exist among our Friends. Nor in our ranks.

The same man later found favour in the hearts of the Czech people for he screwed the Soviet ambassador's wife, but in our eyes his redemption is only partial, because deliberate stupidity is a sin against the Holy Spirit.

Likewise there was also a frequently proclaimed hilarious theory that there were no whores in the countries of Peace and Socialism.

Such a view, as every sane person knows, is certainly untrue in an allegorical sense, rather the opposite, but is also erroneous in its literal, original sense.

By which I am right now referring exclusively to the women who make a living out of selling sexual favours.

They were and are ubiquitous, also in the countries of Peace, Socialism and Progress, although in these they exist only unofficially.

At the time which we are describing they were still as abundant as flies.

The policemen were supposed to swat them, but often they did so only to keep up appearances.

There were of course no official brothels, at least not for ordinary people.

I suspect they do exist now, at least for the occupying forces.

Anyway, it is a scientifically established fact that in the year fifty three, which this narrative is about, whores not only existed, but flourished.

———

A long hillside rises up from the slum area, which has more or less been turned into a park.

It has a connection with a particular period and a certain event in history, when *"Czech men were folk who bore no foreign yoke"* as a chronicler put it – when the Hussites led by Žižka trounced the imperial armies of crusaders.

This is why the shrunken homunculi of today turn to this period with considerable nostalgia and sentiment.

At the peak of this geological formation we behold an enormous equestrian statue of one of the long since extinct members of the original resident race of humans.

His position might nevertheless be seen as degrading, for it seems as if his horse is pulling a gigantic removal van behind it.

At the time of which we write, this removal van may already have been turned in the mind into a sort of mobile panopticon, for it contained the embalmed remains of the recently deceased Archvulturaven.[31]

For a time attempts were also made to turn this outsize crate into a national sanctum à-la Lenin's mausoleum, with frightened citizens compelled to form a queue all the way up the hill.

"... an enormous equestrian statue ..."

After a while, the chief exhibit fell from grace, relatively speaking, and I don't even know whether they still kept him there. It was no longer talked about.

Since time immemorial, however, private prostitution was practised on the slopes of this hill; and this practice continued even after its definitive, though temporary, consecration as the Temple of the People.

Various hostelries can be found below the summit of the holy place, serving as venues for the preliminary transactions connected with the hiring of genitalia.

It is in one of these loci that we now find Zderad, accompanied by the aforementioned gravelark, Kopta, in the role of Mephistopheles.

————

It is not, alas, their first visit.

You see, Kopta had found out that Zderad was well off and so clung onto him like a leech.

Zderad was also willing to finance Kopta's Bacchic and Venereal excesses.

Indeed, his own final descent gave him masochistic pleasure.

Unlike Kopta, he had no need of such things.

Firstly, he was by all criteria happily married, and Sylva had lately been showering him not only with passion but also with love.

And perhaps this was what Zderad despised a little, for his marital bed lacked cynicism and crudeness.

Also, as we know, Zderad was a good-looking young man and not only attractive to homosexuals. With a little more effort he could have provided himself with a better class of mistress, and almost for free.

All he needed to do was to start an intelligent conversation with, say, one of the amphibian credulous youth-union studienettes, or with one of the sophisticated young ladies which he now often met with at concerts of so-called serious music.

But for some reason Zderad preferred cruder pleasures.

Now he didn't even care that he could 'bring something home' – it would all end soon enough, so what?

He showed off, paid for rounds of drinks for the tarts and dropouts, and couldn't give a damn about becoming conspicuous as a result.

Having been desensitised by all the tomb meetings with the Monstrette, he now tried out various heterosexual perversions, about which we shall keep discreetly silent, however, for we are writing a basically decent little story.

He took one whore after another and got through lots of them.

Nevertheless, it did not seem to satisfy him much.

Rather, he had the feeling that for some unknown reason he just had to do it.

The idiot.

———

As we write these lines, our two sleazy companions are waiting for the night to grow older, and for the rocky slopes of the legendary hill to open for business.

It's only April and the hill is still as bare as the buttocks of the whores, only covered with their skirts in order to be instantly ready for action.

Perhaps later they will withdraw to some lair, safer and warmer, within its four walls.

The wolf-bitches are already starting to appear, jiggling their Means of Production.

Zderad and Kopta are drinking rum – après nous le déluge. This batch of rum won't be from Cuba as yet, if memory serves.

A man who bears a striking resemblance to blind Kanner, the proletarian musician from a book by Karel Čapek, is phut-farting on a chromatic accordion. We are tempted to write that the instrument is sparkling like an acoustic torch, but we know that in so doing we actually would be plagiarising Czech literature.[32]

And anyhow, this accordion only seems to be smouldering.

Zderad had already borrowed it on occasion, and having had the bass button system explained by the blind man, he played various pieces.

This also enhanced his reputation.

— If his carcassinging fell through he would now know how to secure a modest existence, leaving the Monster aside for the moment of course.

— He could even supplement his income this way.

— After all, he could now afford an instrument, at least second-hand.

— The Comrades are generally unable to grasp the concept of folk art, and unless some anachronistic left-wing intellectual from the First Republic ruins it for them they are willing to call even the worst kind of kitsch 'folk music'.

— Zderad might therefore enjoy a certain charismatic nimbus with the comrades as an accordion player like the mythical rural bagpiper Švanda Dudák.

— For even the Soviet heroes love this instrument.

— Even the new Comrade President is reported to have been an expert performer on the brickie's organ. Now though, as head of state, having entered the place where he'd once chiselled gargoyles in his shirtsleeves, to use the words of the national bard, it is possible that he would rather not admit to it.

— But also – because of some kind of mystical affinity, which is largely irrational but nevertheless experienced – the accordion player in a pub, in contrast to a stiffsinger, seems to be somehow immune from the adventures that Zderad has had with the Monster. Wouldn't you say?

— Maybe the accordion would magically scare off the Monster, just as Švanda's bagpipes sent the Devil packing in the story.

— And with a bit of practice Zderad could even become a variety artist, and so on.

— But that's rubbish. A fantasy. The freak has him good and won't let go. And anyway, what difference does it make?

———

At this moment, however, Zderad is showing off and applying himself in a different way. His fate of a fallen intellectual, associating with the lower strata and even thieves, evokes in the minds of the well read, – and thus also in his own – certain, though vague, historico-literary associations.[*]

---

[*] We refer to the French poet Francois Villon (1431–1463?) who was also a robber. He created the Villonese Ballad, which has a strict format consisting of three verses, rhyming "ababbcbC" where C is a repeating line, and a short parting stanza 'En Voi', rhyme "cbbC".

The ballad is usually on a reflective theme, typified by the repeating rhyme C, and the main theme is summarised in the envoy. This form of poem was particularly popular with Vrchlický (in its longer form) and Vítězslav Nezval, a major Czech poet of the thirties. This bard invented an eternal student called Robert David, a sort of Zderad, a

Let us recall that the hitherto oft mentioned bard Nezval invented his version of Zderad out of sheer luxury and boredom, as he himself had never been poor, let alone destitute.

Still, the poems were excellent. …

For our part, we cannot let such a great opportunity pass without showing off somewhat, as earlier with the Greek:

In short, Zderad, under the influence of rum and self-styled historical romanticism is now astounding Kopta and other onlookers with some kind of rhyme, jotted down with ink crayon on the false marble tabletop:

---

pseudonym under which he wrote three collections of poems, one in the strict form of the Villonese ballad, without prejudicing his position as a surrealist aesthete. The writer Eduard Bass also wrote a polemic in the journal Lidové noviny against an anonymous journalist from Švehla's "Venkov" (The Country-side), supposedly an imitation of Cyrano's ballad from the play by Rostand (as translated by Vrchlický), but it was rather pedestrian, lacking the balladic form proper.

VILLONESE BALLAD
ON THE UNIVERSALITY OF PROSTITUTION,
AS RECITED BY ZDERAD TO WHORES AND DROPOUTS

Each one of us is for sale yet;
Our thirst for self-destruction slaking:
Thrown to the Devil as his pet,
And at his whim, there for the taking,
Resigned to live as gnats, crushed, quaking,
To spare fainthearted resolution,
Our all, our dignity forsaking:
All around you see prostitution.

A storm of terror, black as jet;
Lost in his grip like leaves we're shaking,
Raise up his tail and kiss the wet,
Fearing that sleep which has no waking.
How aptly Sabbath dawn is breaking,
As we lie prostrate on the cushion,
And give in to his undertaking:
All around you see prostitution.

The Devil having won his bet
Whispers vile nothings in his waking,
Strings up your soul to pay the debt,
Whips you until you're barely aching.
Resistance broken, peeling, flaking,
Complying to his retribution,
Whate'er the pain, whate'er the raking:
All around you see prostitution.

Envoy:

We make a splendid contribution!
Girls, let's join hands in merrymaking!
Devil's own troupe, and no mistaking.
All around you, see, prostitution.

179

———

Kopta is sticking his ruddy snout into Zderad's ear and slobbering:

"Today I'll get you that little girl. She's young, tiny, but quite something. She knows the lot already. She's not been at it long, mind. Her mother's a whore, too. It runs in the family, you know.

Last time me and Josef did it – here in the cooling shaft.

If you bolt the door no one can get in. Or look down.

You'll see: She grabbed Joe by the belt, like this, and I picked up her skirt from behind – epicene – you'll see.

But later, you know – she's under age!

So, watch your step.

Their old man is pimping them both, mother and daughter.

Zderad's eyes, we regret to say, are lit up.

"There, there's the old buzzard now."

Zderad looked up.

— Blast it all, Hamouz!

All his debauchery left him.

Instead he was swamped with tremendous shame.

"Wait" he mumbled to Kopta, "I've got to go to the bog."

He got up, leaving Kopta the bone-crushing bill – and was off.

— So that's the story then!

— Let's hope Hamouz hadn't seen him.

— And so, what if he had? He can't know why he was there. He could have just stopped off for a beer, right.

— Crap! He knows Kopta. And they were sitting together.

— So what if he does! It's all the same now – in another month. Should he go back? No, a thousand times no!

— Not Nadia.

— You bastard, didn't the other whores have fathers, mothers and neighbours, didn't they once do homework and play with dolls, and hopscotch? Some of the ones he'd had already could easily have been under age – though possibly older than she is.

— Looking at it another way, I'm a whore too.

— Anyone watching that business with the Monster would see me as nothing but an ordinary prostitute. Even with the coercion.

— Does that make me any the worse a human being?

With this insight, Zderad's whoring period came to an end.

INTERMEZZO

Not far to the north of the City one begins to encroach upon the outer border zone, theoretically out of bounds for most people, yet inhabited by more or less ordinary folk.

Somewhere in this belt can be found a certain hamlet.

Once upon a time it used to be spotless, as if made of sugar or gingerbread, being inhabited by Germans.

Nowadays, quite to the contrary, it was extraordinarily dingy, as the main inhabitants were resettled Gypsies, magyarons and some species of pseudoslovaks, or whatever.

The village square is adorned by an inadvertently surrealist statue. In the seventeenth century a pillar had been erected there, topped by some sculptor's interpretation of the Holy Trinity.

The sculpture comfortably survived the first three hundred years, but not the great Year Forty Five: Whether it had been subjected to a deliberate act of Scientific Atheism is hard to say.

The fact of the matter is that the Holy Ghost, in the guise of Dove, has vanished, and both the Father and Son have had their heads shot off or otherwise removed.

The result has a certain surreal and infernally blasphemous quality. If we were to include the swarthy ragged figures of the villagers, not forgetting the particularly green and smelly goose-puddle, we would imagine that we are in hell, and that the statuary has always been headless, in contrived blasphemy.

The quaintly infernal impression of the village was momentarily heightened by an incredibly bizarre hunchbacked figure, hopping across the square, resembling the popular Quasimodo.

The hopping was not in this case the expression of Constructive Socialist Joy.

Having one of his legs shorter that the other, there was no other way to run.

He was running away from a bunch of grubby Gypsy children who threw mud and shrieked: "Buckelhanes, Buckelhanes, Crooked Jack ..."

To crown the illusion, the escaping cripple was carrying a sack on his back.

He weaved through the houses until his pursuers dropped back.

Grimacing and cursing, Buckelhanes lamely climbed the steep slopes of the Sudeten foothills.

Buckelhanes was the local cripple and simpleton, and therefore had not been shunted out with the other Germans.

He had not been a Nazi of course, nor even a soldier, so the collective Guilt of the German nation extended to him only marginally and imprecisely, in a purely legalistic way. It seemed logical to let him be.

In the event, he was worse off among the Gypsies than he would probably have been among the exiled Germans.

At least we can think of it that way.

Otherwise his sentence might seem fair, which would be at odds with Progressive Justice.

Of Buckelhanes' sibs and parents, some had died, some were exiled and some didn't stay around to be caught. One or two were already holed up in South America. Naturally enough, they did not look for, or care about Buckelhanes, since it would have given away their identity.

Buckelhanes lived in the old family chalet, a remote, crumbling place.

He was widely regarded as an idiot, but was more probably touched by chronic schizophrenia. Nobody knew nor cared, and a doctor hadn't been around the headless village at least since the Germans. Theoretically speaking there was some district doctor, but the Gypsies probably knew nothing of it.

The other things known about Buckelhanes were, that he was religious, that he prayed by the headless pillar and other places and that he had once been some kind of servant at the vicarage and used to drive the bellows for the church organ.

Now the church was no longer in use and the vicarage stood empty.

So, Buckelhanes hobbled uphill.

The tree blossoms were already out.

Inspired by the sight, Buckelhanes squawked into song in his maternal dialect:

Es fengt oh zu treppel
ei Schiene plien tie Eppel
ei Preschke pliet ta Majaron
*ta Sef, ta wie tie Anna hohn.**

Translated from the Sudeten dialect, a variant of German almost as extinct as Zderad's Homeric Greek, it might go, roughly: *"The sky begins to spit with rain, Schonau apple trees bloom again, in Proschken marjoram's in flow'r, Sef wants to have Anna (in his pow'r)."*

Later, when they reintroduce teaching German in the schools, the dialect will have died out, I suspect. Unless the deported Germans have formed some closed community. Even so, whole languages disappear in a foreign linguistic environment, never mind dialects.

Buckelhanes was clearly some kind of linguistic fossil, like the solitary speaker of the Manx idiom from recent British history.

Having hobbled home to his smelly and decrepit hut, Buckelhanes shut the door and emptied the contents of the sack onto the ground.

Out fell a live dog which crawled under a nearby bench-seat with his tail between his legs. The dog was a mongrel, about the size of a fox terrier. His appearance gave a hint of his partial descent from a French bulldog. He had a blunt muzzle, and pale eyes, like those described earlier in chapter three.

The dog curled up under the bench and watched Buckelhanes with a mixture of fear and anger.

Clucking in his ethnic German, the hunchback stretched his arm under the bench, but quickly drew back as the dog snarled and went for him.

"Na kummjah, kumma hienl," appeased the hunchback circling his birdlike claw about the dog's head.

Seizing his opportunity and the dog by the scruff of the neck he dragged him into the light. The dog yelped in terror and wet himself. In his attempts at self-defence he tried to bite the hand that held him, but Hanes whacked him with the other and the dog desisted, whining.

Buckelhanes now set about stroking the dog and talking to him, and

---

* As with the dustman's Hungaro-Czechoslovak utterances earlier, our transcription is orthographically loose.

the dog began to calm down. He writhed humbly under the hunch-back's hands and wagged his tail, though it was still between his legs.

Buckelhanes crowed happily.

Taking the dog under his arm to make sure he didn't go back under the bench, he made his way to a cupboard. He took out a clammy bottle, uncorked and tipped it to his lips.

He then poured some onto the dog's head saying, in dialect:

"I' taaf te Julisch…" I baptize thee Julius.

The dog thrashed about, as if rabid. Like an uncorrupted child, a dog regards alcohol on his first encounter as filth. Equally, you can accustom a dog to drink, like other animals, whether mice, or bears, or humans.

In trying to wipe himself the dog inhaled and licked some of the liquor. After a short while he seemed to be inebriated. He staggered about with a puppy-like good humour. Buckelhanes played with him, laughed, stroked him. *"Kumma ja, Julisch, Julisch, ehwuydiga hea, na kut,kut, Julisch, Julisch,"*

He began to scratch the dog's fur more and more vigorously. Finally, the lunatic cripple began to masturbate the dog. The dog clasped his forearm with both front paws and gave in to the perverse pleasure, eyes bulging. Buckelhanes reached behind him and produced an axe. He struck the dog with the blunt end, hard across the nose. The dog didn't utter a sound. He crashed to the floor, blood pouring from the nostrils. Death was sudden and enjoyable.

Buckelhanes laughed and clapped his hands.

"Julisch, Julisch," he crowed. *"Ta sehste"* … there you see. That's for what you did to Anna. And a lot of good it did you. And now, Julisch, Julisch, now I'm going to eat you.

Buckelhanes took the dead animal to the woodshed, and hung it up by the hind legs. Skilfully he disembowelled and skinned it.

Shortly afterward smoke rose from the chimney, accompanied by the aroma of a roast.

CHAPTER

XVI

Nadia is missing. She's vanished.

It's been almost a week.

Mrs Hamouz is distraught.

Sylva deals with the matter at first (Nadia goes to her school).

Even comrade Burda gets involved.

For some reason Mrs Hamouz doesn't want to involve the police. Maybe Nadia will turn up soon, why make a fuss, etc.

Comrade Hamouz is also upset:

"That's what comes of having people interfering in how parents bring up a child," he shouts plaintively, apparently referring to Zderad. "You have to be cruel to be kind with some kids. I should know, I used to teach in a borstal. So, now she's gone and whose fault is it?!"

He's so worked up he might even believe in what he's saying.

He even goes as far as an anti-Soviet remark, denouncing the much publicised educationalist:

"To hell with your soddin' Makarenko!"

He's in tears.

Zderad can't make him out.

Oh the complexities of the human heart!

The Police arrive, investigate, interrogate and come up with a big fat zero. The Hamouz couple are very imprecise as to place and time of her disappearance.

After much obfuscation the pseudo-Mrs Hamouz finally blurts out, (oblivious to the sharp, unsettled stare of her husband) that she saw Nadia standing, at about three in the afternoon, with some fine looking lady, who, she can't be sure, may have taken her off in a car.

"No, you stupid cow," Mr Hamouz interrupts.

"Wait, citizen!

And this Lady, what did she look like?"

"Well, she was quite tall, about forty, blonde, with pale eyes."

The copper proceeds at his leisure. There's no point interviewing everyone in private, I mean, the number of people who go missing these days!

Something prods at Zderad.

— Could it be?

— But He said He'd be away.

— From what we know already, it was hardly likely to have been in the afternoon.

— The Hamouz women used to show up quite late. Since Nadia was under age they had to be more careful.

— Or maybe, I don't know. Maybe old Hamouz rented her out to the better classes in broad daylight.

— Kerb crawling.

— Well, maybe we'll find out.

— Why bother? Under the circumstances –

———

"Odóli hi e Hučka," Góno o Graj introduces the young Gypsy girl to Zderad.

This is Hučka.

Zderad is surprised at the name, which he has hitherto associated with a kind of hat. It seems his ex-army knowledge of Gypsy is pretty limited.

Still, he gives the hand with the cheap rings a squeeze.

Hučka is a mightily pretty young Gypsy girl.

"I am black, but comely, o ye daughters of Jerusalem" the Song of Solomon goes. Gypsies often look like Jews, only darker. Indians in general do.

"E Hučka hi jek l'ubni," Góno says simply and to the point, as if he was telling the world that Hučka sells ice cream: Hučka is a prostitute. A somewhat irreverent association of Zderad's.

"Joj džánel i ráni pchárne jakengero."

(She knows the Lady with the pale eyes.)

Of course, the Gypsies know the underworld inside out.

According to them *"o Dzerádo hi jek rom"* (Zderad, whose name has been turned into "Hairy," is a Gypsy) so they'll tell.

He'd have less chance getting any sense from the white sluts.

Those aren't as bright, either. The ordinary girls who turn to prostitution (the real stuff, not Socialist Realism or Marxist Science) tend not to be too bright.

Among the Gypsies it's different. As we see, it is not considered an untoward profession. Different background, different morality. Take India, or Japan.

Zderad starts in Gypsy but Hučka speaks some weird dialect. Góno seems to understand her all right, Zderad can only catch a word or two.

They lower their voices and the conversation proceeds in Czech.

Hučka knows Czech just like any other child of the slums.

She probably grew up there. But Góno speaks with the distinctive lisping accent of eastern Slovakia.

Yes, she knows the Lady.

The Lady goes looking for young girls, but not often.

She takes them off in her car.

Nobody wants to go with Her anymore. Berta went once and said She took a whip to her. She promised to pay a lot, but —

She took her into some kind of chapel. Berta took off, she fought her off and ran.

Berta is strong.

But she was lost in the woods for ages after that, couldn't find her way back.

Then somebody gave her a lift in a lorry, but Berta fell asleep, so she doesn't know the way.

She said though, that the Lady," the Gypsy dropped her gaze and darkened visibly – "had, well – *o kchárik hár jek murš*," she added quickly in Gypsy.

(A prick like a man.)

Zderad wasn't the least surprised that a whore could blush. There was no need to explain that, not to him.

"So where's Berta now?"

"That's just it, Berta disappeared. Who knows. But somebody said she had plans to go to Ostrava."

"The other girls, before her, vanished too. The Lady doesn't come by often, maybe once a year, once every two years."

"You did tell the cops."

"No, we didn't do that," Hučka went on. "The old girls said that in their time, when there were houses and they had their booklets, the police used to look after them. Nowadays it's actually illegal," she adds knowingly.

(There, what did I tell you about her being smart.)

"So it's worse now?"

"Actually, now and again, for old time's sake, they – but really they're supposed to catch us and take us to Apollinaire's.[33] It's tricky, see?"

(So that's how it is.)

"Me už džáha. Parikérav tuke, Hučkije." Zderad tries to salvage his linguistic reputation with a Gypsy farewell.

(I'll be going. Thank you, Hučka.)

"Dža mro Devleske" – (go with God), the Gypsies devotedly take their leave.

———

— So that's how it is.

— The Monster. No doubt about it.

— Omnibus ille viris mulier, mas ille puellis.
Or rather:

— Omnibus ille viris mulier, mulierque puellis.[*]
Or better still:

— Omnibus ille viris spectrum, monstrumque puellis.[†]

— He goes around in drag as well.

— But he seems to be even more horrible to women.

— Can it be? It would seem that way.

— Is it to avoid being recognised? Hardly. They say prostitutes are wary of lesbians. When they're nasty, apparently they're worse than the men.

— Well, that Monster – He's not a man really – He's a pathetic freak of nature. Grotesque.

— He's not even a decent normal queer, like Krůta for instance.

— He probably gets an extra kick from women's clothes. Zderad recalls reading about that somewhere – that some sadists are into drag. Come to think of it, the idea of one woman beating another is kind of tickling. (So, you too, eh?)

— Ah – shut up!

---

[*] Zderad'a paraphrase of the quote: 'A woman to all men, and a woman to all girls.'

[†] A Spectre to men, a Monster to girls.

— He fits the bill: The Hamouzes were in the whoring business only part-time…

— Hamouz is with the militia (does he work in the factory or just do the militia bit there?), and Mrs Hamouz is a cleaner somewhere.

— They had little contact with the real professionals.

— When they brought Nadia in they had to be very careful so they didn't mix with the hookers at their jamborees, just crept around. They probably knew nothing of the "Lady with pale eyes".

— Nadia was a novice, and it seems she didn't have much contact with the others.

— The Monster, for it must have been Him, could turn to them with all confidence. He most likely paid Hamouz in advance, took the girl and – never brought her back.

The other side of the story was probably that time when Zderad turned to him for help, for protection from Hamouz. The creep got interested, and being experienced and shrewd soon found out what was what. But he saved it for later.

———

Zderad pondered whether he shouldn't speak up.

But then he thought better of it, it was just too risky.

Maybe this was another of his mistakes in the whole affair. Now that the Georgian Moloch[34] had left the scene it might have been possible, but, Zderad couldn't have known that.

Let us also observe that the Monster's connection with the secret police was uncertain and will remain so to the end. It's quite possible that His contact with the Comrades was marginal – but equally, He might have been a high ranking officer among the "organs". He was able to skate along on this uncertainty principle and bluff his way out, even if He wasn't a high ranking agent. Even so, He was a creature of the régime and of the secret police.

After much thought, Zderad decided to take no action. It also became clear that there would be no way out for him and that, regretfully, things would have to be resolved in the previously determined way.

Zderad was utterly devastated by all this.

Even his pre-quietus consumerism ceased to be enjoyable.

XVII

A golden May morning pecks its way out of a shell of light mist.

The slopes on the left bank of the River are a riot of blossom.

Up there somewhere sits a young couple, a man and a woman looking down at the City whose beauty is indestructible.

"A City of Glory never waning" – as Seifert wrote…

They are, of course, Zderad and Sylva.

The day before Sylva had decided to put on some kind of celebration, just out of the blue.

First she took Zderad down to the City and kitted him out from head to toe with her own money.

It seemed to have escaped her notice that Zderad's economic base had itself improved – he tried to hide it from her – and they didn't see much of each other during daylight hours.

Zderad left her to it.

Then they went to a concert, it was the Spring Season.

Then down to a wine cellar, to a nice candlelit dinner with wine. Sylva was paying, though she gave the money to Zderad so he could act the gentleman.

Afterwards, they didn't go back to the coffin-dwelling.

They spent the night in a decent flat with a view of the blossoming slopes, and a real bathroom. Sylva had most probably borrowed the flat from some girl friend of hers – the flat bore the hallmark of a single woman.

Sylva was extremely charming, cheerful, but somehow a little over-solemn and hiding her melancholy.

Zderad may not even have noticed.

His own mood was very similar, and we know why.

There was only a week to the Monster's deadline.

They talked as they had not done for a long time.

They recalled the lake, and how they used to meet there, mysteriously and beautifully, once upon a time. And then they ventured out to look at the City, holding hands.

Then Sylva spoke.

Sylva was a teacher and always spoke properly, grammatically, so as not to 'spoil her diction'.

At the time, this kind of teacher-speak was already in decline, but Sylva, who had been brought up in the Ram's house, had been raised to respect the language in which their Bible was written and for which her forebears had risked their necks.

Sometimes she sounded quaint and overdone, but this morning it was strangely appropriate.

Thus speaks the mermaid of the fairytale, once having left the water and followed a mortal man ashore, about the magic and the curse that binds her.

"Zderad, do know that I shall always love you.

Nevertheless, our ways must part.

Zderad, I have been unfaithful to you. With comrade Burda. For a long time now. I could not have kept my job otherwise. I do not like him, he disgusts me, but a woman can yield even when her heart and body are protesting.

The money we were celebrating with was from him. I have to take it. He would destroy us otherwise. You see, father did not want to join the collective.

He has conceded now.

And then you. For some reason you are not in their good books. I do not even know why.

I mainly worry about little Záviš.

Now, he wants me to marry him. His divorce has come through.

It will be better this way. For the child.

The place where we live is no fit environment.

And the weekday nursery, you know yourself what they write about it abroad.

If I resisted, we would all be finished…

It will be better for you, too.

Burda promised me he would see to it that you can finish your studies.

You are wasted. You have such talent.

You will forget soon enough.

Men are different in these things.

I know that you – have visited women who sell themselves. But I am not complaining. I am no better.

Zderad, my dearest Zderad, – "

Sylva burst into tears.

Zderad wasn't really surprised by any of this, as if he'd known for a long, long time. After all, the way she was always off somewhere, the way she seemed suddenly prettier, more appearance-conscious, and the way she embraced him lovingly – and that time he met them by the lake.

— Sylvie, even I –

— What you are telling me is nothing, by comparison.

— My spell is more evil, more like a fairytale, more monstrous.

— I'm in the clutches of a creature from the tomb.

— And now, now it is reaching out for you too –

He told her everything.

How could he have been such a fool, to think it couldn't be done?

———

When the first passers-by appeared in the park, they stared in surprise at a young man and a young woman crying bitterly in each other's arms.

Later, when the sun had climbed up high, the passers-by thought they could guess the reason.

The young couple were dressed in dark and formal clothes.

They must have just come back from a loved-one's funeral.

XVIII

——"Do we – have to do it? —

Couldn't we just – disappear somewhere?"

"We can't. He's a Monster.

He drove Zdeněk Brva to suicide, possibly killed several women, and Nadia, He might even have destroyed my own sister. Perhaps even some men.

He's even after Father Plicka.

And He can get us, too. Even little Záviš.

First He was a priest, then He was with the Nazis, now He's got some connections with Them.

At least this way we can put off the inevitable.

There's no other way.

Burda has no chance against Him, believe me.

He'd destroy Burda as well.

I know, it's revolting but – we've put up with a lot already.

We can cope with this, too. We'll live."

Zderad and Sylva are lying in their coffin-slum, embracing.

Not erotically.

Just so, protecting one another from the world out there.

They whisper very quietly. Záviš is at home, in his little bed.

They brought him home because he has a cold, so the others at the school wouldn't catch it.

"Killing ourselves is no solution."

"We'll have to."

———

They sat under the weeping willow and waited. They had arrived too early. The sun was slowly setting, and a swarm of midges danced above the tombstone.

A bird called out its stereotyped lament in the thicket.

Nature's unconcern seemed a deliberate cruelty.

The Monster appeared on the stroke of the set hour.

Zderad had long since become accustomed to Him, but now an electrified shock of fright ran through him. Involuntarily, he and Sylva grasped hands.

The Monster, seeing Zderad's fear, and naturally, Sylva's, was delighted. He was in the sort of mood that the Germans call 'kreuzfidel'.

The disposal of the Moloch's high priests had passed Him by for the moment, and it seemed that the danger was over.

Besides which, His appointment to full professorship was well in the pipeline – aided by the declarations of many convincing comrades on His behalf, that the Comrade Assistant Professor had never participated in the Personality Cult.

It wasn't the money, he had enough from elsewhere.

But the prestige!

And so, to celebrate how well He was doing, He had prepared a roast feast, with choice of meat.

He carried a basket of delicacies, covered by a raincoat.

We shall celebrate in all opulence.

He approached His victims jovially and bid himself welcome.

We will not repeat what He said: We've seen a short example of the Monster's style in the passage about the photograph of the Parson.

They climbed into the tomb carefully and locked the door.

The damp mouldy stench assailed their nostrils.

The Monster lit the usual candle, and produced a bottle of Champagne and three glasses from the basket. He no longer had the missal cups, and we know why not.

They drank.

Then the Monster ordered them to undress.

There was nothing for it.

The Monster stared at them with glee.

They were in His power, to do with as He pleased.

Darting His eyes from man to woman and back, the Monster experienced a duality of desire which you, ordinary mono-sexuals, cannot even dream of. His lust for man and woman was equally strong, but it was characterised by a particular difference in quality which could possibly be expressed by means of music, the counterpoint of the sound of two instruments, though such can surely not exist anywhere in this world.

The prostituting duo had progressed in their disrobing down to the skin and the pupils in those pale irises dilated like those of a cat watching a bird on a branch.

Inadvertently, He concentrated more on Sylva, for He was already very familiar with Zderad's body.

Behold, His new trinket, terrified and obedient.

The Monster ogled as her curves slid reluctantly and slowly out of her discarded garments, flickering white in the greenish gloom of the tomb. A huge and grotesque shadow faithfully followed her every movement.

He had ordered Zderad beforehand to ensure that Sylva wore black stockings with old-fashioned round garters, (like those painted by the lecherous barber Clovis Trouille, in vogue at the time on the other side of the Iron Curtain) and He was appreciating the fact that His wishes had been followed to the letter.

With delight, His eyes slid over the girl's body as she was bending and turning before him:

From the ankles to the calves and strong thighs up to the luscious curvaceous and white buttocks and then up the spine to strong shoulders and arms, to the elastically flexing breasts, to her still flat belly and underbelly, shaded by pubic moss.

He could hardly wait to destroy that whiteness, to furrow and open it with the stripes of lashes.

But He would take it slowly, step by step so that they would not suspect: Their gradual realisation and terror will bring added pleasure.

Now He watched Zderad for a while:

His broad shoulders and narrow hips, the arousing hairiness of his chest and thighs, the muscles rippling beneath the skin. He also yearned for this body, but His desire had an entirely different character, flavour, colour and sound; this lust was somehow harder, more angular, more dissonant as if in a major key compared with the minor key and softer harmony of His lust for the woman.

At a certain stage, the Monster was thinking, I'll make them torture each other.

But for that I'll have to get hold of the child first – it should still be possible – though the death of the Generalissimo is bound to bring a token liberalisation, less terrorism, reduced fear, at least for a time, and thus more public bravery and less scope for operational freedom; let's hope one will still have time:

The mere threat of jail will not be enough for mutual torture. Anyway, it's amazing how cowardly people are, what they will let you do to them, they're sheep, sheep is what they are – Nietzsche was right – they are just the extras on the stage which is ruled by the strong – the demigods – like me.

And it would be a shame to waste the chance – such a beautiful, pleasant couple.

But first we'll have to take it slowly, heighten the pleasure step by step – they will endure that for a long time: First mental humiliation, and only then physical torture. And give them money so that they take it, so that they know that they are prostitutes!

I bet this little chick isn't one for any perversions: So first we'll have to educate her a little and shock her.

While He pondered on these matters, the Monster was undressing himself.

The coolness of the tomb tickled His turgid member and around His anus.

Then he ordered Zderad in French to demonstrate the biorally genital position.

Sylva didn't speak French.

When Zderad quietly explained, she immediately began to weep.

That was an absolute delicacy for the Monster.

The prostituting couple climbed on top the altar table and took up the appropriate position.

The Monster borrowed Sylva's slipper: Like almost all sadomasochists, the freak was a shoe fetishist at the same time.

He had almost every possible and impossible perversion going, so as the experts say, He was a 'polymorphic' pervert.

He noticed, however, with some displeasure, that Zderad was not in the mood. This, naturally, made it impossible for Sylva to take part and her humiliation was thus not going well.

The Monster decided to assist in His usual manner.

He knelt and set about His habitual abomination. At the same time He employed the slipper to stimulate himself.

The ecstasy of this monstrous, absurd obscenity enveloped Him completely.

He tasted and sniffed with delectation at what most people would find nauseating.

Grunting, He was falling further into the infernal heavens of His damnation, slurping and gulping like a dog.

A long, viscous string of canine saliva drooled out of the corner of His mouth.

Unvoiced obscene cries were exploding inside His head.

All that could be heard on the outside, however, was His grunting.

Suddenly He stopped, as if cut down.

Air, air!

He dropped the slipper and reached with both hands for His throat. He produced a stifled, spewing glugging for a short time.

Splitting His nails He tore into the flesh on His neck, but the noose had already cut too deep.

He was gripped by a hitherto unknown terror and wrath.

Falling onto His back He felt a callused bare foot stepping onto his chest. A moment later, His mind clouded over.

He no longer felt anguish, or the passionate rage of the struggle for life.

The pain of His constricted throat turned into a grotesque pleasure.

A giant stork-like bird emerged out of His head, convulsively flapping enormous wings.

Simultaneously, an absurd and weird idea flashed through His extinguishing consciousness, that He was going back through the phylogenetic process and that He had just reached the stage of some kind of antediluvian stork ancestor.

Immediately after that there was total darkness and void.

The face of Julius Skomelný became that of an eerie purple gargoyle.

At first He had kicked and tried to open the noose, but He finally splayed out His limbs like a monstrous string puppet.

Standing on the chest of the dragon and keeping the silken noose taut, Zderad saw the jet of the Monster's sperm for the last time.

It was as if He was taking leave of His strange life and nightmarish loves:

> *Silver pallid moon*
> *Shining bait,*
> *In final doom to swoon*
> *At your gate.*

———

The Zderad couple had throttled Dr Julius Skomelný with a silk noose, which Sylva had pre-wound around her thigh above her garter.

The Monster's last wishes had in fact facilitated His execution considerably, for Sylva was able to place the noose around His neck with ease and unobserved.

As soon as the noose cut in, she'd let out a victorious shriek, whereupon Zderad had slipped off the altar to take over the actual execution.

They continued strangling Skomelný for some time, long after He had gone limp. They were afraid lest his infernal essence brought him to life again somehow.

———

Zderad looked down at the Monster's gruesome face, remarkably calmly:

Perhaps at that moment he felt nothing at all, he was like a robot.

What he could not understand was Sylva's immense bravery, as she was otherwise afraid of mice and spiders.

But Sylva was from a farming community and used to the necessary killing of domestic animals.

To her, Skomelný was a deformed, misbegotten beast, to be put down, to be taken out of the breeding stock and put out of its misery. She simply didn't regard him as human.

———

Julius Skomelný lay on the cold floor of the chapel, whose walls were adorned by maniacally repeating gothic rosettes.

His motionless face looked like a demonic self-caricature.

It was purplish-black and swollen to almost twice its size.

The pale eyes, with light blue irises and purple bloodshot sclera were bulging, as on a grotesque mask from a gothic organ console.

The teeth protruding from purple, negroid lips, were pink, where the pulp capillaries had burst with the pressure and forced blood into the porous dentine.

From His mouth dangled a black and unbelievably large tongue.

It was as though the Devil, who had been coming in the shape of the Doctor, had now revealed himself in his true form.

The flickering candlelight played across this dreadful face and it seemed that it was rippling with a strange, infernal life force.

Skomelný's body was thin, with feeble muscles and a concave, slightly rachitic chest, thickly overgrown with pale bristles.

———

Zderad now looked upon the corpse with a mixture of awe, revulsion and compassion.

The hardest thing to comprehend was how quickly, ignobly and unceremoniously the whole thing had ended, after days, weeks or rather, months of constantly mounting tension.

He had expected God-knows-what – and now, this.

How easy it is to kill a person, how fragile is life.

It was almost, simply, like wringing the neck of a chicken, like treading on a cockroach.

He would never have imagined it like that.

———

The Monster stared motionlessly with His terrible eyes, as if in reproach.

A small shiny silverfish insect, *Lepsima sacharina*, ran quickly past his head.

Zderad shivered, and burst into further action.

Not pausing to dress, the couple lifted a stone in the floor which covered the entrance to the crypt itself, and taking hold of the dead Monster under the arms and by the legs, they carried Him inside, by the light of the candle.

He was still pliable and warm and during His transportation he waggled His head and devilish tongue.

Zderad and Sylva placed Skomelný's body into a previously pre-pared, not yet disintegrated coffin, which Zderad had made ready the day before. He had had the key to the tomb for some time now, the Gypsy Vlk – the wolf – had made it for him.

They arranged the bones of the coffin's original occupier around the Monster's body, and placed the skull under His head.

They also packed the doctor's clothes around the body.

Then they replaced the lid.

———

They looked at each other.

Zderad's reason and feelings were slowly returning and he was suddenly overcome by a wave of unbelievable barbaric triumph. He raised his arms above his head and yelled.

His voice echoed hollow and distorted around the crypt.

Then, Zderad burst into a hysterical mixture of tears and laughter. For a moment Sylva looked at him in surprise.

In really serious situations, women have stronger nerves than men, as a rule. As well as this, in our case, Sylva was rustically down-to-earth, whereas Zderad was a decadent intellectual, possessing various luxury talents which are irrelevant for survival.

A moment later, however, Sylva also burst into a convulsive fit of girlish giggles, in a manner quite unexpected of an adult woman.

They both laughed and writhed hysterically for a while.

Then their excitement found another outlet and focal point.

They fell on the coffin, and conjoined.

Their embrace was barbarically vigorous, accompanied by much rattling and thudding.

It was as if the cheated freak was trying to get out, pleading for release with feminine whimperings.

———

Then they emerged, threw the feast basket and the various whips, rods and straps into the crypt, and pushed the stone back into place. They dressed, carefully opened the door, blew out the candle, climbed out, locked the door – and off they went.

The first stars were already glittering in the heavens.

The sky was as clear as spring water.

The cemetery was now officially shut, and they had to climb over the wall.

On the way home, Zderad threw the key to the tomb down a drain. He also threw his "wedding" ring after it.

Now they were both strangely, ceremoniously calm.

———

They got home, collected the sleeping Záviš from widow Hromádková, and began their preparations.

———

Zderad and Sylva had already decided to kill the Monster after their mutual confessions in the park.

Instead of themselves – why not him?

The earlier idea of the razor was abandoned for reasons of cleanliness.

They had killed the Monster at the height of his carnal pleasure, just as Buckelhanes had done with the symbolic dog.

He had even baptised him with schnapps with the Monster's name, hadn't he.

Perhaps this was what is known as Sympathetic Magic; the destruction of a "volt," that is a figure or animal representing the intended victim is said to magically cause or facilitate the destruction of the being represented by the "volt".

The Indians of Central America and even the Russians, (though in secret) to this day regard madmen and cripples as sacred and endowed with magical powers.

Perhaps it had been no mere coincidence.

Someone might even have hired Buckelhanes to do it.

After all, there were Gypsies living in the village.

XIX

Let us begin on a historical note.

Even the ancient Greeks and Romans[35] knew that rivers have their distinctive personalities, and assigned various deities to them.

This idea survived through to Christian Byzantium.

On the mosaics showing the baptism of Christ a male figure with a tail and a trident is often depicted, being none other than the personified Jordan.

The Greek and Roman river-gods were, however, invariably male, because the word "river" in both languages is masculine.

By contrast, Slavonic rivers are very often of the female gender.

This is especially true of the River flowing through the City, and we all know that that is how it should be.

Dear reader in exile, would that we could once again, with dignity and without tribute to the Moloch... but this is no time for such sentiments. –

However, in the south-eastern part of the country flows a river which is of a very masculine character.[36]

'He' has been sung about many times.

Frequently by the Slavs, even those who, it might seem, have never settled by 'his' banks – an interesting conundrum, which our comrade Germans are not very happy about. Also by other nations, including the aforementioned Romans.

So then, as we all know, where this river turns for a while onto the territory of the *"Čichaslavatska gubernia,"* the Czechoslovak province, a pleasant, happy provincial town lies on its banks.

The river is already quite broad here, and surprisingly fast-flowing for its breadth, so that the barges that bring goods upriver, to that unfortunate country still suffering under the yoke of capitalism, only proceed at walking pace, or rather, a snail's crawl.

Here the river is also spanned by at least one bridge, or perhaps two, if not several.

That May, some considerable time after midnight, once the happy little town was preparing for bed after the usual celebrations, a group of Gypsies stood on one of the bridges. It seemed that they too were about to end their *'mulatybinen'* or, as we say, spree.

Everyone would rather stay clear of a band of Gypsies, especially at night, and even the solitary policeman would rather rationalise away to find a good reason to take a different route, because of other duties.

The Gyppos, then, are standing on the bridge, conversing in their Indian-sounding lingo: "čogora-mogora paytáš".

One of the Gypsies is a blonde – that much is evident even in the poor light.

She is obviously *'i pchárni'*, a "white" Gypsy, descendant of some white tramp who sometimes joined up with the Gypsies, or the product of some other racial blending.

In some places, like Britain, there are practically no other types of Gypsy anymore.

On her back she carries a sack, with a sleeping child inside – the uncivilised bastards even take children along to their drunken sprees, just imagine.

It seems the Gyppos are in no hurry to leave. They stand around gawping at the river. Then a convoy of cargo boats appears in the distance.

"*Už džan*" (they're coming), say the Gypsies.

But it still takes the best part of an hour for the first tug to draw near the bridge at its snail's pace.

And it takes a small eternity before they all go by and before the last string of them comes a little closer.

There is a light on one of the boats.

And also one on the bridge.

The Gypsy band huddles together.

Two men step aside from the group, one at each end, looking around.

There is some commotion in the centre of the group. Something seems to be going on, and now it seems they are embracing the blonde tramp.

"*Dža mro Devleske – Sylvije – Dzderadá*" …

Then they all seem to be hauling at something. Down come two big parcels, descending slowly to the snail-paced tug. The ropes fall behind them. There's no time to untie them.

Záviš is fast asleep, the Gypsies have given him something to drink. They are expert at this sort of thing.

Then the Gypsies disperse, quickly, yet without conspicuous haste.

This is probably the way in which the carved baroque saints, once the property of Dr Skomelný, left Joyous Reality behind them.

I sincerely hope that no secret has been betrayed here:

After all, in the intervening thirty years, the Comrades must have got wise to this one.

And anyway, we've told it all wrong somehow.

But some such avenue remained open for a long time, long after the minefields and the border guards, wearing the nationally insulting doggie symbols on their lapels, had been introduced, to protect us from the imperialists.[37]

———

So Zderad and Sylva and even little Záviš are out. They fled, not only from comrade Burda and the potential avengers of the Monster, but mainly from That which had stimulated and enabled the existence of Burda, Hamouz, Skomelný and their ilk.

But their first steps in the free world will be arduous.

In those days they knew even less about us in the free world than now, when we are still taken to be all kinds of Hungarians and Azerbaijanies, and the more educated consider us to be a dwarf Russian subspecies.

But why go on; we have all experienced it.

Let us not forget that in reality Zderad is a nobody.

A student dropout. A gravelark.

Even at home the not-so-bright or older people couldn't grasp that it had never been his fault.

What chance with those abroad?

Much better to be like those comrades who let the Party of the homeland turn them into 'somebodies' before they scarpered.

At the time of this narrative, however, such exodites are still a thing of the future.

———

With the demise of Julius Skomelný, Czech spiritual and cultural life suffered a severe setback.

What am I drivelling on about?

Ah – just letting off steam.

Dr. Skomelný is of course an abstracted fiction, but the material from which he is woven is still running around on the face of our planet.

Quite a few of the Skomelný types became reformists during the Dubček era – (but even a bit before, they have a good nose for change) but some didn't manage to back out in time. And the grateful nation now adorns their brows with laurel leaves.

Let us prefer to imagine that they underwent a sincere conversion. Because if they did not, it would drive us mad, and that would just play into the Comrades' hands.

The body of Dr. Skomelný was never found.

He was so good at hiding his car, that by the time they found it not even the most alert and razor-sharp Leninist superhound could find the trail.

Likewise, it did not occur to anyone to look for Him in a graveyard, in a tomb.

A legend spread, that the Devil took him.

May he take the lot of Them – and soon!

(★)

And into this little town there now descends Mr Sparklighter-Křesadlo, discreetly rattling steel against flint, so as to begin to tell the tale. And you there, Muses, in your Olympian abodes, lend him your helping hands.

JAN KŘESADLO: Vara Guru

Given just a touch of humour, imagination and superciliousness, we might envisage World Literature as a large multi-storey building, an old crumbling mansion with a swathe of rooms, chambers and closets, something along the lines of a cosy old madhouse. The rooms of the mansion resound all day and night with the feverish voices of the inmates.

A detached and dutiful listener, who might place his ear from the outside onto the cool wall of the mansion – not to mention embellishing his hearing by way of a makeshift Helmholz resonator made out of a suitable metal kitchen pot – such an observer can make out at any hour whatsoever the loud interlocution of male and female voices. Quite clearly there are voices here resonant with credibility, voices full of affectation and puppet-like artifice, voices bilious and raging, voices cowardly and defeatist, voices full of enmity and hatred, voices resounding with genuine or devious empathy, voices feeble, deluded, or unstable with excitement. The voices of suppressed sexual deviants, the confused, the shaky and croaky voices of alcoholics of either sex, the oozingly hollow and huffy voices of demagogues and here and there the less distinct, as yet untrained voices of the youngest occupants of the mansion, meekly seeking wider attention.

This mansion is fated to remain forever an unfinished edifice, though its foundations are, or seem to be, robust enough. It has room enough for everyone: for those who helped to build it and still do, for those who have taken up residence in a few rooms (though they don't stay long – not outstaying one human lifespan, sometimes not even that), even those who – as soon as taking up residence in some room – start to break down its walls with a pickaxe to make their way into adjacent spaces.

The mansion can admit and accept them all without batting an eyelash. There are many sprawling storeys and a labyrinth of passageways, rooms and stairways (the higher we rise, the lower the population density per square foot, the less crowded it becomes), till at the top, on the roof we find a luxurious penthouse, off limits to ordinary inmates, which includes a large roof garden. This is the abode of the most esteemed tenants of note.

The mansion has its own basement and even a cesspit.

The inhabitants do not enjoy equal opportunities. Some need only utter a few witticisms and word of them spreads immediately to the entire floor, even to several floors above and below. It is not unheard of – to be heard of – through the whole building. Others waffle on – and on – till they go dry in the throat, but remain audible only within their own room, at best on the corridor or to a few neighbours.

Every inhabitant has their place in the Mansion, but only very few can boast an ability to wander equally nonchalantly anywhere from the sundrenched splendour of the uppermost chambers to the rooms set deep underground; and to be welcome in either place.

The greatest post-war Czech writer Jan Křesadlo is one of the few inhabitants of the Mansion who enjoyed the pleasure of strolling the rose-gardens of the penthouse, while not excluded from the most stifling, bizarre and obscure catacombs, even those to where no doors seem to lead, or into cupboards full of extraordinary devices whose external appearance often leaves us unsettled about their purpose, whether they are intended for some sophisticated torture or some equally refined and arcane source of unearthly delights, intense enough instantly to burn the recipients nervous systems to a crisp.

It is this Janus-like two-facedness of Křesadlo, which jarred with the majority of literary critics, those merciless and unfeeling vivisectors of books. During his life some of them uncritically put him on the very apex, the rose-garden, the penthouse, the Mount of Olymp, next to the divine Marquis and his ilk, Rétif De la Bretonne, Henry Miller, Georges Bataille, Charles Bukowski, Pierre Louÿs, Felix Salten (who, apart from being the author of Bambi, much adored by children, also gave us the figure of the child prostitute Josephine Mutzenbacher) or Ian McEwan (before he became well-to-do), while others uncompromisingly drove him down into the darkest most damp and dank subterranean corner, where, paradoxically, he once again found himself in identical company. The confusion that went on throughout his life continues to this day.

The author himself does not give a damn, and did not, during his life (he died on 13th August 1995). And neither do his loyal admirers (myself among them).

SO WHO OR WHAT WAS THIS KŘESADLO, FLINT-AND-STEEL, TINDERBOX SPARKMAKER?

Going by his own brief autobiography it came into being on the 9th December 1926 as Václav Pinkava into the family of a lesser-calibre Prague merchant and industrialist. Hot on the heels of this family event there came one of the periodic crises of capitalism, such that young Pinkava could not expect his birth to make the rest of his life preferential, but instead grounds for cadre profile problems. Having passed through Grammar School (in addition thereto learning to become a pharmacist and through self-study having entered the secret realms of Church music, Scholastic philosophy, ancient Greek, and mediaeval Latin) he embarked in 1947 on the study of Philosophy at Charles University. Under the prevailing political climate he was in 1949 forced temporarily to abandon his studies, having been investigated by the Secret Police and tried for participating in an armed uprising. Contrary to all the (absence of) logic and laws of probability of the era he was freed (despite two appeals by the prosecutor!) and was sent off to do his military service.

On his return home he embarked on the career of an assistant labourer, alongside which he devoted himself to choral singing partly as a translator of texts, as a capable singer, and composer. Having been re-accepted to higher education, he graduated in 1954 in psychology (a subject which the socialist camp had only just ceased to consider a pseudoscience) and began working at the outpatient clinic for sexual deviations, and establishment affiliated to Charles University. Here he had the opportunity to meet and treat numerous personages of our cultural, political and scientific spheres, confronted with their sexual aberrations.

In 1968 the graduate psychologist Václav Pinkava belatedly got his doctorate, went on to defend his postdoctoral thesis and in the following year emigrated with his family to Great Britain. Here he became Head Psychologist at a provincial psychiatric hospital (in Colchester) spending time on research and publishing in scientific journals. His scientific interest included the theoretical treatment of idealised neural networks and their application to phenomena of abnormal psychology, whereto he came up with a class of multiple valued logics, known among specialists today as the Pinkava algebras.

What Dr Pinkava retained from his former career of an outpatient psychologist-sexologist was a fascination for the various bizarre manifestations of the human reproductive instinct, so that the various comic and not-so-comic sexual deviations present themselves to us among the salient and characteristic features of the literary works of Jan Křesadlo.

The Křesadlo firestarter device itself came into being at the beginning of the nineteen eighties, when 'it' wrote the present novel *Mrchopěvci* (published in 1984 by Josef Škvorecký's émigré publishing house Sixty-Eight Publishers in Toronto), for which he got the prestigious Egon Hostovský prize. The book raised a storm of reaction from critics and readers, something typical of all of Křesadlo's subsequent works. '68 Publishers also published two other Křesadlo novels which were republished later in Czechoslovakia, *Vara Guru* and *Fuga Trium*.

Mrchopěvci was also the first of his novels to appear in his homeland of Czechoslovakia after the change of regime in 1989. It was published in magazine form in the so-called Bestseller edition, by ArtServis, a Prague publishing house, which was later to turn into the publishing house Ivo Železný. Later on it was republished in hardback in Czech and English (as *GraveLarks*) by Maťa. In the

Bestseller format was also published a set of witty short stories about sexual deviations, entitled *Slepá Bohyně* (The Blind Goddess), and a couple of short stories. Ivo Železný staunchly embarked upon, but did not finish, the publication of a 'complete works' edition of Jan Křesadlo writings. He published the novels *Vara Guru* (The True Guru), *Zámecký pán aneb Antikuro* (The Lord of the Manor or Antidaybreak), *Zuzana a dva starci* (Susan and the two old men), *Girgal, Obětina* (The Offering) and *La Calle Neruda* (Neruda street). Apart from these, the same publisher also issued a bibliophile publication, a monumental poetic piece written in Homeric Greek (and the authors accompanying verse translation into Czech), the *Astronautilia-Hvězdoplavba* (The Star Voyage).

The Brno-based publishing house Host published *Dvacet snů* (Twenty Dreams) and *Fuga trium* (which means Fugue for three voices and also Flight of three). The Olomouc-based Votobia published a short story collection entitled *Království české a jiné polokatolické povídky* (The Kingdom of Bohemia and other semi-Catholic tales), and the novel *Dům* (The House). Then Periplum published *Kravex₅* and the first half of an unfinished educational piece on Psychology and Psychiatry for the Layman. Most recently Tartaros published an extended edition of *Slepá Bohyně a jiné příběhy* (The Blind Goddess and other stories) and two other unpublished novels from the author's legacy – *Rusticalia*, and *Skrytý život Cypriána Belvy* (The Secret Life of Cyprian Belva).

Not to be overlooked is the publication of a selection from the authors poetry *Sedmihlásek* ('Sevenvoiced') this being the Czech name of the Icterine Warbler, published by the London-based Rozmluvy; the anthology *Instrukce, insuinace a invektivy* (Instructions, insinuations and invectives) by the literary magazine publisher Tvar; the poetic collection *Vertikální spílání* (Vertical vituperations) from Pražská imaginace; and the collectors' item *Eponymous Verse*, a bilingual publication – poetry selected and translated by the author's eldest son Václav Z. J. Pinkava. And since Jan Křesadlo liked to delve into the realms of so-called pulp fiction, he wrote, and Ivo Železný published in the Rodokaps pocket format, a parodical Western – *Ranč u kotvy a hvězdy* (The Anchor and Star Ranch) which was written under another assumed name, Jake Rolands (Jan Kresadlo, without the accent, in anagram).

Other pieces have been published in literary magazines. Křesadlo's literary legacy is not yet completely exhausted.

Jan Křesadlo is a writer who, had he not lived and worked in the so-called postmodern era, would have had to come up with post-modernism himself. I know everyone has a different and personal idea of what postmodernism is or is not, and there are a number of definitions of it. I confess to having read none of them, although I believe that Umberto Eco or John Fowles have made some proc-lamation on behalf of postmodernism somewhere or other in their essays.

If we accept that one of the features of postmodernism is inter-textuality, i.e. that the author is not so much inspired by the world around him, but by another text that makes Křesadlo a postmodern-ist par excellence; and he confuses the heck out of critics too.

No wonder then, that at the onset they attributed his short story *Dívka v rytmu zrozená* (Miss Rhythm-born) to Josef Škvorecký. In his novel *Mrchopěvci* they found traces of the novel Honzlová by the aforesaid's wife Zdena Salivarová. Jan Křesadlo had it in for Milan Kundera, so that in his novel *Obětina* he not only parodies his style, but this remarkable work devotes much space to a fictional charac-ter whose debased moral and ascribed sexual preferences ostensibly closely match Kundera's. And what of Viktor Fischl, the author of the well known *Kuropění* (Daybreak, literally Cockerel-song), rid-iculed by Křesadlo in his novel *Antikuro*? What of the self-styled "marxist levý", (Marxist lefty) self appointed curious poet, philos-opher, and idiosyncratic Prague intellectual hobo Egon Bondy, whom Křesadlo ridicules in another novel, *La Calle Neruda*?

Above all, yes, high above all these figurines and their goings on, there hovers the all-powerful and appropriately narcissistic figure of the creator, who controls it all with his godlike hands, constantly reminding us that it is just his own text, primarily for his own enter-tainment, and only then for the reader's delight.

Topmost among the works of Křesadlo remains that extensive epic *Astronautilia-Hvězdoplavba*.

Given that Křesadlo was an exceptionally talented (I would say a genius) writer and cultivator of other activities, as well as a gifted linguist, it comes as no surprise that his most significant work purports to be an authentic Classical Greek Epic. The text in ancient Greek (in facsimile of the authors own hand), comprises well over six thousand Homeric hexameters, shadowed by its faithful Czech translation in the style of the old-school translations of the classical Epic poems.

The plot is a kind of spun-off paraphrase of Homer's Odyssey, transported into Outer Space. The protagonist is a cosmic Captain Nemo in search of a special cosmic sheep (again a thematic tie-in to the story of Jason and the Argonauts and their quest for the golden fleece), which magical creature has been abducted by the villainous Mandys (the resemblance to the name of a Czech literary critic and Křesadlo's antagonist Pavel Mandys certainly being no coincidence).

Despite appearing epically serious on the surface, the Star Voyage is a tale glowing with the omnipresent humour peculiar to Křesadlo and a delightful treat for the experienced reader.

SO WHITHER WITH KŘESADLO?

Some (such as the aforementioned Mandys) see no place for him in Czech literature, others unreservedly praise him to the skies. I think that after initially dazzling us with his wholly extraordinary level of talent, Křesadlo has become assimilated as an integral part of Czech literature. In support of which, we see some worthy followers in his postmodern intertextual footsteps. The likes of Miloš Urban with his gothic-toned horrors of Prague new and old, accented by non-conformist decadent eroticism, or Petr Stančík with his novel *Pérák*, would surely have appealed to the old Master, were he still with us today.

Peter Pišťanek
Devínska Nová Ves, 2009

Translated by V Z J Pinkava

TRANSLATOR'S NOTES

Jan Křesadlo (1926–1995) made his debut with this award-winning novel in 1984. Its first English translation was published in a bilingual edition in 1999, though it had been in preparation for some time with the author's endorsement. Being the work of a group it had some issues of stylistic consistency, as well as errors and omissions, some due to relying on the Czech versions published. This commemorative retranslation is revised in form and content, based on the original source typescript. The footnotes in the text are largely those of the author, with some enhancements for the non-Czech reader, including some asides in the text. Gypsy language exchanges are as transcribed, with the author's translations (in brackets), but have been italicised in this edition. These end-notes are entirely supplementary.

1 This motto is a slight variation on Alexander Sergeyevich Pushkin's text from his lascivious poem Czar Nikita, whose original "their" has been changed to "your".

2 A reference to the actor who played the popular TV cop "Kojak" at the time of writing.

3 The novel's original slangy neologism title, "Mrchopěvci" is a calque from "mrcha/mršina" and "pěvci" meaning 'dead(animal)body singers'. GraveLarks, as proposed by Pavel Pinkava (1965–2011), captures the compactness of the original title and its wordplay. Since the author used some paraphrases of this term, you will also find 'carcassingers', or 'stiffsingers' mentioned here.

4 Krůta (pronounced Crootah) is the Czech word for a hen turkey.

5 A reference to Jaroslav Hašek's "Good Soldier Švejk" part four, where a Mr Božetěch finds his clothes to have been stolen during his taking a dip in a river.

6 Jozef Lada (1887–1957) A popular Czech illustrator with a distinctive 2D style.

7 In transliteration (with thanks to academics Stefan Weise and
Han Baltussen):

Στᾱλιν ἄναξ, ἄγαμαί σε· σὺ λευκολίθῳ ἐνὶ Κρέμλῳ
ἑζόμενος κρατέεις πάντων Ῥώσσων Τατάρων τε
καὶ πολλῶν ἐθνῶν ξείνων ἀμενηνῶν κράτων.
Ἕρποντες κονίῃ σε θεὸν ὣς εἰσορόωσιν.
Σοὶ δὲ μέγας στρατός ἐστι βροτοκτόνος, ὅς τ' ἐνὶ χώραις
ἀλλοδαπῶν φορέει γ' οἰζὺν καὶ κῆρα μέλαιναν·
Ἄνδρας συλεύουσι βιάζουσίν τε γυναῖκας,
ὡρολόγους γὰρ κλέπτουσιν, τοὺς ἄνδρες ἀγαυοί
ἐν καρποῖς φορέουσι· τὸ γὰρ μέγα θαῦμα ἰδέσθαι.
Ἄλλοι γά λλοι γάρ ῥ'ἐκάμοντο ἰδυίῃσι πραπίδεσσιν,
σὺ δ' ἐλθὼν αἱρεῖς, ὅτι τοι κράτος ἐστὶ μέγιστον·
Χεῖρας βεβριθὼς παμπόλλοις ὡρολόγοισιν
ἑζόμενος γ' ὀράας χρονοδείγματα κύδεϊ γαίων.
Πάντες δειδιότες κυνέουσι πόδας πυγήν τε,
Αὐτὸς γὰρ κρατέεις καί γ' οὕστινας οὐκ ἐφίλησας,
πέμψας Σειβιρίηνδ' εἰς λάγερα, ᾗ ψύχωνται
δεσμοῖσι στυγεροῖσι δεδημένοι ἠὲ θάνωσιν.
Ῥωσσιακῆς γαίης πάντες ῥ'ἄνδρες τε γυναῖκες,
εὐχόμενοι στυγέουσιν, ἐπεὶ θεός ἐσσι μέγιστος·
Ἥλιον δ' αὐτόν φασιν σόν τ' ἔμμεναι ὄμμα μεναι ὄμμα
καὶ Στάλινος πορδήν φασι ψολόεντα κεραυνόν.

8 Aleksandr Isayevich Solzhenitsyn (1918–2008) was arrested in
1945 and interred in labour camps, after his mildly derogatory re-
marks about Stalin in private correspondence.

9 One of the many salutations of Joseph Stalin.

10 Fritz Haarmann, the 'Butcher of Hanover'

11 Rougly translated: "Where a wooden cross marks the start of the
road to God, lined with sad little appletrees, going on indefinitely,
two-by-two."

12 "A tall steeple like a flowering onion."

13 English spelling pronunciation precludes using the original location "L", which might be misconstrued; hence "X".

14 Although a made-up location, Mlno happens to be an outdated
Czech word for electricity, related to an old word for lightning.

15 sit venia verbo – 'if you'll pardon the word'

16 The painter Lukáš Marold (1865–1898)

17 Petr Bezruč (1867–1958) was a distinctive nationalist poet, though there is some controversy about his major piece, "Slezské písně" ('Silesian songs') being all his own.

18 Václav Kopecký was a key communist journalist and politician of the worst sort.

19 The "Čest práci" slogan predates Communism, appearing as it does in a poem by Svatopluk Čech (1846–1908), here translated as a bonus. The greeting was also adopted by the Baťa shoe factory workers in Zlín, between the Wars.

> Eternity has swallowed countless ages,
> Where falsehood, sham with violence had reigned,
> To wrench and hold the mace of worldly sages,
> For their own pleasure keeping others chained;
> Vainglory pomp and wealth basked fist, upraised,
> Till darkness heard the cry: Let toil be praised!
>
> Has history upheld that fame misguided?
> Parchment scraps marked with mould and blood congealed.
> But oh! The legacy of work confided:
> Here, dark green meadows, yonder ripened field;
> Village trees, blossom flaming, bustling town marketplace,
> And buildings tall, proclaiming: Let toil be praised!
>
> A worthy call, solemn and worth revering,
> Shaking off surfdom chains of wretchedness,
> Scattering golden idols, hollow, reeling,
> Winning out over hate, and feigned success;
> Above raised heads, new dawn's portent, ablaze,
> World unison, reborn: Let toil be praised!
>
> Praise toil of every kind that brings well-being,
> Though wielding hammer, or behind the plough,
> Wading through mud and dust in strife unseeing,
> Or lofty penned, uplifting care-worn brow;
> Unsteered by selfish dictate, lust, greed-crazed –
> Toil of pen, file and spade, alike be praised!

20 The "Socialism with a human face" slogan of the Prague Spring of

1968, thus dating the given events to 1952.

21 Emanuel Moravec, the Nazi collaborator, who argued that St Wenceslas laudably exemplified the notion of lasting compromise with the Germans.

22 The dual-mode "amphibian" lifestyles of those who participated in church singing as well as communist society.

23 Alexander Solzhenitsyn's 'Gulag Archipelago'.

24 An obscure reference to features in the vicinity of the Prague police station in Bartolomějská st. One human-headed stone bollard is at Liliová & Zlatá streets, in fact.

25 A reference to the way the Communist anthem *The Internationale*, when sung in Czech, acoustically seems to combine the ravens and vultures into 'vulturavens', albeit more literally raven-vultures. ('Vransup' from " ... vran, supů hejna kroužící").

26 A transparently veiled reference to "Schovávaná na schodech" ('hide-and-seek on the stairs') by Vítězslav Nezval (1900–1958).

27 A reference to the novel "Honzlová" by Zdena Salivarová, wife of J. Škvorecký.

28 A word remininscent of 'blessed', as in the old religious greeting. "Pochválen buď Ježíš Kristus" ('Blessed be Our Lord Jesus Christ').

29 Karel Škréta (1610–1674), a leading Czech baroque painter.

30 The proanimabus office looks after the capital bequeathed to a church or parish to posthumously finance the welfare of one's relatives.

31 Klement Gottwald, who loyally followed Stalin, even to the grave.

32 A reference to "Pole orná a válečná" by Vladislav Vančura (1891–1942).

33 A reference to the clinic for sexual and other delinquency near St. Apollinaire's church in Prague.

34 A reference to Stalin.

35 A reference to a traditional phrase in Czech schools.

36 Evidently the Danube.

37 A reference to the historic Czech-Bavarian Border Ranger ("Chod") emblem of a guard dog, usurped by communist border patrol insignia.

Also available from Jantar Publishing

A KINGDOM OF SOULS

by Daniela Hodrová

Translation by Véronique Firkusny and Elena Sokol
Introduction by Elena Sokol

Through playful poetic prose, imaginatively blending historical
and cultural motifs with autobiographical moments, Daniela
Hodrová shares her unique perception of Prague.
A Kingdom of Souls is the first volume of this author's literary
journey — an unusual quest for self, for one's place in life and
in the world, a world that for Hodrová is embodied in Prague.

KYTICE
CZECH & ENGLISH BILINGUAL EDITION

by Karel Jaromír Erben

Translation and Introduction by Susan Reynolds

Kytice was inspired by Erben's love of Slavonic myth and the
folklore surrounding such creatures as the Noonday Witch and
the Water Goblin. First published in 1853, these poems, along
with Mácha's *Máj* and Němcová's *Babička*, are the best loved and
most widely read 19th century Czech classics. Published in the
expanded 1861 version, the collection has moved generations of
artists and composers, including Dvořák, Smetana and Janáček.

CIRCULATING STOCK PUBLIC LIBRARIES

BLOCK LOAN

19·7·14   W·D. 15/3/24